Eliza Meteyard

The Lady Herbert's Gentlewomen

Vol. I.

Eliza Meteyard

The Lady Herbert's Gentlewomen
Vol. I.

ISBN/EAN: 9783337249366

Printed in Europe, USA, Canada, Australia, Japan

Cover: Foto ©Andreas Hilbeck / pixelio.de

More available books at **www.hansebooks.com**

THE LADY HERBERT'S GENTLEWOMEN.

BY

ELIZA METEYARD,

("SILVERPEN,")

AUTHOR OF "MAINSTONE'S HOUSEKEEPER,"

&c., &c.

IN THREE VOLUMES.

VOL. I.

LONDON:
HURST AND BLACKETT, PUBLISHERS,
SUCCESSORS TO HENRY COLBURN,
13, GREAT MARLBOROUGH STREET.
1862.

THE LADY HERBERT'S GENTLEWOMEN.

CHAPTER I.

THE HALL.

THE clock is striking twelve as Mr. Quatford, the chaplain, closes the customary service read on Wednesday mornings. Pausing a few moments, he thus adds, according to ancient rule :—

"Peace be to the memory of Lady Catherine Herbert.—Amen. Let her bounty ever cherish those of good rearing but low estate.—Amen. Let her name be remembered by her gentlewomen evermore.—Amen, Amen."

He then descends from his little movable pulpit, which on all other days in the week stands in a distant corner of the hall, and retiring to an adjacent closet, takes off his gown. Coming forth again—his hat in one hand, a book and some flowers in the other—he crosses the tesselated marble floor towards the great doors, which, the first time this year, stand open to admit the sun. Its rays have poured in cheerily all through the hour of service, till now the air is warm and laden with spring odours from near gardens, orchards, and far-off fields.

Passing through a lane of little mob-capped girls, twenty in number, in ages between six and sixteen years, and whom, brought up humbly and fittingly for domestic servitude, this noble charity supports, Mr. Quatford descends the sweeping flight of steps. Here he is amidst such of the aged ladies as have attended week-day service; and though they have already begun to pass right and left, or across the lawn-covered quadrangle, to their respective rooms, he has a word or a bow for all. Little Miss Thorne—who is eighty and greatly bent, yet who, nevertheless, wears a fashionable cap of spotless white, leans on an ivory-headed stick, and has a gold chain and dangling eye-glass—returns the bow stiffly and passes on; for she is severely Calvinistic, and considering herself one of the "elect," differs with the tolerant chaplain on learned questions of predestination, baptism, and free-will: whilst Mrs. Rutland and Miss Simpkins just give flippant nods—for the first he offended by making prior loan of "John Halifax" to her neighbour Mrs. Smith, and the other by calling her parrot "Billy" a noisy fellow. But the rest of the old ladies, fifteen or sixteen in all, cluster round him

like happy bees, for their wise chaplain is, as they
have proved, their tender and sincerest friend.
Be they ill and in trouble, he is ever by their
side—confidant of their joys and woes, they have
him to speak to, whether they mourn or rejoice.
So he has a kindly word for each one. Has this
one seen her daughter?—has this other heard of
her far-away son?—is this one better?—the other
less depressed?   Then he speaks on general
topics—some piece of public news, some festival
in the neighbourhood—and reverts at last to the
weather as he prepares to go on.

"Our first true morning of spring, ladies. In
such balmy air and divine sunshine our hearts
should indeed rejoice."   And he bares his
noble head, covered by its shock of iron-grey
hair, as he speaks, so that the sunshine falls full
upon it.

"It is, indeed," they answer; "a morning
when the old feel young."

Then severally they speak of their gardens—
the springing peas, the budding gooseberry bushes
—and end by telling him that Mrs. Hutchinson,
the matron, had allowed the children to go into
the woods that morning; and the result is that
each room is at this moment—according to ancient and annual custom—gay with its first vernal
nosegay of violets and primroses.

"Ha! one of those old things of Shirlot, that,
were I a poet, I would put into verse. Well,
spring is the time for birds and children. This
mention of flowers reminds me of my own gar-

den, what I gathered there two hours ago, and what I hold here. My bouquet is intended for Miss Hazlehurst. How is she?" Bowing and saying, "Good morning!" to the other ladies, he by this last question has specially addressed a most pleasant-looking old gentlewoman, who, timing her steps to his, now walks beside him. She is a mother you can see by her looks, for the divine sanctity of motherhood sits so lovingly upon her face.

"Better to-day," she answers, "though still a sad cripple. But as this is the happy anniversary of my coming here, I keep it as I always do—and she will be good enough to take her tea with me and a few other friends. It is but a step along the gallery, Mr. Quatford—but a step, sir; and with a little aid she will travel the small journey, I daresay."

"Ha! most kind of you; the little change will do our old friend good. Some of you live too much alone, and solitude in excess is not good for us, Mrs. Boston. But I am going up-stairs to my old friend—I shall not intrude, shall I?"

"Dear—no, sir. She will be glad to see you; she was already seated by one of her sunny windows, as I called in on my way to service. She seemed to expect you, for she was talking of a book you had promised to lend her."

"Here it is, and a few of the first flowers my garden has produced this spring. Whilst I walked up and down there in the sun this morning, I could not help thinking what a long winter hers had been—so here is the first offering of my flower borders."

Whilst the chaplain and the old gentlewoman have been thus talking they have stepped into the left cloister of the quadrangle, and passing through a wide opening or passage at the side, there lies before them a very broad staircase, with low steps, vast landings, and oaken balustrades; one of Pickford's largest waggons and half-a-dozen waggoners might pass up it easily abreast. It leads on to a very long, wide gallery, running above the cloister beneath; one wall looking out by many sunny windows on to the lawn-covered quadrangle, whilst in the other are set oaken doors at even distances, which shut in sacredly some few of the homes of Lady Herbert's Gentlewomen.

Bidding Mrs. Boston "good day and a pleasant evening," the chaplain, pausing for a moment in the rich sunlight that pours down from the gallery windows on to the spotless floor beneath, opens the book. It is a volume of Tennyson's, and contains the sweet poem of "Lord Burleigh."

> "Weeping late, and weeping early;
>   Walking up, and walking down;
>   Deeply mourn'd the Lord of Burleigh;
>   Burleigh House by Stamford Town."

Thus much, and more, he reads, the verses having, as it seems, an attractive charm which makes them irresistible; then, putting the marker in the book again, he closes it and knocks at the door before him. A gentle "come in" invites him to enter, and in another instant he has closed the door upon the gallery, and is within a very large room, and in the presence of an aged lady, who, seated by one of two sunny casements, has her little work-table before her. On it lie divers small bags and parcels, from which she is selecting gay-coloured strips of silk, and placing them together in a little heap of radiant hues. But now, pausing in her task, she makes a poor attempt to rise in courtesy to her visitor, who, repressing her intent, shakes her kindly by the hand, looks with interest on her venerable face, and takes a chair beside her.

"Here is a little offering from my garden," he says, as he lays down his exquisitely-perfumed bouquet of early flowers; "and here the book I spoke of when I saw you last. It is a fortnight since then, and you are better, eh? I hear so."

"Yes, thank you, Mr. Quatford; I am even going to step beyond my room this afternoon, the first time for seven months. To speak the truth, I would rather be quiet here, but my good friend and neighbour, Mrs. Boston, has a grateful heart, and thus keeps the anniversary of her coming to Shirlot. I, on the contrary, think that these festivals are best hallowed in the sanctity of our own hearts. But this is a matter of taste; and so, with a little aid, I hope to get along the gallery to her room by four o'clock, for the party begins thus early."

"Who are the ladies?" And there is an arch look in the chaplain's face as he asks the question.

"There is Miss Simpkins, I fear—"

"And the parrot?" interrupts the chaplain, with a smile.

"I hope not. Mrs. Boston told me she had made it a proviso that Billy was not to come; but Miss Simpkins is an audacious sort of woman, and cares little for others' wishes or feelings. Then there is Miss Gregg—"

"And Spark, the poodle," again interrupts the chaplain, still more merrily.

"As a matter of course, Mr. Quatford, Lydia Gregg goes nowhere without her dog."

"Well, I wish you joy of your gathering. But Miss Thorne!—I forgot Miss Thorne—is she to be there?"

"Miss Thorne! Mr. Quatford, you forget the woman! Why, we might as well expect the Archbishop of Canterbury, or a Presbyter of the Synod of Geneva! She join a set of primitive old women, who drink tea at five o'clock, and begin knitting afterwards! Oh, no! She hasn't even dined at so vulgar an hour. For of late, I am told, since some visit she paid in the summer, her pride and state have greatly increased."

"Yes, I fancied her bow and manner more stiff and distant than ever to-day. But it is a lamentable picture, Miss Hazlehurst—the saddest, I think, that Shirlot holds. Pride, false pride, sits well upon none of us, more especially if we are poor, old, and dependent; and here, where it is joined with the utmost ignorance and bigotry, the case is still worse. Such a nature has no charity for others; in its profound ignorance of what *is* truth, it judges itself immaculate, and is thus deaf and blind to what might teach. Happy for those who have to come in contact with such diseased, badly organised, and literally degraded natures—happy for themselves, and happily for the advancing weal of humanity, Death at last steps in—Death, that sublimest of the divine mysteries which surround us —if only for the power inherent in it, of removing stereotyped and imbecile opinions from amidst advancing truth, as weeds from springing corn."

"Yes, Mr. Quatford, I think with you that the aged are too apt to be narrow and prejudiced, and that they leave the stage not an hour too soon for younger and wiser actors. I often reason with myself when I cannot quite bring my mind to think, or my tastes to agree with, the opinions and things of the present day; and when unable to rule my judgment, as is, I confess, sometimes the case, I recollect that it can matter but little what *I* think, whose race is so nearly run. Thus I gain charity of thought, at least, by remembering that opinions, like their professors, grow obsolete through time."

The chaplain has been watching the sweet old countenance, and he can but gaze at it still. It has been comely through its youth and womanhood—it is made comely even now by the presence of the serene peace of a well-spent life. It is a face which has looked upon that of Washington—upon those of the heroes of American independence—upon man in his savage state—and upon the forests, the rivers, the lakes of one of the noblest countries in the world. It has passed through the scenes of a troublous and hard-fought life—a life whose human joys have been so few as scarce to deserve a reckoning; and yet here it is at last irradiated by the great light of the kindly heart and peaceful soul within. He can but look, he can but venerate, seeing her seated thus—amidst the blessed hush of this sunny, vernal noon.

"Before I left home—" he begins.

"Excuse me, Mr. Quatford—one question; I have been longing to ask it since you first entered the room. How did you speed on the errand for which you left us? How did you leave your nephew? I take the privilege of an old and honouring friend in being so inquisitive."

"Mary Hazlehurst," he says, "is at all times privileged. Why, I found the poor fellow dying, as my letter of summons said, but eminent medical skill and unceasing care at last saved him. Two days ago, I journeyed with him into the south of Devonshire, where he now is, in the house of a tender friend. When he is sufficiently recovered, he will come here for a time. Poor fellow, he had been overworking himself, bodily and mentally, as young men will, and had been living too parsimoniously, in order to spare me. Yet it is only like him. Islip cannot act otherwise than nobly."

"That is true. Even when a child he was

manly and straightforward. I recollect his first coming an orphan to you, Mr. Quatford, as though it were but yesterday; and you well know how in years succeeding he grew to love me and my old room. But it is a long time now since I saw him—five years at least."

" Quite; but youth and idleness are incompatible, and there were boyish associations in the neighbourhood that were best severed. Next year he leaves me for a long time, or—as fate perhaps has it—for ever."

" Surely not; I thought his appointment a good one, and engineering work in this country abundant."

" So it is comparatively, and ordinary minds might settle down to its routine, but not so Islip. He is ambitious, and his nature is such as to need free space for action. A civil appointment, connected with railways in India, of great value, though of extraordinary responsibility, that would awe most men, has been offered to his acceptance in the ensuing year, and with my consent he takes it. I had made my mind up to have my only sister's only child within reasonable distance, so as for us to meet occasionally, and have joy in the deep friendship which is ours; but I found that his spirit had been vexed and chafed by narrow circumstances and narrow controlling causes. So I have consented to his acceptance of the appointment, even urged him to accept it, though it will leave me friendless and alone; and thus, when he is recovered, he will come here—

stay with me some months—prepare himself in several ways for his duty—and next spring or summer leave me and the old parsonage of Shirlot for many a year. It will be hard parting with one so truly noble, and the only near relative I have; but it will be for his good, and that is sovereign over every other consideration to me. In this life, those sacrifices have to be made more or less by all of us, Miss Hazlehurst."

"They have, indeed, sir," she replies, with deep feeling, as though remembering the many she has made.

"Now," he says, after a moment's pause, "let us speak of more cheerful things. Here is the book I told you of, before I was called away so suddenly from home; and here, where I have put the marker, is the poem I referred to, when we were talking one day of Lord Essex and Sally Hoggins. You were telling me some particulars of their romantic story, never yet correctly narrated, and here you will find a version of it by our greatest living poet. There are other glorious things in the book, which may make its perusal a joy of joys; but 'Lord Burleigh' is a noble story, set to eternal music by a great singer. I daresay, if we only knew them, it is not the only romance of a like kind that our century has known. Not that I think such romances in the abstract desirable, for learning and education form together the impassable barrier between rank and rank. No lady, I believe, ever married her footman without living to bitterly regret the act; and few educated men ever married dairymaids, or simple country girls, without results that soon changed romance into sad prose. But there may be occasional exceptions. Lord Essex's case was one; and there may have been others, where nature was affluent in gifts, and the heart of the woman unselfish and loving."

"I heard of a case once, Mr. Quatford, and its details were most interesting. It is quite a story, the particulars of which became known to me whilst I was making a brief stay in London some years ago."

"A story, Miss Hazlehurst? Why not tell it over the tea-table this evening? It would be better than Miss Simpkins' scandal."

"It would, indeed, sir; but I am such a poor story-teller, and many of those invited are such quizzes. To you I can talk without embarrassment, because I am accustomed to you, and you are good enough to make excuses for age and infirmity. I could read it if it were written, but my power of consecutive narration is, I fear, all gone."

"Shall I ask our clever friend, Miss Morfe, to write it?—I am going to call upon her."

"She is from home. It is Amy's Easter holidays, and she is gone to London to spend them with her there. To my great pleasure, the dear lady will be back again next week."

"Ay, to all our pleasures; for Amy Morfe, the elder, is the shining light of Shirlot. Well, shall I write it?—I will do so much to spare the parrot and scandal. There will be time between this and five o'clock, and Peter, my man, shall bring the paper to Mrs. Boston's room. Now, take up your knitting, you will talk less embarrassed then, and tell me word for word."

She obeys him like a child; and so, with bent head, and moving fingers, she tells the story of the " New Lord Burleigh."

When she has ended, the chaplain thanks her, and takes his leave. In twenty minutes more he is quiet in his ancient study—the pen glides across the paper—the sun shines in—the ripple of the little river, as it passes by the oaks of Shirlot, makes music, if he heard.

CHAPTER II.

THE KITCHEN.

THE twenty wooden platters are set on the great oaken table in the kitchen, and dinner is about to begin. The twenty little maids are ranged on either side—the matron at the head—the teacher at the foot of the table, and a servant, bearing great dishes from the capacious fire-place, sets on the meal. There are large joints of veal, a piece of boiled bacon, batter-pudding and potatoes—for none who partake of Lady Herbert's bounty know what parsimony is. There is wise moderation—but nothing which is mean.

"Rhoda!"—and the matron, a gentle but mournful-looking woman of fifty, thus calls a little maid seated some way down the table. This summons, as though expected, gives instant motion to the prettiest of girlish figures; and in another moment the little mob-cap beauty—for the sweetest countenance is set in this Puritan garniture—curtseys before the mistress's chair.

"A dinner to Miss Hazlehurst." This is said sententiously; but its meaning is fully understood.

Hereupon Rhoda fetches warm plates from the fire, a tray, and dainty napkin, and again standing before the mistress, curtseys humbly.

"Tibb," says the matron—this time calling to a bent and aged woman—who, having helped to serve the dinner, is now about to take her place at an adjoining table, with the old porter or serving-man and another female servant, "a pint of best ale for Miss Hazlehurst;" whereupon Tibb, taking a jug from a rack, departs to a distant cellar. By the time she returns the dainty meal is carved, and Rhoda ready to go.

"My respects to Miss Hazlehurst," says the matron. "I send her a dinner of which I hope she will partake—I shall be glad to hear if she is better to-day—and add that to-morrow I will call upon her." Thus commissioned, Rhoda curtseys and goes. Across the vast kitchen—so vast as to be like a baronial hall—through a wide sunny passage—through the heavy door opening on to the head of the cloister—whence stretches the long vista of arches, pavement, light and shadow—thence into the great passage, through which is seen a prospect of near and rugged hills—and so to the stairs'-foot, up which, with her hospitable burden, the little mob-capped maid begins to go. Then suddenly there comes in from the garden, on the outer side of the hall, a man's heavy step—and a voice calls softly, "Rhoda!"

The little maid glances down through the balustrades, and sees young Mr. Clayton—a farmer living near at hand. He is a wild-looking young fellow; but Rhoda is somewhat in awe of him—for he is said to be rich, and his sisters dress grandly on Sundays—so she drops a little curtsey —and, blushing red, stays a moment.

" Rhoda! come back."

" I can't, sir, I am going to Miss Hazlehurst's."

" Will you be long? If not, I will stay till you come back."

" Please don't, sir—if Mrs. Hutchinson should know I talk to you, she will be very angry. We're all at dinner, and I shall be missed if I am long. Please go! Miss Jones gave me a heavy task last Monday—for what I don't know, unless it was because you looked at me at church."

" Miss Jones!" he exclaims angrily. " What care I for her? Because my sisters take her up— and she's always pestering at our house—that's no reason why she should sit judge over me. I'll look where I like, and when I like; and now, as you can't stop, will you be by the shrubbery on the outer lawn by four o'clock. I've something to say to you—you play at that hour ?"

" I don't, sir, nor none of the bigger girls. We're going to stay in the hall, for we've some things to make for Mrs. Hutchinson's birth-day." She goes on now, but again he detains her.

" Rhoda! I will speak to you, come what may! . I'm very fond of you, for you're lovely. See here what I brought you from the town when I last went;" and he exhibits a little glass and pictured work-box, such as might be bought for sixpence, but which is dazzling to the eye of a country-bred and unsophisticated child.

"Do come, Rhoda, and this shall be yours."

It has been one of Rhoda's school-girl dreams to buy such a little box, and, seeing it, she hesitates.

"Do come, Rhoda, it shall be yours then— so don't say no."

"I can't come at four o'clock."

"Later, then, before it's time for bed."

"You won't keep me very long?—you won't tell anybody?"

"Not I; then we'll say seven—by the shrubbery on the outer lawn."

She scarcely says "yes," for she is conscious she is consenting to what is wrong; but the young man, interpreting the answer his own way, nods his head and goes. Less quick of foot than heretofore, she ascends the stairs slowly, for a shadow seems to go before her, and a weight to lie upon her hitherto happy spirit. "If I take the box," she thinks, "I must tell a story about it, for all the children will be asking me where I got it." Thus pondering, she gains the gallery and taps at the door.

When she enters, the old lady, moving with pain and great slowness, is spreading a little table for her frugal dinner. The cloth is on, and going to and fro to two capacious closets, one on either side the fire-place, and as large as the rooms of a small-sized London house, she is bringing things thence; she has also recourse to two safes, which, ornamented with paper, and somewhat out of keeping with a lady's sitting-room, are nailed against the wall. After the manner of the bed in Goldsmith's " Deserted Village " they are,

> An escritoire or box to view—
> In truth, a pantry fit for mutton cold,
> Or even dainty stew.

But we have not yet seen the aristocratic rooms in Shirlot—in due time they will be open to our entrance. Nevertheless, Miss Hazlehurst's room is large and vastly comfortable. Walls as thick as those of a Norman donjon keep out all cold; they are neatly papered, and a carpet bespreads the floor, little queer amateur watercolour drawings of the Minerva-press school, framed in paper, and the gift of loving nieces, adorn the walls. There is a roomy sofa, and tables with oil-cloth covers, and a set of hanging bookshelves, decked in yellow muslin to keep out dust and flies; and there are comfortable chairs and the bed-place, or recess just large enough to hold a bed, a chest of drawers and washstand, is hidden from view by a sweeping green curtain. There is old china on the mantel-shelf, and a glowing fire in the grate. But the old lady herself is the gem and prize of her room : well-bred, gentle, simple, unsuspicious, affectionate—a noble woman, made nobler by a life of many tears.

"If you please, ma'am," says little Rhoda, dropping her habitual curtsey, "Mrs. Hutchinson has sent you a dinner, which she hopes you will enjoy."

And Rhoda, uncovering the plate, shows the nice viands, and then stooping to the fire she places them before it to keep them warm. Miss Hazlehurst is very fond of pretty Rhoda, and this thoughtful act adds to her tender feeling.

"Thank you—you're a good child, Rhoda. I am sure it is very kind of Mrs. Hutchinson thus bearing me in memory, for it was only on Monday that I had a nice dinner of roast beef. Pray, give my grateful thanks."

"If you please, ma'am, I was to ask you how you do to-day."

"Say better, if you please, and that I am even going out to tea this evening to Mrs. Boston's. How is Mrs. Hutchinson—more cheerful, I hope, this sunny day?"

"No, ma'am," replies Rhoda, innocently; "she was crying bitterly last night, and this morning too—indeed, she was too low-spirited to attend service. I think it is some fresh trouble about her son; for Mr. Shugborough, the druggist, came over from the town yesterday, and he spoke very sternly, and said he could bear it no longer. In reply Mrs. Hutchinson said that he should leave, and she would try and get him a place in London. I was going into the room with some ale and glasses, and heard this."

" Well, let it go no further—with me it is safe, but there are those at Shirlot who, I am sorry to say, though they eat the divine bread of charity, are not kindly when another's woe is in the case."

Thus saying no more, for she is too rigidly conscientious to ask questions or elicit gossip, Miss Hazlehurst moves aside to the little table by which she sat when Mr. Quatford paid his visit an hour before, and, taking up the little shining heap of silk, gives it to the little beauty in the quaint garb.

"Here, Rhoda, these are all for you. I know Mrs. Hutchinson's birthday is near at hand, and that her scholars make her needle-books and pin-cushions for the occasion, so I have been looking up my treasures. They are pieces of the dresses and ribbons I wore in days when I was not as old and as troublesome as now. So take them, Rhoda —you are so good a child to me."

Rhoda is entranced — the riches seem so infinite. None but those who know the heart of a school-girl can tell the exquisite pleasure these little vanities give. No Eastern despot, with his jewels round him, has half the joy.

"Oh, dear, ma'am," says Rhoda, dropping the gratefullest and profoundest curtsey she ever made, "I cannot thank you enough — I never saw such beautiful silk in my life before. This very morning Caroline Brown and I were saying that if we had some nice silk we would make Mrs. Hutchinson a bag. And here's enough for a bag and many things beside. I am sure I cannot show you how grateful I am!"

"Yes, Rhoda, by being always a good child.

Never tell a lie, nor let others persuade you to do deceitful things. They lead to suffering and evil, my dear; and your remembrance of my words will be precious to you when I've long passed away."

These words are spoken in no particular sense, but they wound a tender conscience as though they were.

Faltering "no," and trembling as she falters, the aged eyes, were they less dim, would see that evil, in some one of its countless shapes, had already touched the heart of innocence. The keenness of her joy has waned—fear molests her peace—and hurriedly rolling up the little heap of silk, she puts it into her pocket, makes her curtsey, and goes.

"Rhoda," calls the old lady, as the door is about to close, "give my respects to Mrs. Hutchinson, and say if she will permit you to come after school to hook my dress and pin my brooch, I shall be obliged—for Mrs. Stephens, my woman, has gone to hoe her potatoes to-day, and will not be here till evening."

"Yes, ma'am." And the little trembling maid goes forth in the shadows which lie before her.

Her nice dinner partaken of, part of the ale bottled for the morrow, the things cleared away, her nap taken, her best dress laid forth, with quaint lace and ruffles, and other little adornments, it is just four o'clock. Rhoda coming again, the old gentlewoman dresses, and then locking her door, goes forth along the gallery, assisted by her pretty friend and Mrs. Boston, who, watching for the purpose, hastens to assist her. Thus, in the sweet shadows of the evening, she treads the gallery—the first time for seven long months, and looking, as in some Rembrandt picture, the perfect lady which she is.

CHAPTER III.

MRS. BOSTON'S ROOM—THE NEW LORD BURLEIGH.

A MINOR episode must have space ere we enter
Mrs. Boston's room, and approach the tea-table,
charmingly set forth with the best china and
the sweetest cake.

Right gallery—room nine—does not in the
least look as though it belonged to Shirlot, or
Lady Herbert's gentlewomen. Miss Sophia Simpkins is frigid, censorious, and parsimonious. To
save is the great end of her being—to malign the
great joy of her heart. Born in the rank of a
gentlewoman, she is a lady neither in principle,
education, nor spirit. She is at war with all the
world ; and, as she supposes, all the world with
her. Hence her intense bitterness of spirit :
she loves nobody, she cares for nothing—except—
except Billy, her parrot. On this sage gentleman she expends all the little warmth of her
frosty nature, and two-pence a week for seed.
He is the sole companion of her solitary days.

It is approaching four o'clock, and Sophia is dressing. Just at this moment—perhaps we ought not thus to intrude into the mystery of a lady's boudoir, only truth, as the axiom has it, is truth—she is robed in her petticoat, which is a defunct dress, still enriched with furbelows; her neck—"tall as a poplar-tree"—is bare, and her locks, scanty and unadorned, are gathered together on the top of her head by a comb. She is thus what *gamins* would call "a reg'lar fright!" But being alone, and unconscious of critical eyes— except they be those of Billy, who, reposing on his perch, seems to wickedly regard her—she leans against the fire-place; whilst before her, on the table, lie three dresses, but lately produced from an ancient box beneath the bed. They are amazingly old-fashioned, and dingy in hue, for they formed part of the wardrobe of a very old aunt—dead at least thirty years—but this is of no account to Sophia, who, so she saves, is perfectly content. To her fashion is nothing, for in her bitterness of spirit she habitually contemns everything modern or new.

Now, as she deliberately chooses to pass her days in solitude—except when she can take tea, and talk scandal, at others' expense—she has fallen into a sad habit of talking to herself, and, forgetting the adage that walls have ears, confides the tenderest secrets of her heart to Billy. That twinkling-eyed gentleman, thus treated to so much human speech, is learned therein, and treasuring up vast stores thereof in his pate, asks questions and makes replies, often at seasons most inopportune. But then, for the major part of his days, his mistress is the only listener.

"Which *shall* I put on?" soliloquizes Sophia, for the fourth or fifth time, as she stands regarding with great veneration these antique treasures of her wardrobe; "shall it be the brown, the black, or the yellow?"

"Put on!—put on!—put on!" screams the parrot.

" Billy, if you talk thus, I'll leave you at home, sir; you'll be making some dreadful mistake, I'm sure."

" No, no!" croaks the gentleman; for he is cunning enough to see that his mistress is cross.

"Hush!" she says; and having thus, as she thinks, silenced her loquacious friend, she again communes with herself thus:

"I think I'll put on—I think I'll put on—"

"The yellow!" screams Billy.

As this advice coincides with her own opinion, she only shakes her head, by way of monition, as it were; then losing no further time, she arranges herself in the yellow stuff gown, and a cap gaily trimmed with brilliant red; this done, she stores away the precious gowns as though they were pearls of price; rakes out her little scrap of fire, and prepares to go.

"Now, sir," she says, as, approaching Billy, she takes him off his perch, "you're going with me, though Mrs. Particular said not. But I *do* hope you'll behave yourself. I shall leave you with one of the children for half-an-hour, then she can bring you to the door, and say you won't be good alone."

Billy, who understands enough of human speech to know that the antithesis of good is bad, screams out,

" Bad, bad !—I'll be bad !"

" No, you'll be good; and you shall come just as we're in the middle of tea, and have some sugar."

This is a musical word to the parrot's ear. "Yes, yes !" he croaks, " Billy likes sugar !"

"Ay! my dear," comforts his mistress, "you shall have the biggest lump in the basin. Poor dear! you don't often taste it, for missis can't afford it."

"No!" croaks Billy.

"But it shall have a nice lump to-day. Why, that's why I accepted the invitation, for there'll be little enough entertainment, and nothing better than a crisp biscuit and ginger-wine, before one comes away, unless it be a sermon from that old woman, Hazlehurst, who's only been ill in order to get charity dinners. Not take you! Mrs. Particular shall see that Sophia Simpkins is not to be dictated to." Having thus delivered her opinions of her friends, Sophia takes her familiar on her finger, and, locking her door, goes.

Passing down the gallery and staircase, and thence to the outer lawn, which is in fact a small park, dotted with oaks once forming part of the ancient forest of Shirlot, and divided from the highway, towards which it rapidly slopes by a shrubbery, a wall, and a lodge, she summons one of the children from her play, and delivering Billy, with divers threats if he is not taken care of, she bids that he be brought to Mrs. Boston's door in half-an-hour from that time, with information to the effect " that he's screaming himself to death, and has had to be brought."

Returning to the hall, by a route through the shrubbery and gardens, Miss Simpkins at length reaches Miss Boston's room, where she finds the ladies assembled. Including herself they are eight in number.

" Well, my dear," says Mrs. Boston, welcoming her bitter friend with great cordiality, " it is very kind of you thus to come, and help me to keep one of the happiest days I ever knew. I only wait for you to make the tea. And, my dear, it is really very good of you not to bring that parrot, he is so very noisy and troublesome."

" Oh," answers Sophia, tartly, " I find him a good creature. But, alas! I fear he'll pine himself to death, so if I am summoned away, or he's brought here, you must forgive me."

Then, assuming a lugubrious air, she takes her seat.

A little vexed at this prospect of Billy's visit, the good old motherly lady makes tea; and her company gathering round the table, they are soon enjoying the pleasant meal. The tea being of particular excellence, Mrs. Boston relates to them how it forms part of a small chest her good son in China sent her a while before; and this topic of her children entered upon, it proves a fertile one, for she has much to tell about her newly-married daughter in Northumberland, and of another who is a Government schoolmistress in Cornwall. But this innocent sort of conversation, not being relished by Miss Sophia, is interrupted after a short interval.

"Can any of you tell," she asks, "what that young Clayton hangs about the hall for? I saw him last night, and I saw him again to-day, when I was in my garden sowing mustard and cress. He's after no good, I'm sure of it."

"I see no harm in it," replies Miss Hazlehurst. "Perhaps he had to speak to Mrs. Hutchinson—or to old Harris. It is best not to judge our neighbours, Miss Simpkins."

"Perhaps not, but I keep my opinion still. After one of the bigger girls, I daresay. That Rhoda, or Lucy, or Julia. Pretty impudent they're becoming — never curtseying to *me*, though they do so to others like slaves."

"Well, for my part," speaks Miss Salway, a sweet and true gentlewoman, "I do not court humiliating reverence from any one."

"Nor I, but I like due respect," replies Sophia, tartly, "when I am one of the ladies longest here. As to that fellow Clayton, we all just know what he is—and what happened last year to the dairymaid."

"Well, we'll talk of something else," says Mrs.

Boston. "For once, Miss Simpkins, we'll not blacken our neighbour's character."

An altercation would in all probability ensue, but there comes a divertisement in the shape of a knock at the door; and Sophia, being conscious that Billy is there, keeps the Queen's peace.

"Please, ma'am," says a little treble voice, as Mrs. Boston opens the door, "the parrot's making himself ill with screaming. He would be brought, it wasn't to be helped."

Waiting till this is said, but no longer, Sophia hurries to the door, in a pretended flutter of surprise mingled with pity, for she fears a negative which she will not be able to gainsay.

"Dear, dear! I am very sorry! Billy, you should have been good! But, poor thing, it mustn't scream itself to death—it must come in and have a lump of sugar."

"Yes! yes!" croaks Billy, "a lump of sugar!"

Waiting, therefore, for neither dissent nor assent, Miss Simpkins brings her favourite in, and, perching him on the back of her chair, dives her hand into the sugar basin, selects and gives him the biggest lump, and resumes her seat and her tea—whilst the good-natured mistress of the room, judging, perhaps, that peace is the wiser policy, makes no comment, and hides her fears by busy hospitality.

Chat is resumed—pleasant chat upon divers innocent topics—when again the bitter drop is infused.

"What's Mrs. Hutchinson so miserable about?

Her eyes were as red as poppies when I went into the hall kitchen this morning. Is it that ne'er-do-well son of hers again?"

"I suppose it is," replies Mrs. Rutland, an old lady who loves gossip as boys love gingerbread, that is, will make it theirs when they can; "old Shugborough was over here yesterday, for his gig was standing in the stable-yard, and after that I saw him cross the inner lawn."

"Oh, yes, it's pretty easy to guess why *he* came," says Sophia; "for that boy, George Hutchinson, is as bad as can be. When I last went to Temeford I heard of his always being at the 'Swan;' and as for debts, it was wonderful how a lad not more than nineteen could have contracted so many. That wasn't all either, for his master had been losing books and other things in a very strange way, and—"

"A bit of sugar—a little bit of sugar!" cries the parrot.

There is a sweet needed elsewhere—the honey-drop of charity; and there are hearts there who judge so.

"I would rather not, Miss Simpkins, that we spoke of these things," remarks Mrs. Boston; "women who have been mothers know that they must make allowance for their children's frailties. Mrs. Hutchinson is a sincere and worthy woman, our true friend without exception; and that she has an only child who is wild and reckless is a matter for our silent pity, and not our bitter comments."

"We eat the bread of Lady Catherine Herbert," says Miss Hazlehurst, a little stiffly, for the old gentlewoman is rather inclined to assume a Justice-of-the-Peace air when she reproves—"and her head minister for eighteen years has a right to our charitable thoughts, if nothing more."

"She has indeed," adds Miss Salway; "for good judges consider that she has filled a difficult position very worthily; and we all of us, when we open our doors, have some skeleton beyond the threshold."

"I suppose so," is Sophia's tart reply. Then not a whit abashed, she mollifies her humour by a fresh dip into the sugar.

As tea is now over, Mrs. Boston—prudential motives connected with her sugar-basin partly inducing—hastens to remove the things. When this is effected, the table is drawn near the fire, the candles are lighted, though it is yet a little early, and the ladies, gathering round, produce their needlework and knitting.

Just at this happy moment, and when Miss Hazlehurst is dreading a recurrence to topics best left unmeddled with, there is a knock at the door, and at the words "Come in," a smart young fellow enters and delivers a packet, or large letter, to Miss Hazlehurst.

"Master's very sorry to be thus late with what he sends, but the writing took longer than he expected."

As Peter, the chaplain's servant, makes this speech, all the ladies look wonderingly, except the

three initiated in the pleasant secret—to whit,
Miss Hazlehurst, Miss Salway, and Mrs. Boston.

"My grateful compliments to your master,"
replies the former, "and say I am extremely
obliged."

When Peter has made his respectful bow, and
is gone, Miss Hazlehurst opens the packet.

"Ladies," she says, "here is a story you may
like to hear. Mr. Quatford has been good enough
to write it out from my narration, for the greater
portion of it is perfectly true, and was told me by
the landlord of a house where I lodged some years
ago, in London. I might have been unable to repeat it to you pleasantly from mere memory, for
that, old as I am, is at times a little treacherous,
but thus written in worthier language than is mine,
the beginning will flow on evenly to the end.
Ladies, whilst listening to this little history we
shall be innocently employed—the sorrows and
trials of our neighbours' lives will be kept sacred
from unworthy comment, and the time may pass
pleasantly by. With your leave I will now
begin."

Delightedly they all say "Yes," with the exception of Miss Simpkins, who, bending her head
down to her knitting, gives a little derisive sniff—
implying thereby as plainly as may be, "Go on
with your nonsense, but I'll have *my* laugh, won't
I?"

So the story is read.

THE NEW LORD BURLEIGH.

After a low knock, which remained unanswered, she entered the bedchamber, for it was ten o'clock, and the gentleman had risen. Yes, to fill anew the porcelain ewer, fold the rich silk curtains, spread the laced pillows of the bed, and with poor, coarse, hireling hand, minister, again and again, to the luxury and comfort of the unseen and the unregarding. As she looked round the room with natural curiosity—for the gentleman had only arrived at this " Jamble's " fashionable west-end hotel the night before—there was, instead of the ordinary display of gorgeous waistcoats, many coats, pipes, sticks, gloves, nothing more than a very old portmanteau, still strapped up and locked, and a foreign cap and Turkish pipe on a chair near it. The little housemaid stood surprised by these signs of poverty ; for poverty was a thing against which Mrs. Jamble herself, and Millicent her niece, and Gloss the head-waiter, and Miss Dust the upper-housemaid, all severally and in combination waged war; therefore, to suppose that it could by any chance cross with its cold foot the aristocratic steps of " Jamble's," was about as much a probability as to expect an elephant tucked up asleep in its richest silken curtained bed. As it was but a glance from the poor portmanteau to the cap, and the pipe, on to the toilet, on which swung the rich mirror with its waxen lights, she saw with new surprise a vase of purest marble standing there, fashioned in the shape of a rustic pitcher, held up by a tripping Naiad of the fountain. But it was not the lucent marble, or the goddess, or the pitcher, or the ivy leaves, or the drooping vine, or the Bacchanals sculptured thereon, that she regarded with surprise, for the untaught heart knew nothing of these things, but that some hand, whether rich or poor, whether young or old, had not scornfully trodden down a flower she had dropped the over-night, when performing some little offices about the room, but had carefully placed it with water in this beautiful fountain. It was nothing more than a simple bit of gilliflower, which most would have trodden down unregardingly. Whose foot was thus gentle?—whose hand was thus graceful?—whose heart thus loved the beautiful? What country did this garlanded pitcher come from?—what story did it involve?—was he stern, or old or young? Who was he? What was he? As in this way she thought busily, Meg, the little housemaid, tripped quickly and lightly about her duties, and never did poor coarse hand, yet withal woman's, spread more carefully pillow and curtain and cloth; for the flower, not trodden scornfully down, linked something new of interest and duty to the daily round of indifference and hireling service. As she came back to and fro to where the vase stood, she saw a pair of strong leather gloves lying beside it; and as was very natural, she took them up, and saw that one was rent. Out from her pocket was quickly brought the little huswife, and a thimble and black thread, and turning her back to the door, lest Miss Dust, on her governing perambulations, should peep, and discover, and cannonade, busily needle and thread went to mend the rent ; it was but small duty for the grace of the untrodden flower. Thus standing, with her ear quite alive to Miss Dust's progressions, a stifled sound from the adjoining room was followed by another and another, till these deepened into a man's low cry of pain. Her first impulse was to open the separating door, and she had made a step towards it, when the recollection of Miss Dust's suspicious and tale-bearing propensities, and the lively clamour that would arise in Mrs. Jamble's parlour were such a circumstance known, stayed her hand, and, after a minute's hesitation, she passed from the bed-room on to the corridor to call a waiter. Miss Dust was safe in her little soap, candle, duster, brush, and linen-bedecked room, and in full depth and logic of a towel argument with one of the six housemaids ; and looking down over the balustrades, she saw Shark the waiter, who attended to the " southern suite," leaning napkin in hand over the bar window. She called, but as the one portmanteau had already been a matter for deep consultation between himself and the hall porter, he merely made answer with a cool " presently," and went on with his gossip. Going back quickly to the bedchamber, the same low cry of pain met her ear, and without thinking further of Miss Dust or Mrs. Jamble, she opened the door, looked, and, without stopping, went in. It was the richly

furnished ante-chamber of a drawing-room, partly
darkened by the sun-blinds outside; for it was
summer time and the height of the London season.
On a table placed near one of the windows an
untasted breakfast was yet spread, for the tea,
though poured out, had grown cold in the cup, and
neither knife nor fork had touched the rich
dishes; but some of these had been pushed aside,
to make standing room for two or three fragments
of marvellous Greek sculpture, and beside the
teacup lay a very old volume of Greek poetry.
But the little housemaid might have been blind
for what she saw of these—the whole spectacle
within the room was the gentleman lying insensible upon the low couch beside the table. Trembling and hesitating, she lightly touched his cold,
rigid hands; then bolder grown as fear was
absorbed by sympathy, she gently raised his dark-
hued face upon the pillow, and stepped back to
the toilet for a glass of water. With this she
lightly laved his lips and hands, thinking that
if he were suddenly to recover and look up, he
might take this small act of mercy to be large in
self-interest, or otherwise evil from one so poor
and rude. Yet it was pure and womanly. As
she stood thus, her fear increasing as she looked
down upon this man's stern and haughty face, the
door opened and Mr. Shark slipped in. His first
care, after shaking his head and glancing at the
girl, was to make a pirouette round the breakfast-
table, and after duly peeping into the cream-ewer
and sugar-basin, and counting the silver forks, he

gave a yawn, put his hands behind him, and stepped up to the couch.

"Bad in the night, I b'lieve; bad agin now," mused Mr. Shark coolly, as if some very important idea had just come to mind; "but with one portmanteau, too—that'll never do. Jamble's ain't easily done, and so, my dear, you'll put on your best bonnet and take a walk next Sunday—that you will."

"I'm sure," replied the little housemaid, trembling still more, "I only came in because I supposed the gentleman was ill, and then only——"

"You *will* walk—it's quite settled that, my dear," winked Shark significantly, "or Dust and Jamble 'll be a-putting their precious heads together about you doing sich a thing as stepping into the gentleman's room, eh?—won't they?" And so saying, and making a very strange hieroglyphic with his nose and fingers, possibly implying some further private opinion respecting the solitary "portmanteau," he slipped again from the room, and soon returned, not foremost, but in the wake of a large fat pompous man, and a tall, shrivelled, long-necked, woman, whilst rearward of himself were three or four junior waiters, and a crowd of wondering housemaids, most of whom were armed with some insignia of office, such as a duster or a brush.

"One portmanteau and two or three small boxes only, I think you said," coughed Gloss significantly, touching the lifeless hands of the sick gentleman with his flabby fingers, "and came at seven last night in nothing better than a hired cabriolet?"

"Yes, sir—and had a bottle of soda water, sir—and went to bed directly, sir."

"He—m!" coughed Gloss, still more doubtfully. "Of course——."

"I'm sure," interrupted Miss Dust, drawing up her figure as if she were shouldering a musket, "illnesses as is doubtful paying doesn't do for Jamble's, and to add'em gratis to the superintending of linen and candlesticks 'll never do, for a hotel isn't to be got through as if it was a private house, where works is reg'lar, and times and seasons the same, so——."

"I think, ma'am," spoke little Meg, who, true to her womanly nature, still stood behind the couch with the glass of water, "that the gentleman is exceedingly ill, and ought to have a doctor."

Miss Dust looked at little Meg, and Mr. Gloss looked, mob-capped housemaids looked, and Shark winked at the preposterous suggestion of supposed unpaid charity.

"The imperance of lower housemaids," gasped Dust, "shows that wickitniss is a thing as grows as fast as gooseberries, and suggesting a doctor instead of being a-cleaning and making No. 14, is——"

"A doctor," reasoned Gloss, drowning with his deeper bass Dust's shrill treble, "involves responsibility, and a doctor might be safely called in to a carriage and an imperial, but to a hack cab and one portmanteau, it's doubtful."

"Let him have a cab and be drove some-where," commanded Miss Dust, "so it's not having sicknesses as is unpaid for at Jamble's; and sheets and laced pillow-slips, No. 37, Jamble's, 1852, equally——"

"But if I might respectfully suggest," said a little stout waiter, rising on his tiptoes, so as just to get a glance of the gentleman over Miss Dust's shoulders, " portmantoes and boxes isn't al-ways——"

" Full," interrupted one of Miss Dust's favourite satellites; " as in a si-ti-a-tion where I took and left upper works, five big boxes, as were particu-larly heavy, turned out nothing but stones, so that the——"

" Of a banking-book," continued the fat waiter, respectfully; " and as for the sick gentleman, he may have been on foreign travel."

"He—m," coughed Gloss, a little ashamed that this sagacious idea should have been lost sight of by himself, during the carrying out of the suspicion respecting the portmanteau, " pro-bably. In that case, why——."

"There!" exclaimed Miss Dust, stopping her official colleague full short, " don't let an imper-sition be a-coming over you ; it wouldn't sin-ni-fy, Mr. Gloss, as the young womens here knows if you could take and leave upper works yourself, but when it's the sheets and laced pillow-slips, as well as——"

"Hush, hush !" spoke Gloss, with an imperious wave of his hand, for the idea of foreign travel now fully occupied his mind; and during this last Dust-interruption he had looked round upon the breakfast-table, and noticed the fragments of sculpture standing thereon; " them spinx-ses and arms there, look something like it, so it may be such a thing as a well-paying gentleman travelling. Jist therefore be sprinkling his face carefully, whilst I step to Mrs. Jamble."

Intent upon this praiseworthy and cautious resolve, Mr. Gloss stepped from the room, leaving little Meg to renew her foregone act of mercy; but Miss Dust, now rather shaken in her opinion of " impersition," undertook the Samaritanal office herself, with such enthusiasm as in a few minutes to exhaust the whole contents of the water-bottle upon the face of the sick man, and to have dismissed Meg to the official duties of No. 14, with an intimation that she should speak to her in private.

Mrs. Jamble's sitting-room, though somewhat dark, and placed at the rear of the house, was excessively snug and well-furnished. It was indeed over-furnished, being clearly the receptacle for any supernumerary sofa or table from more exalted regions. It had two sideboards, two sofas, a taper-legged pianoforte, a large desk with innumerable small drawers, and round its top little brass hooks, with prodigious bunches of keys hanging thereon; all duly labelled and ticketed, and conveying notions of remote cellars brimful of excellent wine; of chests where plate was hoarded

up; of deep closets crowded with all sorts of luxurious dainties; and, as a climax, of a well-filled
cash-box over and above assets and Three-per-
Cents. Mrs. Jamble was seated at this desk,
already dressed for the day in a matronly cap and
rich satin gown, occupied in transferring into a
large green-backed ledger before her the blotted
hieroglyphics of divers little books lying at her
left hand; and Millicent, her niece, a young lady
dressed in very airy muslin, was seated near,
knitting a purse, and occasionally assisting Mrs.
Jamble to decipher the aforesaid hieroglyphics.
Miss Millicent gave a little affected cough, and
simpered, "Pray, come in," when Gloss knocked
and entered; for Mr. Wiggs, the wine-merchant,
was expected on business, and this circumstance
might account for the taper-legged piano-forte
being already open, and "Tell me, my heart,"
conspicuously set forth—Mr. Wiggs being musical, and a supposed admirer.

The head-waiter, after some circumlocution,
got out his doubts about the sick gentleman, the
responsibility of a doctor, the hired cab, and the
solitary portmanteau. In spite of a very tolera-
ble heart beneath the black satin gown, Mrs.
Jamble, imbued with due caution, was rather
inclining toward the Dust-opinion, when Miss
Millicent, totally irreverent to Mr. Wiggs' supposed admiration, exclaimed—

"I'm sure, aunt, if it's the one I accidentally
saw from Dust's room last night, with a beautiful
dark, intellectual, yet, alas! melancholy face, I'm

sure he's a gentleman. Perhaps a foreign prince in disguise."

"Well, miss and ma'am," spoke Gloss, with a dignity that implied that this idea was originally his own, "though I ain't got up quite so far as a prince, this is jist my opinion; and, of course, if he's bad, we must nat'rally try to find his friends; and as I felt he'd got a pocket-book as I was untying his neckcloth, why—why—why, we'd better open it, and this, ma'am, in your presence."

After some little hesitation—for there was good, as I have said, in the worldly heart of Mrs. Jamble—she consented to visit the sick gentleman's room; and accordingly, after adjusting her gold eye-glass and chain, and unfolding a very white and fine cambric pocket-handkerchief, she proceeded leisurely up the grand staircase, followed by her niece, the head-waiter, and even by Mr. Wiggs, who had just arrived.

The sick gentleman still lay insensible upon the couch, the group yet standing round him, with the exception of little Meg, who had been summarily dismissed to the duties of No. 14; the only alteration being in Miss Dust, who, on the approach of Mrs. Jamble, had now assumed a neutral aspect of face, as well as position, near the couch, so as to be ready, at a moment's notice, to express either charitable commiseration or her full idea of "impersition."

After a cough, and a look at his mistress and the wine-merchant, Mr. Gloss drew forth the gentleman's pocket-book. It was a large Russia leather one, bound by a strap—nothing in it to rivet every eye as it did; but on its opening depended whether there should be laced or plain pillow-slips, or none at all; whether the far-down cellar should produce its richest wines; whether Mr. Gloss should be profoundly respectful; whether Mr. Shark civil; whether Mr. Wiggs should give a favourable opinion; whether Millicent should still entertain the same sentimental idea of beauty; whether there should be a physician grave and learned; and, lastly, whether in extremity should minister the poor coarse hireling, yet withal tenderest-fashioned hand of Nature's woman, and bring in action once, and once again, the true and touching story of Lord Burleigh.

In a moment all was solved; out dropped upon the lifeless hands a roll of bank-notes, and in an inner pocket lay, with a cheque for a large amount upon a London bank, a diamond ring of immense value, just thrust carelessly in as if its price were of no account. There were no cards, no address, no private papers, except what were written in some foreign language, and no other name than the one the gentleman had given the over night of Verdun, plainly written "John Verdun" on one of the leaves. But the bank-notes were quite tangibility and name enough; for here lay princely resources, were the sickness to be lengthened out to days, days into weeks, and weeks into the monotony of months.

Like the changes of a magic lantern from dark to light, every hue was now upon the rosy side of charity and love; the only one left upon the dark side was Mr. Wiggs, in the opinion of Miss Millicent. The one that commenced directly the new overture of charity was Miss Dust, the rest having sense enough to feel that a pause and line of gradation were necessary. Therefore, whilst Mrs. Jamble and Mr. Wiggs talked aside as to the several merits of learned physicians in Saville Row, Hanover Square, Old and New Burlington Streets, Mr. Gloss listening respectfully, so as himself to act in a moment on their decision, Miss Dust was deep into the matter of the very finest sheets, such as were only now and then used for the service of a marquis or a duke, the very shadiest night-lamp (I verily believe, too, in her charitable enthusiasm there was incidental mention of a warming-pan, though it was the very height·of June), with divers other minuter matters, concluded by a pretty copious summary of her own tender and "blissid-babe-like feelings," and how "dooty in sicknesses was, as every one knew, a part in her nature." Acting promptly upon these charitable intents, she proceeded forthwith to the bedchamber to undo all which little Meg had so lately done; and exorcise the gentle spirit that hung around the spring of wall-flower. Added to this, her staff of maids were dispersed hither and thither upon immediate service for the sick gentleman; a peremptory message sent down to the kitchen respecting the probability of needed gruel; whilst in person this Samaritanal Dust kept coming back every five minutes to the drawing-room on tiptoe, to look over the couch, to sigh, and put her ear down tenderly as if she were listening to the breathings of a babe.

The physician decided upon soon arrived, and was received by Mrs. Jamble, the room being now cleared of all but herself, Mr. Wiggs, and Gloss, who had hastened back from his important mission with astonishing celerity, considering the usual pomp and slowness of his movements. The very first words the physician uttered, when he had taken the rigid hand of the sick gentleman into his own, were expressive of regret that he had not been sent for earlier, as the syncope was of a most dangerous character. This opinion becoming more confirmed, another physician was sent for, the attendance of a neighbouring surgeon required, and in a few minutes the unknown gentleman, whose life or death had, to a certain extent, hung upon the condition of his pocket-book, was surrounded by all needful care and skill. After expressing much sympathy, and promising that every attention should be given, Mrs. Jamble retired to her parlour, to find Mr. Wiggs much discomfited, and going over his own "List of Prices" by way of amusement, and Miss Millicent in a meditative humour, as she was just then in the full concoction of a pretty little romance of marriage, in which she figured as the heroine, and the sick gentleman as the hero.

Far nearer death than any episode of life, however fraught with human interest, was the unknown gentleman.   He lay still insensible, though
bled, though resting on the extraordinary laced
pillows, though watched over by the noble and
disinterested physician first called in; and still
was lying whilst the glorious summer's day waned
on; whilst evening deepened into night; whilst
this night seemed faster to roll on to the unknown
and mighty ocean of eternity.   By this time one
of the " Gamp " sisterhood had been duly inducted
into office, Miss Dust's earnest entreaty to fully
undertake its duties having been negatived by Mrs.
Jamble.   But as she reasoned " that superinten-
dency after other works was a Christian's dooty,"
she about 12 p.m. entered the sick chamber, duly
robed in deep-frilled nightcap and "sitting-up gown,"
and armed with a large prayer-book and rushlight,
having first spent an hour, as was her custom, in
Miss Millicent's bed-room.   The great subject of
confabulation had been of course on this particular
night the sick gentleman, his pocket-book, and
the doings of the small housemaid, whom Miss
Dust denounced as " bold and artful," and "much
too awkward for a sick chamber;" whereas the
simple reason was her determination that there
should be no extraneous participation in the rich
gifts that might flow forth from the marvellous
contents of the sick gentleman's pocket-book.

But quite unconscious of the mercenary hopes
and fears that were active round his pillow—of
the relieved guard of the " Gamp " sisterhood,

morning and night—of Miss Dust's bobbings in and out, sweet and tender expressions, and small ministry of various kinds—lay the sick gentleman for many days. Not wholly neglected either by Mrs. Jamble, who every day at noon, in her richest black satin, made personal inquiries, she having by this time, from certain small circumstances, invested the unknown gentleman with a mighty heirship, which investiture, duly related and commented on to her niece, went far to enrich the Millicent romance and the Dust enthusiasm. In fact, this alteration in ordinary Dust-tactics soon completely took the domestic household by surprise, of a very pleasurable kind most assuredly, for the peepings, the plottings, the war of words, the tattlings, were reduced to a minimum, and never before had the six lean housemaids found "Jamble's" such a paradise. From the morning of the rare upraised fountain, and the untrodden flower, number fourteen and thereabouts had been the allotted land of the small housemaid, who, besides any entry into the sick gentleman's chamber, was forbidden, by the sternness of Dust-morality, to make even inquiry of any sort or description.

But Truth and Nature, small housemaid, are divine qualities, never to be wholly submerged in the ocean of Dust-tactics and cunning; therefore the hours waned on for thee and thy pure life's comedy of tenderness and truth!

The gentleman had now been under Dust and Gamp-sister ministry some ten days, when one morning, about 2 o'clock a.m., Miss Dust was aroused from a deep snooze behind the curtain by the nurse, much to her mortification and displeasure, for she had instilled into the household, that such was the intense wide-awake state of her sympathies and feelings, that she never winked an eye, much less dropped off into uncharitable slumber.

"Well, my dear," said the old woman, with somewhat of a satirical grin, for she neither liked her nor her sharp system of governance, " I'm glad to see you a-dropping off a bit at last; for even them as has had rig'lar edication of sitting-up can't help it sometimes. But it's come at last, my dear. He's got the fever, and a precious catching one it'll be; but on course you don't mind it, my dear, as turns the pillow with such kristin patience ? "

Yet though Miss Dust made some answer in keeping with the vigorous nature of her foregone charity, the additional pallor that spread itself beneath the deep-frilled nightcap showed that her harpy greed had never once taken into account burning, wasting, death-giving fever. Heretofore she had zealously led in all the Samaritanal duties of the sick chamber, but at the word "fever" it might be observed that she by degrees removed to a remote part of the room, and there remained till she withdrew at an unusually early hour. That such a low thing as fever should have curtained itself within the aristocratic "Jamble's" filled the good landlady

with the greatest consternation. All the servants
were called together and enjoined to silence; for
the merest whisper that such an enemy was in
the house would at once have put to flight its
overflowing company. Mrs. Jamble was at the
same time informed that Miss Dust was much
indisposed, and that the full conclave of housemaids had one and all agreed, with the exception of the smallest and most defenceless, that
besides having other duties, they would not risk
the danger of the sick chamber, but devolve
it on Miss Dust, who had already given much
offence by her enthusiastic charity, the nurse, or
anyone else who might like to undertake the
office.

This was exactly what Dust policy had
planned. It would be convenient for her to be
ill whilst grim fever hung above the unknown
and the uncared for; it would be convenient that
the youngest, and smallest, and most unrepining
of her slaves should serve and wait whilst the
balance lay with danger and with death; it
served her purpose, because *this* smallest and *this*
least would do her ministerings faithfully and
well; and *when* all fear was over, she, Dust,
great paramount chambermaid at "Jamble's,"
could recover in a day, and thrusting forth the
dear nature that had seen not, nor thought of,
fear, or death, or self, watch the halcyon moments of recovery, and reap the golden harvest.
And what if this small fragment of humanity
perished? She was but an orphan, from a far-off

County Union!—and who would shed one tear over her unknown parish coffin?

Blessings on thee, small Meg! Be light of heart, be light of foot, be light of hand; he thou watchest has a divine spirit, and God and Truth are for thee!

Without consciousness of Dust policy, she entered on her office. Now no rough hand upon the curtains, none to snatch the pillows, none to roughly speak or roughly serve—and this not because the gentleman was rich, or might be great, but because THE HEART OF THE WOMAN WAS GENUINE!

Yet within the fever worked and raged; the throes were not less deep for being inarticulate; nor the tide of the mighty ocean of life less perilous!

Two days passed on; the third night came! The gentleman had sunk to sleep, the good physician had left some time, and the nurse had dropped off into a little preparatory nap after her first modicum of gin. Though worn by several nights' watching, in addition to her daily round of duties, small Meg sat within a few paces of the bed, in the very trimmest and tightest of brown stuff gowns, and in a very little cap with one pink bow. She had but lately stepped to the bed, and seen how deep and calm, for the first time since his severe illness, was the sick gentleman's sleep; how less the fever raged, how a gathering dew hung round his forehead and within his before scorched hand, that for hours in the delirium of fever had moved round and round on every side, as if in search of some cool space, however small, whereon to rest; and now she moved lightly again about the room, to place many small things in order, that the nurse had displaced or Miss Dust "settled" with a taste peculiar to herself. She had come back to her seat some minutes, thinking of a small plot just brought to mind by moving the vase into the place where it had first stood—which plot was no other than that the fat waiter should buy her a choice bunch of flowers for it next morning; when, hearing the curtain move, and turning quickly round, she was startled to see the sick gentleman awake from his deep sleep, sitting upright in bed, and regarding her attentively. In a moment she was by the bed, with her bright face looking into his haggard one, and asking if he were better.

"Yes," he very faintly said. She would awaken the nurse. "No!" was somewhat energetically said for one so very weak that he dropped back on to the pillow; then more faintly asking for some tea.

She quickly, though more lightly than ever, moved about; going to and fro into the ante-chamber, making the little kettle boil in no time, toasting a very thin round of bread, having the tea ready by the time the toast was done, then coming to the bed with all so nice on a tiny waiter; pouring out the tea to cool, then propping up the gentleman with pillows, and putting her own shawl, that hung on a chair, round him, lest he should take cold, then standing modestly by to hold the saucer; she might have been a nurse all her life, from the way she set about the matter. Presently the nurse woke up, and seeing the gentleman was better, and the process of tea going forward, undertook her official duties immediately, and dismissed the small housemaid for the remainder of the night.

Before, however, the nurse was aroused, or the gentleman awake next morning, she was there again, about her duties, and made everything neat and nice, even placed the flowers, which the fat waiter had brought up-stairs secretly, in the vase, by the time, which was early, the good physician arrived. Pleased to see his patient better, he sat down by the bed, and talked to him, though in a very low voice, when, presently, Meg coming into the room—for they had been alone before—the physician motioned her to the bed.

"To this good girl," he said to the gentleman, "rather than to me, you owe your life, for one more gentle, careful, tender, I have never seen; and one, I feel morally certain, who has acted from no mercenary motives." She blushed, and moved away. The physician's glance, following her, saw the vase upon the toilet—"What, even flowers this morning, housemaid?" She blushed still more.

"She thought the gentleman might like to see

them, now he was better," was her short answer as she quickly left the room.

As soon as the physician was gone, the gentleman asked the nurse for Meg; would have her come and place the vase on a little table beside the bed, and through all that day and the next, if she were near, and could be found, he would take everything from her hand, in preference to that of the nurse. This proceeding, and the absence now of all danger from the sick room, soon reached the ears of Miss Dust, who recovered forthwith so speedily from her "illness," as to be enabled the very next morning to undertake, as heretofore, her Samaritanal duties, with such prodigious enthusiasm and tenderness as to quite throw the nurse into the shade. As a matter of course, contingent on this state of affairs, Meg, whose "awkwardness was quite dreadful," was dismissed to even more remote regions of the house than number fourteen; and whenever inquired for by the sick gentleman, was either busy or not to be found.

Things went on thus for some days, Miss Dust in the meanwhile much chagrined that to her talkings and officious doings hardly came answers, and rarely more than coldest thanks. As soon as he could leave his bed, the sick gentleman was moved on his couch into the drawing-room, on which occasion Mrs. Jamble paid him a formal visit, delivered up the long-sealed pocket-book, digressed much on the aristocratic patronage bestowed on her hotel, and even treated him with small episodes concerning her marriageable niece and the late Mr. Jamble.

"You would confer a further great favour," said the gentleman, when they had thus talked some time, "if you will allow your small housemaid to continue her services. She is silent, and that is at all times a thing I covet."

Mrs. Jamble, who had suffered much from Miss Dust's loquacity, readily assented, and some half-hour after she had withdrawn Meg brought in the basin of beef-tea. More than that he was glad that she was come back again, the gentleman said little. It seemed to him a delight to lie, and have the vase brought in from the bed-room, its dead flowers removed—Miss Dust's hand had been forbidden to touch them—fresh and very choice ones sent for directly from Covent Garden, with an order for a fresh supply every morning; when come, to see Meg dress them forth, to have them put upon the table, and his books placed beside him on the couch—all of which time, few words being said, Miss Dust, whose ear was at the bed-chamber key-hole, was not much the wiser. In fact, Mrs. Jamble's command for Meg to resume her customary duties came like a thunderbolt upon the head chambermaid, who, after a good, hearty cry, resolved that, either through the agency of Miss Millicent, Gloss, her own, or all combined, the reign of the small housemaid should be short. To carry out this admirable resolve, she immediately commenced an elaborate system of espionage, in which she was ably and heartily assisted by Shark, who, having had a deaf ear turned to his own ardent suit, was sufficiently spiteful and vicious to make an admirable ally. There were, therefore, quick comings into the rooms whenever possible; following her steps in every direction, and a continuous ear at the various accessible key-holes. One thing, however, wholly defeated any success that might have arisen from listening. The gentleman, by habit taciturn, scarcely ever spoke to Meg, though she might be for a whole hour about the room, or even waiting by his side. Yet he would look up into her face often if she were standing by, not rudely, not haughtily, not as the high might look upon the humble, but ever as one owing much that could not be repaid by money gifts, and as one whose best homage to purity was silence. Yet, too, he would watch her all about the room, laying down *then* the newspaper or book by which he had shaded his upturned glance, liking to see her arrange the morning's fresh bouquet, his books, his papers; yet all this in silence. Still withal, small Meg knew her services were gratefully received; it was pleasant to her to feel that for once hireling duty was worthily received, and pleasurable, to her womanly and most genuine nature, to be convinced that this same duty and service were estimated in the same spirit as that in which they were bestowed.

Wonderfully debilitated by so severe an illness, it was nearly a month before the gentleman could leave his couch to walk, by painful steps, across the room; and through all this time Meg had waited tenderly and well, Miss Dust listened, Mr. Shark "popped in" on tiptoe, and yet not one word had been heard satisfactory to Miss Dust's ears, or one blush, with all the "poppings-in" seen upon small Meg's face. One night, however, after a pretty long confabulation in the brush-and-duster senate-house, the mighty chambermaid and Shark took up their usual position by the most admissible key-hole. Meg had just gone in with the evening's letters. There was, as they could hear, some wine and medicine to fetch from the ante-chamber. When brought, the gentleman spoke, and asked Meg why she never wore the brown gown now, and the cap with the pink bow. Meg's voice trembled very much—even Miss Dust could distinguish *that*.

"I thought, sir, it had grown too shabby to wait upon you, and the pink in the cap, sir, is quite faded."

"Wear the gown, though, Meg—it will never be old or shabby to me; but—but—the time will be quickly here, Meg, when I shall be able to talk of that and other things, with full justice to you."

He seemed to take her hand, which must have been quickly withdrawn, and that without a spoken word, for she went again into the ante-chamber.

"Well, there," whispered Miss Dust, absolutely gasping with delight, and touching Mr. Shark significantly on the shoulder, "it's jist what I thought! Yes—the time is coming, I daresay, but it shan't be at Jamble's, as never had yet a breath upon its private character, nor public neither, up-stairs nor down-stairs.   No, miss, missis may be kind to customers and humour their wishes, but it shall never come to *that*, or else a respectable young woman like me (she was above fifty) as has a character to maintain, shall pack up her four boxes and her two trunks, and put a quarter's wages in Mrs. Jamble's hands and say, There, ma'am, it's a sacrifice on course, but it's what a modest young woman is driven to by an unnameable miss, as shall be buried in silence. Yes, and a pretty taste he must have, as has had a Christian-spirited upper housemaid to wait on him."

The point thus broached in the latter part of her speech made Miss Dust so uncommonly indignant, that she was necessitated to retire to her senate-house, and there give her wrath its due vent; after which explosion she put on her best cap, produced two wine-glasses, and a little something from a corner cupboard, sent down a private and confidential message to Mr. Gloss, who, arriving, was closeted with her, till Miss Millicent's bell rung, as signal for attendance on her toilette.   As this young lady was much given, as I have before mentioned, to the concoction of romances, the mystery that still hung round the sick gentleman, his long illness, the many reports that had reached her of his generosity and kindness, and, moreover, her settled belief that she

was born to great and romantic things in the way
of marriage, inclined her not merely to lend a
willing ear to all Miss Dust had to communicate,
but also to pass many unjust and severe remarks
upon Meg's pretty face and humble fortunes.
For it was mortifying to consider that whilst she,
the sole niece and heiress of Mrs. Jamble, must
manœuvre and plot to obtain peeps and abrupt
glances, this small housemaid, whom she always
passed with such supreme indifference, could talk,
and look, and wait upon this gentleman, and this
with effect, if the matter of the brown gown and
pink cap might be taken as a guarantee. Accordingly next day Miss Millicent took care to
inform Mrs. Jamble of certain particulars concerning Meg, how long she stayed in the sick
gentleman's room, how much she talked, and so
on. But the landlady, on the whole, having a
good heart, and liking Meg, and feeling assured
that she was a good as well as virtuous girl,
looked much more favourably upon the matter;
but when from day to day, after this time, Mr.
Gloss would give significant shakes of the head,
Miss Dust drop astounding hints, not daring
wholly to speak that which had no truth within
it, and Miss Millicent say that "it was a pity
some people were imposed upon," Mrs. Jamble
began to think that there must be really something in the matter. She therefore, after due
consultation with her niece, sent for Meg, much,
be it remarked, against Miss Dust's desire. When
come, and taxed with her sins, Meg, as she could

truly, denied them with many tears, and in such earnest, honest sort of fashion that Mrs. Jamble believed her from the very bottom of her heart.

"It is indeed true, ma'am," confessed Meg, "about the gown and cap, but that could only become known through listening. Otherwise the gentleman rarely, very ·rarely talks, or as for giving me money, ma'am, he never in his whole life offered me so much as one sixpence, or the value of it."

"Indeed I believe you, my good girl," said the landlady, much touched, "but as a gentleman, probably of high station, and really so wealthy, can have no honourable ——"

"Indeed, ma'am," interrupted Meg, "he never has offered one insult, or even made approach to one—indeed, ma'am, never."

"Possibly not, Meg; his meaning may be not less dishonourable for being hidden. To prevent this, and save you many bitter years, the more especially as I think you a very good and honest girl, and should be sorry to see any misfortune fall upon you, I forbid your further attendance upon Mr. Verdun, strictly forbid it, and must never again hear of your carrying flowers into any chamber of my house. It is a fault I never had to find with Dust."

True! O Jamble, Dust *was* quite incapable of much beyond a lie. But be of good hope, small Meg, he thou hast watched over has a divine heart, and God and Truth are for thee!

Thus prohibited — and there were plenty of

watchful eyes to see that this prohibition was not in-
fringed upon—Meg's services were again apportion-
ed to her in a distant part of the house, and Miss
Dust resumed her sway, assisted by Mr. Shark and
a minor satellite.   Everything for some days pro-
gressed through the same clock-work round, only
it was observable that the flowers, when brought
each morning, lay to fade upon the table, and that
every time the doors opened, whether he were
walking, lying down, or sitting at the table, the
gentleman turned round as if to look for some
one.   On the fourth evening he abruptly asked
Shark why he was not waited upon as usual; and
when that worthy, with an obsequious bow, declared he did not know, the gentleman wrote a
note, sealed it, and dispatched the waiter with it
downstairs.   As, of course, was necessary, Mr.
Shark could not pass without stepping into the
Dust senate-house; and the worthy owner, after
inspecting the note on every side, fully convinced that it was on some affair touching small
Meg, declared she would be its bearer.

It was eight o'clock in the evening, and Mr.
Wiggs, somewhat low in hope and heart, was taking a "friendly cup of tea" with Miss Millicent
and her aunt—that admirable young lady, not liking the worthy Wiggs wholly to depart, though
the before-mentioned small romance absorbed
her much, kept playing with the passion of her
admirer as a cat does with a mouse—giving him
now a little hope, then pouncing upon him with
extraordinary cold looks and icy words, while

Wiggs, looking at both the Three-per-Cents. and the ready cash, as well as at Miss Millicent, bore on with much fortitude.

Mrs. Jamble brought the candle much nearer to her, for it was dark always at an early hour in her parlour, read the note over very carefully two or three times, then, to Miss Dust's astonishment, after looking absorbedly at the tea-pot, into the sugar-basin, and up to the ceiling, said—

"Let Shark immediately present my dutiful respects to Mr. Verdun, and say that, as I cannot give a written answer to his note, I will wait upon him to-morrow at noon precisely."

After receiving this message, Miss Dust lingered for a minute or two to see if anything further would be communicated, but Mrs. Jamble remaining silent, she left the room, closed the door, and listened outside.

"Only think, my dear sir," spoke Mrs. Jamble, when Dust had closed the door, "of Mr. Verdun actually writing about Meg, asking to have her wait upon him again, and says his motives towards her are most honourable, as he shall prove. What do you think?"

Mr. Wiggs looked doubtfully at Miss Millicent, but his better nature triumphed.

"He really *may*—such romantic things have been."

Miss Millicent glanced with supreme contempt upon her admirer—

"What! as handsome and rich gentlemen marrying ugly servant-maids? I'm surprised at your offering such an opinion, Mr. Wiggs; but, of course, aunt can but act in one way, that is, dismiss the girl altogether."

"This is really what I must do," spoke the landlady after a moment or two's reflection, Miss Millicent's humane suggestion not having presented itself to her mind; "a disgrace must not fall on 'Jamble's;' and I shall be able to say with perfect truth to Mr. Verdun, 'the servant you inquire after, sir, has left this respectable west-end hotel, and I'm not at liberty to say where she is gone.'"

This determination so elated Miss Millicent, as it did much towards the furthering of her romance, that instead of remaining to play divers touching songs to Mr. Wiggs, as she had promised before tea, she presently adjourned with Mrs. Jamble to her bed-room. From thence she was deputed with much solemnity and secrecy to search out Meg, whilst Mrs. Jamble concocted a small moral sermon ready for delivery, and determined to add an extra pound to the quarter's wages which were due. Small Meg, in morning cap and gown, was busy in a suite of apartments just vacated, and received Mrs. Jamble's summons with much surprise. She begged to remain and change her dress, but of this Miss Millicent would hear nothing, so just as she was found they descended to the landlady's bedchamber. Mrs. Jamble was there ready with her sermon, and the wages screwed up in a piece of paper, and, intermingled with the delivery of the first, she gave in detail certain portions of her reason why Meg should then, that very night, pack up her few clothes, receive her wages, and depart, without further communication with the rest of the servants.

"For, my good girl, gentlemen in these days are full of evil designs; and it would be such a disgrace on this respectable family hotel, and would always grieve me to think that I had allowed you to remain in harm's way. I have no alternative then but to dismiss you, without giving any information to the rest of my servants, and with the gift of this extra pound."

"I'm much obliged," replied the little housemaid, bursting into tears, "but it's late to-night, and I haven't a relative or friend in London, and know no one, except an old woman with whom I once lodged. And as for Mr. Verdun, he never——"

This evident desire to remain, and the denial of evil word or look from the sick gentleman, seemed so much like guilt in the eyes of Miss Millicent, and presently in Mrs. Jamble's also, that Meg was somewhat peremptorily dismissed to pack her solitary box with as much haste as possible, whilst a cab should wait for her in a back street that ran in the rear of the hotel. To see that she held no further communication with the servants, Miss Millicent followed Meg to her humble garret bed-chamber, and sat down on one of the beds whilst the small box was packed. At first the heavy things were put into the box, next the gowns one by one, at last the brown one, that had been so often watched and looked after when Meg little thought or knew that it was more precious than costliest velvet or richest satin ; that linked long years of care, of stern and solitary thought, of life without a home or one endearing tie, to a new spiritual life that seemed like youth again ; that was the sign of a new life, a new world, a host of new enjoyments, the signet and the seal of a new appreciation of nature, and the divine human heart !—that was the outer covering of one that with poor, coarse, hireling hand had yet ministered with the faith and tenderness of an angel ! Touch it lightly, Meg, be careful of it ; he that has looked upon it has a divine heart, and God and Truth are with you !

Miss Millicent, however, looked at it with eyes askance, little dreaming of these things; though had she known its coming day of destiny, she would have verily torn it into little pieces and scattered them to the winds. But it went into the box, other things with it, all locked ; the pink cap in another box, that corded, Meg in her shawl and bonnet, the cabman came up the back stairs and took them down, Meg following, and with no more adieu than a haughty nod from Miss Millicent, she has quitted Jamble's Hotel, and is gone on her lonely, tearful, unregarded way !

*   *   *   *

Soon after this event, there commenced, in most of the daily papers, a series of advertisements, to the effect that if a certain M. who through the months of June and July lived as under-housemaid at J—— Hotel, —— Street, Piccadilly, would call upon a certain solicitor in Lincoln's Inn, she would hear of something much to her advantage; or any one discovering the present residence of the said M. should be handsomely rewarded. It was soon evident, however, by this advertisement appearing from week to week, that M. had never applied for this something so greatly to her advantage; possibly she was not a reader of newspapers, or had removed a long way off. The police, too, began to remark and talk it over at the various station-houses, that there was scarcely one of a division that had not been addressed by a gentleman, more particularly if they were on duty in by-streets or unfrequented districts, and always respecting the same person—a girl some eighteen years of age, and a servant, supposed to be out of place. The description of dress and features was always the same. Then, perhaps for some weeks, the inquiry would die away, then be made suddenly again in districts of London most remote from one another, with always the same negative and failure.

At last, one very cold November night, a cab came westward into Russell-square, and driven to its eastern side, out jumped a gentleman very lightly clad for so cold a night, followed by a small fat man, with very low quarter shoes, and with a very great habit of bringing his right hand up to his left arm as if he were tucking something under it. The gentleman turned into Bernard-street, followed by the small fat man, and stopped the first policeman; there was the same old question put as heretofore, only now with more certainty.

"I think I have seen such a person as you describe come up the area step of one of those empty houses, a few yards down on the other side of the way." In a moment the policeman had crossed the street, and stood with the gentleman before the house. It was a gloomy-looking place, evidently long shut up; the windows, through the interstices of dust and cobwebs, showing blank distances of wall and ceiling, more cold and dreary than the street outside. There was light, however, through the basement windows, which danced and flickered on the area wall like a sprite of cheerfulness. As they were about to ring, an old woman with a small bundle on her arm issued from the door and came up the area steps. She did not appear to heed the group, but, closing the gate, was moving onwards, when the fat man, pushing back the gentleman, said almost breathlessly,

"Is Meg down there? I'm an old friend."

"Yes, you'll find her; the door's on the latch." And as if her heart was full of sorrow, or her errand an earnest one, she passed as quickly onward as her feebleness would allow. The gentleman was quicker, for he was already half way down the area steps, till stopped by the small fat man.

"Bliss ye, sir, jist let me step one minute before. If it shouldn't be Meg, it will be the old sorrow and disappointment over again." He had passed the gentleman before an answer could come, had looked in at the window, and was back again. The fat waiter's whole heart was in his voice when he said—

"Yes, yes, yes, sir, it *is* Meg, and looking blooming too, God bless her!"

"You'll wait here," added the gentleman.

"Oh! yes, sir, I understand—a situation of the kind don't need company."

Mr. Verdun softly opened the door and entered the kitchen. It was bare of all furniture excepting two chairs, a table, and an old dresser; the fire was very scant and dull, and the girl was seated by it, with her head bent down, and some work lying idly in her lap. He had looked at her, was by her side, had spoken, before she saw him; then it was with a sort of paralyzed wonder of pain, fear, sorrow, liking, all combined.

"Meg," he said again. She turned very pale, partly rose; needed not wholly to do so; for she was raised and in his arms.

"Dear love, and is it you, after all these months!"

Some thought of Jamble seemed to come across her mind, for she flinched away from his manly grasp.

"Not so, not so, Meg, unless you will not be what you shall be to-morrow morning—*my wife.*"

"Oh, sir," she faintly said, as her face drooped beneath his passionate kisses, "recollect what I am, only fit to wait upon you, and be what I am—your servant."

"Fit to be my wife, Meg, no man shall gainsay it. If I loved you then, if I admired your tenderness, if I worshiped your womanly purity, I do much more now, knowing the circumstances that surrounded you. Meg, it is small payment, but it is the best I can give you to make you *mine.* God bless you, Meg, and thank you for your angel service."

And then like a child, a very little child, the stern man wept and knelt beside the girl. Ay, Meg, was I not right, he thou didst watch had a divine heart, and God and Truth were with thee!

Yet, without comment on himself or his private circumstances, he sat beside Meg, still with his arms around her, and told her of his many interviews with Mrs. Jamble, how on all occasions, and on moral grounds, she had refused to say where Meg was; how he had advertised and searched, and paid for the services of others; how, when all hope seemed lost, he had accidentally met with the fat waiter, who had been expelled from "Jamble's" on account of his advocacy of Meg, and the tale-bearing propensities of Mr. Shark, and how some clue to Meg's abode had been gained by the observance of the post-mark on a letter to Mrs. Jamble.

"Yes, sir, I have been trying for a place ever since I left."

" And have got one for life, Meg, and for which
your character is not written upon paper, but
upon a human heart; but where's the brown
gown?" She coloured very much and drooped
her head.

" Not gone, I hope, nor given."

" I have been living on my clothes, sir." At
last Meg faintly said, " I kept it to the very last,
but it was obliged to go to-night, the poor creature who has so long and so kindly given me shelter
had no bread."

" She who opened the area-gate?"   ·

" Yes, sir, the last thing I possess; it was in her
bundle."

" More noble still, Meg, to have kept some
thought about the gown. But I shall leave money
with your friend, not with you—it shall not be
said that you ever took money of mine till *you
were mine*. So let the gown be yours again, have
it on by ten o'clock to-morrow morning, and I
will be ready to give the trust you shall keep."
In this sort of way, but with no explanation, letting Meg take him for what he was, the " rich
gentleman at Jamble's," he sat and talked till the
old woman returned, to be astonished to see a
grand and well-dressed stranger sitting in that poor
place, and more so when he gave her so much
money as five pounds. But she had heard Meg
often speak of the " kind gentleman," and partly
perhaps guessed the truth, for she presently digressed into small episodes concerning Meg's
kindness and sad struggles of late with poverty,

but needed not to guess when Verdun, presently going, said good-bye in words that told so much. The small fat waiter would have liked a second glance at Meg, added thereto possibly an explosion at the cost of Miss Dust and Gloss, but as this was not permitted, he was soon once more westward with the gentleman.

Brightest of November mornings was it when the good people of Bernard-street, Russell-square, looking up from their breakfast-tables, and coming to the windows immediately, beheld a noble carriage and pair standing before the long empty house. It was more a marvel, too, when a crowd began to collect, and passers-by talk out that there was going to be a wedding. The people opposite had never seen any one issue from the house, except an old woman and a young girl from the basement story; and conjecture was added to their wonder, when, the crowd parting, they saw a grave middle-aged gentleman lead this same young girl, clad in the identical stuff gown they had so often seen, up the area steps, and place her within the carriage. The girl had on a straw bonnet, but no shawl; when once within the carriage, however, and the gentleman had followed, he took up a costly one from the seat and placed it about her shoulders. But even then she did not look up, but sate with her face buried in her hands, as if she dared not look round upon the grandeur that had so suddenly encompassed her. Two footmen closed the door, and as the carriage drove off, the crowd, catching up some portion of the truth, huzzaed with hearty voice.

All the while the carriage was on its way to a church near Portland-place he sate with her hand within his own; the once hireling hand that had spread his pillow with tenderness, when all else was mere heartlessness and money service. Another private carriage waited before the church, out of which now came some gentlemen, one of whom took small Meg's trembling arm and led her into the church. Never once yet had she looked up, never once since she had left the poor kitchen. Scarcely did she when she reached the altar; but knelt down as if half unconscious. There was another couple waiting for the holy office, others arriving: amidst this crowd, however, she knelt, neither looking to the right nor to the left, but straight up with tearful eyes, when it was asked, and she said, " Yes," not doubtingly as if it were a word of bondage, but gratefully, purely, truthfully from the heart. And when the ring was on, the last word said, he raised her proudly up and whispered " *Mine!*" Who in the wedding-party just arrived saw and heard this? To whose eyes was it surprise and wonder? To whose heart envy and bitterness? To whose heart a pleasure? Why, to no less than Mrs. Jamble, Miss Millicent and Mr. Wiggs—Miss Millicent in richest satin—but a weed beside the human flower, as pure and natural as the one which had not been trodden, but raised and placed within the garlanded pitcher!

For a moment the haughty man dropped the little arm within his own, spoke to Mrs. Jamble, took the small arm again, and swept loftily down the aisle. Mrs. Jamble whispered to Miss Millicent, Miss Millicent to Mr. Wiggs, Mr. Wiggs to Gloss, who was there in his blackest coat to see the ceremony, and all eyes followed the small stuff gown, and the little drooping figure within it.

The strangers were parted with at the church door, and the carriage swiftly bore the bridegroom and the bride to the Euston-square station. All that day they travelled through the rich counties of England, stopping at Birmingham to dine, and from thence proceeding again in the carriage. Nightfall was early, and little could be seen, but by eight or so some gates swung back, then came a softer road, then a continuous ticking noise on the carriage top, as if from the dipping branches of sweeping trees. She clinging to him closer; lights were seen, the carriage stopped, he lifting her out, taking her arm, leading her up a step or two, through a lofty, ancient hall, by clusters of servants, into a magnificent old library, in which a great fire glowed, in which the night meal was spread in costly plate, in which, on another table, placed by a small low chair of richest velvet, stood the well-remembered rustic pitcher filled with fragrant flowers: they together thus alone, he clasped her to his heart, and whispered, "Meg, thine—all thine!"

"Oh, sir——," she lowlily began to say.

"Not sir, Meg—never that again, but *husband.* And now so long kept back, let me say what you are, and what I am—the wife of Sir John Verdun, in this his Leicestershire home. Not merely Meg then, therefore, but Lady if you will, though that, love, cannot add one glory to your sweet, womanly nature. If you have been humble, Meg, by chance of circumstance, it is henceforth my vowed duty to raise this humility to the height that is its own from God—as raised I up, unconsciously, thy flower and placed it in the fountain. And now, by God's good grace, a happy life with thee, not knowing me for what I was, or the wealth that's mine: but was merciful, gentle, tender to one you knew not, to one so long solitary, to one long neither too well nor too happy. But now to supper, sweet bride, sweet love, sweet life!"

She clung to him faintly, still whispering something of her own unworthiness.

"Not one word more, Meg—but boldly look on me, and then around—*all is thine!*"

The night closed in, and earth was richer for this true and touching story of the New Lord Burleigh.

Twice or thrice during the reading of the story, Mr. Billy's obstreperous cry for sugar has disturbed the little company; but silence happily reigns, as the last words die upon the ear.

"I hope, ladies," asks Miss Hazlehurst, a little spent and worn by reading, "that you have been amused, and that the time has passed agreeably?"

"It has indeed," they say, simultaneously—that is to say, six ladies out of seven, for Miss Simpkins only shakes her head—"we much wish we had oftener an opportunity of passing it in so pleasant a manner."

"Well, ladies, when our dear friend, Miss Morfe, comes back, I will speak to her, as to some stories I think she knows. She has been a writer, and must have ample stores."

"For my part," chimes in Sophia, "I think the time might be much better spent in chatting a bit socially about one's friends and affairs. As to that Meg you have been just reading about, I think that she was an artful baggage; and if I'd been that old, foolish Mrs. Jamble, I'd have sent her where she would have never seen that man again. That girl turned into 'my lady!'—I really hate such sentimental stuff."

"People's tastes differ, Miss Simpkins," replies Mrs. Boston. "Now we'll talk no more, but have a little refreshment."

"Oh, thank you," snarls Sophia, "I must be going, ginger-wine and crisp biscuits don't agree with *my* stomach."

"But, my dear," begins Mrs Boston.

"Oh, thank you, I must be going." So hurrying across the room, she begins to put on her shawl. When it is on she returns towards the fire-place.

"Do stay," entreats the hospitable old lady,

"the tray is set all ready. It isn't ginger-wine this time, but a pair of fine fowls my sister sent me, as well as some boiled custards and raspberry puffs of my own making." So saying, the old lady repairs to her little storeroom.

Miss Sophia, being passionately fond of boiled custards, would now give her ears to have said nothing about going. However, delicacy of thought or feeling being unknown to her, she has murmured a consent, and is ready to take off her shawl, as the delicious viands appear. But good luck is wisely against her.

"I think I'll have—I think I'll have—" begins the parrot in an ominous sort of croak.

Knowing what will follow, and guessing rightly that her favourite is in a particularly obstinate and vicious mood, through being aware that a well-filled sugar-basin is in the cupboard, she shakes her hand at him fiercely.

"Hush, sir!—hush, sir!"

But the sage bird affects not to comprehend. Only winking his dull eyelids, he goes on—

"I think I'll have—I think I'll have——"

Lifting him off the chair-back, she shakes him well. Still he croaks on—

"I must go," she says hurriedly, and with a sigh, as her eyes fall on the supper. "I may be wanted—and—good night, ladies." Thus, in a sort of breathless terror, which all can see, she hastens to the door; but uselessly—her familiar is even with her.

"I think I'll have," he calls in his loudest

voice, adding *sotto voce,* as she is closing the door behind her—*" a little drop of rum !"*

The effect is so transcendantly comic, that none can resist a merry laugh. It being well known that the parrot only repeats what his mistress says, and that this is a phrase he nightly hears when she is about to indulge in those sweet drops of which she has been long suspected, though disclaiming to the world all drink stronger than very mild beer.

The little pleasantry over, Lady Herbert's Gentlewomen gather round the table, and sup none the less happily for this exorcism of an evil spirit from their midst.

CHAPTER IV.

A MOTHER'S WOE.

THE sun shines pleasantly into the matron's parlour—lies without in golden glory on the crocus-covered flower-borders—whilst the mistress, sitting near one of the windows, is busy at her writing-table with the daily accounts she has to keep. But the beauty and warmth of the sweet spring evening sun seem lost to her perception, for when she pauses in her task it is only to listen intently, as though for some distant sounds, or to glance at the time-piece upon the mantel-shelf. When it is five o'clock Rhoda brings in the tea-things, and, busying herself about the table, places them with neat dexterity. She is thus employed when the door again opens, and a squat, plain-featured girl of about twenty, dressed in tawdry finery, presents herself. Approaching the matron's chair, she announces, whilst fastening a band and buckle about her waist, that she is going out to tea.

The matron asks where.

"Oh, only to the Claytons'," she answers quickly, and colouring as she speaks. "Agnes sent up for a crochet pattern about four o'clock, and as I could not find it just then I thought I would take it myself, and have a cup of tea. I will be back by prayer-time, and as I have made Julia Stanton monitress, the children will take no harm. Besides, as you expect George, my going will leave you undisturbed."

"True—but George will, I hope, stay a few days; and thus there will be time enough for us to talk over our affairs. I only hesitate at your going to the farm so much, for the reason of what may be said. Village people will talk, Mary, especially at your going there uninvited so often as you do. The old mother is surly, and likes people's room better than their company, and the daughters' civility goes for little, whilst young Clayton is only half master of the house."

"Well, at any rate," she answers flippantly, "I don't go to see him. He's scarcely civil to me, though there are those that ought to be learning their catechism and knitting stockings instead, that he's always seeing after, and not uninvited. It is well I don't find them out, as perhaps I may."

Saying this she glances at the girl, who, bending down her face, takes up her tray and leaves the room.

"Miss Jones," says the mistress, severely, as soon as the door is closed, "I will not have this sort of conversation held in presence of the children. Rhoda and the elder girls are, as far as I know, innocent and good—dear Rhoda particularly so. A teacher should hold her self-respect, and this cannot be if she places herself on terms of womanly equality with those whom she has to instruct. As to your seeking young Clayton as you do, it is much talked about, for he has never given you, I understand, any reason to think he prefers you to another, or shown you other than such common-place civility as he might show any woman. In this case a girl with a spark of self-respect would keep aloof, however cordial the young man's sisters may be. I have noted this foolish weakness with much regret, and I must say if it is not more judiciously controlled, I must supply myself with another teacher. Neither your uncle's reputed wealth as a neighbouring farmer, nor the pressing recommendations you brought from two neighbouring clergymen, will avail if this conduct is persisted in."

"I don't want to go," she answers angrily, "and I won't go now. I always guessed the elder girls were more favourites than I, and now I know it. I should have only been absent two hours at the most. I have presided at the children's tea, and I should be back ere they go to bed; and I thought an hour or two with my friends would be better than moping alone in the hall whilst they were at play."

"As you decided upon so doing, go," says the

matron, concisely; " but another time recollect my permission is necessary first. As you say, a quiet hour with my son will be agreeable." And speaking thus sententiously, the matron resumes her pen.

Closing the door rudely behind her, crossing the wide hall or passage with its massive oaken-balustraded staircase, and entering the baronial kitchen, she looks round for Rhoda. The pretty maid, assisted by two others, is preparing toast, bread and butter, and other viands for the parlour—it being the office of the elder girls to assist Tibb, and the other woman-servant, in all such duties as will prepare them fittingly for domestic service.

" Rhoda," says the teacher angrily, as for the moment she approaches the table where the pretty maid stands, " if you go out to play you'll not stay later than six or a little after. You have to finish that fine hemming for me before you go to bed ; and mind, if it is not attended to, I'll punish you severely to-morrow."

Saying this, and waiting for no reply, she hurries from the kitchen, and thence, by a passage, to the sunny cloister.

Weary at length of her duties, of watching the timepiece, and listening for some expected sounds, Mrs. Hutchinson rises, throws on a shawl, and going forth by a private door into the garden, takes her way by the hall-gardens to the outer lawn, and so to the white gates that bound the highway. Here stands old Harris, porter and gardener combined, smoking his pipe in the evening sun—and near him Nanny, Miss Morfe's faithful maid. She was once on the foundation of Shirlot, but now for two years has been the dutifullest of handmaids to a noble-hearted woman.

"Are you expecting your mistress, Nanny?"

"Yes, indeed, ma'am, and gladly enough, too," replies Nanny, with the habitual curtsey to her ten years' honoured mistress; "for the time seems to have been so long since Miss Amy and Miss Morfe went. The latter sent a letter to Miss Hazlehurst this morning, and so I've been preparing all day; and as the kettle boils and tea is ready, I've just run to the gate to look for her."

Even whilst Nanny thus speaks, carriage wheels approach, and in a moment more one of Temeford's yellowest and tubbiest "flies" stays before the lodge gate, which old Harris prepares to open. A little woman with a large nose, but kindly face, has been looking out of one of the fly windows with divers nods and smiles, and now descending as the carriage stops in the wide drive, greets the matron warmly, for they are friends of the sincerest kind. She has also loving words for her servant, who, gathering up carpet bag and box, hurries off to her mistress's quaint home in the left cloister. In age Miss Morfe is about fifty-two—for gentlewomen are eligible for Lady Herbert's noble charity at the age of fifty—and Amy Morfe has been a recipient of its bounty two years. She is also deaf, as is soon known by her producing a marvellous trumpet from her bag; but, this hindrance and bodily feebleness apart, she is the brightest and happiest of human souls. The heroic little woman has fought the fight of life more grandly than a hundred Herculean men.

"Peace be to Shirlot," she says, with a moved voice, as with upraised face she casts her gaze across the lawn, and upon the fine old pile, now gilded on its western side in all the splendid beauty of the setting April sun. "Peace and loving-kindness be within its walls, say I, who return to it with a grateful heart." Then after a moment's pause she adds, "It is very good of you, Ann—you see I will call you after your great namesake—to be thus at the gate to welcome in this humblest of your large household."

"No, dear lady," replies Ann, "I must not take a credit which is not mine. I expect my son from Temeford, and came thus far to look for him, as he is late. Not but that our kindest gentlewoman is welcome home."

"I know it," she answers; "every leaf and bud seems to welcome me, and I am sure it is so with my friends. But what is the matter? No further trouble about George?"

"Not much," she replies evasively. "He has left Shugborough's, and is going up to London, to a situation there."

"Left Shugborough's! That's ill news—the old man is one of the best and most enlightened men in Temeford."

"Yes," rejoins the mother, with unconcealed pain, "it is a pity. I say so much to you, Miss

Morfe, to whom I can speak unreservedly—but they have not agreed, and so it is best they should part. George may be steadier with new masters, and away from old associates."

"But London, Mrs. Hutchinson, is a sad place for those easily moved to temptation. You do not know it as I do, who lived there many years."

"Perhaps not, Miss Morfe," she answers sadly; "but as things are, his going cannot well be helped. I must hope for the best. Mothers must pity and forgive, though all the world frown."

"Yes, indeed, and so must sisters—and indeed every woman who has selfish and reckless men to deal with. I have had my share of this sort of woe, God help me! But it is best to hope through all, for the lad may yet thrive, in spite of present selfishness. Now I will run away and leave you to your tender watch; and if you can spare a few minutes through the evening, come in and speak to me, and recollect my sympathy is yours at all times."

Thus saying, the worthy gentlewoman hurries away to her cloister and its classic room; while Mrs. Hutchinson, opening the gate, goes forth into the winding highway, and so onwards a little distance, till where the road, sweeping down a steep declivity, crosses the narrow valley that lies below.

It is a lovely country—a land of hills—that region of north-western England once covered by the forest of Shirlot, that forest lost amidst mightier forests, when over the country in her

young days were spread what Matthew of West-
minster, in terror, calls "the dread woods." The
nearest town of Temeford twelve miles away—the
little rustic hamlet almost hidden by the acclivity
on which the hall or hospital of Shirlot stands—
the highway but a mere thread crossing the green
distances—the country opposite the gates a broken
sweep of forest land sloping to the brawling river,
still forest land beyond that—beyond that again
upland farms and fields, till the hills rise up in the
far distance, and form a skyward wall against the
darkening sky. Altogether it is a lovely environ-
ment—solitary, peaceful, grandly picturesque—a
fitting setting for the manifold hearths of a blessed
human deed!

Shrubberies and gardens, rising slightly behind
the hall, slope downward in a lawny tract to the
river, which, thus winding partly round the acclivity
on which the hall stands, forms a peninsula on
the other side. In the arc of this lies the hamlet,
two farms, eight or nine cottages, the parsonage,
the church, the ale-house and general shop combined. These neighbouring the little ford consti-
tute the hamlet of Shirlot.

The matron's vigil is but a short one, for soon
there comes towards her a light-stepped youth;
nearer he comes, and you see his dark hair, his
small, degenerate, cunning eyes, his low forehead,
his sensual mouth, his braggart air. He has
spirit enough of a certain kind; yet, when his lips
return his mother's passionate caress, they might

touch stone or wood, so cold and heartless is their motion.

"Dear George!" she says, in her warm, idolatrous way, "I am so glad to see you! I hope we shall have some happy days together. I have got you a bed at the 'Shirlot Arms,' and you can take your meals in my room. But you are late, I have been expecting you since four o'clock."

"I daresay; but a fellow can't be as punctual as a girl in a school-room. The truth is, young Honeyman, and a few others, gave me a bit of dinner at the 'Swan,' and we did not separate till near four. I then went to Jedman's stables for a horse, and so came on."

"A horse, George? That's at least half-a-guinea. And who'll take it back?—and where is it? You should be more careful, seeing the debts I have to pay."

The irritability of his criminal nature is aroused at once: "Come, there, mother, I've had enough of that! I'm past the days of catechising. As to the horse, I left it at a farm below there—I shall want it again."

"What for?"

He hesitates a moment, and then he says in a quick, off-hand manner, "Well, the truth is, mother, I'm going back to-night, and to London early in the morning."

"To London, George!" she says, stopping short in her walk, and looking up with blank and agonized face into his. "What do you mean?— You're surely not in earnest?"

"Earnest? Yes, I am. You must find up the coin, and give me some tea—or, what's better, a glass of brandy, and then I'll rid you of a plague."

"George, you are harder and crueller than ever! To London! What do you need there?—Who is urging you to go? Your engagement does not commence till ten days hence. What will you do in the meanwhile?"

"Why, enjoy myself," he replies, with a flippant laugh. "I'll then become the 'good apprentice,' and stir pestle and mortar with all diligence!"

She is so disgusted at his flippant raillery, so wounded by his heartless oblivion of all she has lately suffered for his sake, as to make no reply; and so, as far as conversation goes, they proceed onward in silence. But he is not otherwise dumb; he hums snatches of popular songs, plucks at the hedge, or raps his boots with the switch he carries; and when at last they reach the lodges, he turns in at the white gate, to hail old Harris and the flyman, the latter of whom has stayed to refresh his horse in the stable-yard of the lodge opposite to the one occupied as a dwelling.

Taking her way through the gardens, the mother gives vent to her bitter tears, and her eyes are still red with weeping when she enters her pleasant room. Here ringing, she bids old Tibb wait at tea, and then inquires after the elder girls.

"Why, all on 'em, missis, be gone out to play,

except Rhoda, and she's got doing some hemming in the hall the teacher set her."

" Really, Mary Jones pushes her authority too far," replied the matron, a little angrily ; " and as Rhoda is one of the best and most industrious of children, I will not have her deprived of her small pleasures."   Speaking thus, Mrs. Hutchinson repairs to the hall by a flight of stone steps leading from the passage, and there, solitary on a form, and within full sight of Kneller's noble portrait of the Lady Catherine Herbert, sits the pretty maid at her silent taskwork.   The shadows of the evening have partially fallen on the tinted windows, and settled round the lovely, earnest face; and yet there are also gleams of light stretching away along the distances of the tesselated marble floor.

The matron is very fond of little Rhoda; there is a link of sympathy between them, that through their long association has found its outlet in a thousand ways; and now, as the girl's quick ear recognizes the beloved footsteps, she rises, and awaits the matron with her habitual reverence.

" There, put by that work, Rhoda, and run out and play.   Why did Miss Jones keep you in ?— why has she set you this fine work to do at this late hour ? "

" I do not know, ma'am.   She's always setting me tasks during play-hours."

" This shall be seen to; now run and play, you have my authority to do so."

Rhoda obeying at once with a light step, the

mistress closes the great doors behind the girl, and returns to her room.

By the time tea is poured out, her son comes in. He says but little during the earlier part of the meal, and, satisfied with one cup, asks for wine or brandy. At first she gently dissents, but when he is urgent, and mutters something about being off to the 'Shirlot Arms,' she fetches him a wine-glass full of spirits from the private store-closet which lies at the end of the room. At the moment she sets the glass on the table she is called away to attend to some small matter of business connected with her office.

"I won't be ten minutes, George," she says; "old Mrs. Smith is worse, and the doctor has called in to speak to me."

It is curious to watch the youth the moment the door is closed upon him. His listless indifference vanishes as though by magic, and an intense acuteness of eye and ear is at once his. He loses not a moment, but rising, steals with the tread of a cat to his mother's writing-table: this he examines—then her capacious key-basket—then he repairs to the well-filled book-shelves between the windows, and deliberately extracting six or seven valuable books—some of them handsomely bound, for they have been gifts to his mother—he places the rest so as to make the abstraction not readily discernible. He next opens one of the windows, with fingers which betray their vocation, and hides his prize amidst the leaves of an adjacent oleander. Hurrying next to the storeroom—the window still open—he brings forth a bottle of wine and a bottle of brandy, and hiding these also, has closed the window, resumed his seat, and assumed his usual listless air by the time his mother returns.

"I'm sorry to have kept you, my dear," she says, in her kind way, and forgetful for the moment of the cruel indifference of him she addresses; "as you know of old, the duties of my place must be attended to. But Tibb shall soon remove the things."

He waits impatiently till this is done, and then rising he walks to the window.

"Mother," he says, as he affects to look out upon the evening, "it's getting late, and I must be going—I really must."

"George, you're surely not serious. I wanted to enjoy a few happy days with you, and I really have not money for you to spend in idleness and pleasure. I had thirty-five pounds to pay Mr. Shugborough, in order to stay his intended pro- secution of you; and then there are the Temeford debts hanging like a millstone round my neck. If you go on in this way the little savings of my life will soon be gone."

"Mother, I must go—I have promised young Black to start with him by rail in the morning. For the rest, I'll be steady, that I will—and try to keep my place. So give me twenty pounds and my father's watch, and I'll not trouble you again for many a day."

"Twenty pounds, George?—it is impossible!

You seem to me to have no idea of the value of money, nor of the sorrows and difficulties through which it is often earned. If you would stay here, as I wish you, till the day previous to your engagement, five pounds would suffice for all expenses."

"Five pounds, mother!—you may keep them. If I can't do as other young fellows one way I will another."

In this fashion he proceeds, till at last, by mingled threats and an affected penitence, a compromise is arrived at, and he obtains fifteen pounds—for his mother is, alas! weak in respect to him, and blind to his real character. That he has been the despair of schoolmasters she forgets; the follies of youth will, she thinks, presently pass away. And thus the dread hour has yet to come when the bitter truth has to enter her soul, when the blindness of affection will be removed, and she will know him for what nature made him—a hopeless and irreclaimable villain. Poor mother! that day has yet to come!

"But I cannot, George," she says, when she has laid the money on the table, "part with your father's watch—it has ever hung at my bed's head since he died, a long eighteen years, and I should miss it like an ever-present friend. There is an old one of your grandfather's you can have, and you cannot consistently ask for more—for I gave ten pounds for the silver one I bought for your eighteenth birthday, and that you know you said you lost, though Mr. Shugborough assured me you had raffled it away at skittle-playing."

"He's a liar!" answers George, vehemently; "he's poisoned your ears with lies enough to fill a sea." Thus he proceeds, till vehemence is softened into cajolery, and bland interminable lies fall again seductively upon the unhappy ear which listens.

Presently Mrs. Hutchinson rises to fetch her son his grandfather's watch, but as she opens the door he follows her.

"I may just as well come with you," he says, "and see what sort of a thing it is—for if it won't go I might as well carry a turnip." Thus speaking he follows his mother up-stairs to her bedchamber.

It is a charming room—large and daintily neat, with the fresh evening air blowing through the yet open windows. It is, however, dusk, so that when she has unlocked an old-fashioned escritoire she has to bring one of its shallow drawers to the window. In it lie, besides the watch, family rings, a few old brooches, and some silver spoons. One of the rings is valuable, a relic of better days. To see this has been his motive in coming up-stairs. What else there is surprises him—it is so much more than he expected. But he makes no comment.

"The watch is better than I imagined," he says, poising it in his hand; "but it will want a guard—where is the one of hair you used to wear?"

"It is here," she answers, as for an instant she sets down the drawer on the toilet-table, and turns to a small ornamental box. "It is here—you can take it." Handing it to him, she next goes with the drawer to the escritoire, locks it, and proceeds to pack a carpet-bag with new shirts, handkerchiefs, and socks she has been preparing. All this while he is in a hurry to go—more in a hurry as the minutes wane.

Once down-stairs, he puts on his hat and outer coat and prepares to go directly.

"Your haste to get away, George," says the mother, sorrowfully, "makes me quite nervous. But you'll write—you'll keep from bad company—you'll take care of the money."

"Tut, tut—have no fears, I'll be as steady as a judge. Now, bye! bye!" and he kisses the weeping woman in his flippant way, and is gone.

Weeping, yet hungry with unsatisfied love, she repairs again to the garden, resolved to watch his last footsteps as he winds down the hilly road. Even if there are shadows, if broadening twilight does not lie fair upon the scene, her ear will gather up his lessening footfalls; hard and thoughtless as he is, he is still dear to her—she loves him—and she must cleave to him, though all the world should fall away.

As she emerges through the white gate once more, thick shadows lying athwart the shrubberies, she sees that the children have left off play, and are gone in for the night. But as her surveying glance comes back again, it is attracted by the outline of a woman's figure standing in a listening attitude at no great distance. It strikes her that it is that of the teacher, and that she is covertly watching some one; but anxious to get one last lingering look of her departing son, she does not stay to learn further, but hurries into the highway, where the twilight lies soft and low—spreading itself across the broken forest land, and touching the sweeping waters with its fading gleams.

She has not advanced many yards, when she is startled by seeing a man climbing across a distant gate that leads from a field of mangelwurzel belonging to the hall. It lies outside the great kitchen gardens at the rear of the right wing, and from it access to the building may be obtained. He seems trammeled with what he carries, which he lifts over the gate with a careful hand—though, no sooner has he set foot in the road than he begins to run onward with rapid feet, and is soon lost to sight in the deepening shadows. Partially as she has seen him, she is conscious that it is her son; and wondering what it could be which had thus led him back to the hall, and what it was he was burdened with, she retraces her sad and thoughtful steps homeward.

Prayers have been read—the children are gone to rest, and the servants say that Miss Jones is in her own room at work; so, as there is thus a quiet hour, Mrs. Hutchinson thinks she will pay Miss Morfe a visit. There, there will be a wise head and a sympathising ear—and her heart seems to hunger for some voice that will speak to her in sincerity and with truth.

She is about to put out her lamp and go, when Tibb comes in for some port-wine for the sick gentlewoman. The doctor ordered it, and Lady Herbert's noble bounty affords such medicinal things when needed. Unlocking her store closet to get the wine, Mrs. Hutchinson misses at once the unopened bottles of brandy and wine, and she questions Tibb, who only brought them from the cellar that morning.

"Bless me, no, ma'am—I know nothing of 'em, you keep the closet locked, and since you were at tea I've been rubbing the stairs, so no one could have come in without my knowing. As to the children, they went straight from prayers to bed, and there was nothing amiss, except a rumpus about Rhoda's being out later than the other children, and for not having kept at her hemming."

"I'll see about that to-morrow. As to the loss, Tibb, say nothing about it." Thus counselled to silence, which she is sure to keep, for she is the faithfullest of creatures, Tibb departs. Suspecting her son—for she recollects leaving the closet-door open during her absence—Mrs. Hutchinson has thus a fresh proof of his baseness. It must have been for this that he retraced his steps to the hall, though she cannot think how he smuggled the bottles from the room; but then he is clever at expedients, as she has had already cause to learn.

Needing sympathy still more—for what wounds

us so much as to discover baseness in those we love?—the matron seeks Miss Morfe's room in the right cloister.

But friends are already there—Miss Salway, Mrs. Boston, Mrs. Cranworth, and one or two more ladies. So there is no opportunity for confidential talk, though there is for much which touches general subjects in a genial manner; and Nanny, at Miss Morfe's request, producing presently from a hamper a bottle of choice port-wine—one of a dozen given to her by an old London friend—and from the store-room a plum-cake Nanny has made to welcome her mistress's return—there is simple festivity as well.

The subject of Mrs. Boston's tea-party is introduced, and warm are the ladies in its praise, never did they remember an evening that passed so rapidly by.

"A proof you were interested as well as happy," says Miss Morfe.

"True," replies Mrs. Cranworth; "but we have not escaped scandal and reproof. Miss Simpkins has been satirising us in every direction; calling us a parcel of chattering old women, though forgetting to hint the secret her parrot blabbed. While Miss Thorne says we should have been much better employed had we had recourse to impressive and saving prayer, or read a soul-healing sermon she could have lent us."

"Never heed these scandals, ladies," says Miss Morfe; "Shirlot no more than any other place is exempt from the bigotry born, as all bigotry is, of selfishness and ignorance, or from the bitterness of evil tongues: it would be a paradise indeed if it were. Keep on the course of your innocent enjoyments, and be sure that they are blessed things in their hour and season. The truth which spares a lie has sterling worth in it, though its formula be not one approved of by small hearts and narrow minds."

"Indeed, we intend to do this," replies Miss Salway; "especially if you will co-operate, dear lady, and enrich our ears with a few of the many things you have delighted the world with in your time."

"I do this? You should have excepted me, Miss Salway."

"On the contrary," says Mrs. Cranworth, "Miss Hazlehurst has told us to look to you for many a pleasant hour by our winter fires, as beneath the trees in summer. This afternoon was warm and very lovely; if to-morrow be as pleasant, could we not meet on the terrace beside the river, and enjoy the sun, whilst listening to whatever you might choose to read or tell us? You will recollect that we are old gentlewomen, and not critics."

"Well, ladies, well, what you wish shall be, if not so early as to-morrow. My days have had many sorrows, and on these it has been easy to raise fictions the repetition of which may interest."

There is one there who has living sorrows, for a sigh, which seems irrepressible, speaks more than words.

"Are you ill, Mrs. Hutchinson?" asks Miss
Morfe, in her tender way; for she has already
noticed the matron's haggard looks, and now sees
that some sudden emotion has deepened the
pallor of her face.

"No," is the answer, "I am tired and a little
depressed. I think I will be going."

As she speaks thus she rises, and bids the
ladies good night. But Miss Morfe follows her
out into the cloister.

"What is the matter?" she whispers. "Do tell
me, that I may comfort you."

"I had come to tell you, but I cannot now.
Another time. Good night." She returns the
loving pressure of the hand, and goes.

"That son," says Miss Morfe to herself—"that
son, more worthless than his mother knows.
Through him, and of him, more woe *must* come;
for that which nature made defective and crooked
no education or entreaty can radically cure."

CHAPTER V.

BENEATH THE BOUGHS—THE STORM.

WHEN the domestic duties for the morning are over Mrs. Hutchinson always repairs to the hall, to see how the lessons are going on, and how the scholars behave. This morning she is later than usual; for there have been callers, and extraneous business, so the last lessons are being said as she takes her seat.

When these are over, and the children only wait the signal to run wildly forth to play, she says, in her mild and quiet manner,

"Miss Jones, why was Rhoda kept in last night, and why was she set a task which could have been done another time?"

"Because," replies the teacher, who has been in a particularly ill-humour all morning, "she is a very bad girl. I was coming into your room to speak to you after school, and I will do so."

"Whatever you have to say, you can say it here, Miss Jones. When we accuse another it should be at least before their face."

"Oh! that as you please," is the flippant answer, though in a voice which trembles with deep passion. "Look into Rhoda's bag, and ask her where the glass work-box you will find there came from."

"Rhoda, bring the bag. I always object to intruding even on children's privacies, but, as you are accused, bring it."

So agitated that all can see it, the girl brings the bag, and lays it on the mistress's knee. When emptied, it contains the usual miscellanies that school-girls hoard—apples, pictures, shreds and patches—and amongst these is the sixpenny work-box.

"Where did you get this from, Rhoda?"

"If you please, ma'am," falters the little mob-capped beauty, and there she stays, and says no more.

Rhoda's manner betrays that there is something wrong; so, in a severe voice, the matron repeats the question.

"I've had it some time, ma'am—I——"

"I do not want to know how long you have had it, but who gave it to you. I insist upon knowing."

"Miss Hazlehurst, ma'am—a long while ago."

Rhoda's voice and face betray untruth; so, calling to her a stolid-looking girl, Mrs. Hutchinson bids her take the work-box up to Miss Hazlehurst's room, and ask if that lady gave it to Rhoda Danvers.

The reply soon arrives, and is in the negative.

Miss Hazlehurst never saw the box before, and is truly sorry that Rhoda should tell so great a story.

"Now, Rhoda, as you have told one flagrant untruth, do not repeat it. Who gave you the box, I say?"

But Rhoda hangs her head, and, full of shame, will not answer.

"Miss Jones, I must appeal to you—who gave the girl the box?"

"I could have told you before, had you chosen to ask me," is the pert reply. "Why, young Clayton, to be sure. The girl is always after him."

"I'm sure I never am," weeps Rhoda, entering on self-defence now truth is spoken; "I never, of my own accord, spoke to him—he always follows me."

"When did he give you the box?" is the sternly-put question.

"The week before last," says Rhoda, weeping bitterly.

"And how did *you*, Miss Jones, discover it, or learn who gave it?"

"What right have I to be interrogated?" is the answer.

"Pray reply to my question."

"Why, instead of remaining at her hemming last night, as she ought to have done, she came out to play with the other children; but disappearing from their midst as the dusk grew, they all supposed she had returned to the house. Thus,

as I came home through the gardens from Clayton's Farm, I heard a whispering amidst the trees,
and listening, I learnt the history of this box—
and much besides."

"This is just what I thought, Miss Jones, and
why I questioned you. I had occasion myself to
pass the lodge as it grew dark, and saw you standing in a listening attitude. I was too absorbed
by my own business just then to make myself
known, and when I returned you were gone.
Now, I look upon your conduct as quite as blame-
able as Rhoda's, in its way. You must have been
fully aware that such meetings—between a girl of
Rhoda's age and position and a man well-to-do
and twice her years—could only lead to evil.
Your duty, then, instead of meanly listening, so
as to entrap the foolish child, was to have at
once called her away, and, leading her to my
parlour, have lost no time in acquainting me with
her guiltiness. I shall say no more now. I hope
you will think over what I have thus said, and
leave to me her punishment."

Unmindful of the teacher's anger, or the looks
of spite and hate she casts upon the girl, the
matron bids Rhoda go before her. Thence re-
pairing with her to a large solitary room—one of
two built apart from the hall, in the gardens, and
used in cases of contagious illness, and for punishment—she questions her, and, amidst many tears
and pleadings for forgiveness, elicits much of what
young Clayton has said, and how many times she
has seen him. Rhoda is innocent enough to con-

fess everything—but her little vanity at being loved, and, what is of more account, of loving in return.

"But you must never transgress so again, Rhoda."

"I never, never will!" sobs Rhoda.

"Because a child like you," says the matron, gently, "cannot be aware of all the evil which would assuredly follow.   In case this occurs again, I must dismiss you from the school; and you can understand, being an orphan, how friendless and desolate you would be—besides, giving great grief to me, to whom you have always been so good."

Rhoda is tenderly fond of the matron, and this appeal to her affection touches her more than all.

"I never will listen or stay again," she says, as she stretches out her hands appealingly, "if you will forgive me."

"I will, but you must remain here till evening, as a punishment for the untruth you told; and I hope you will think seriously over what has occurred, and what I have said.   This afternoon I am engaged, but in the evening I shall carry home the work-box, and speak to the young man myself."

So saying, the matron locks the door, and leaves the girl alone.

The sun shines out still more richly this afternoon.   Towards five o'clock several of Lady Herbert's gentlewomen may be seen wending their slow way up the garden paths behind the hall. Beyond its lawn-covered summit they cross the highway, and, descending to the little brawling river, pause beneath the budding boughs. For a time the little company chat together, and walk leisurely up and down in the blessed sun, though by-and-by its beauty is suddenly dimmed by gathering clouds, and rain begins to fall; but the ancient forest trees make an impervious roof, and so they linger for a time. As they do this, the matron comes hastening towards them.

"I am the bearer, ladies, of a message from Miss Morfe, as also from Mr. Quatford. Our kind friend feels too tired this afternoon to be present here, or to read the story she intended, though at an early date she hopes to have that pleasure. Meanwhile, Mr. Quatford, regretting your disappointment, hopes you will adjourn to the parsonage and take an early tea with him in his study. He has some photographs, as well as his collection of old china, to show you; and it is not unlikely that he can find a book upon his library shelves which will afford some entertaining subject for an hour's reading, if not quite so much so as Miss Morfe's promised story."

The ladies murmur an assent to this kindly invitation; for few have ever entered the bachelor's home, and curiosity thus adds to the worth of the courtesy offered. But true to the little vanities of their sex, six or seven of the nine gentlewomen present begin to ejaculate *sotto voce*, or whisper to each other, as to the absence of best caps and holiday gowns; and their repinings and regrets are not ended when they reach the parsonage door.

Passing along the terrace and the brawling river bank, the little company go onward till where the belt of forest land opens by a wicket into the highway crossing the ford; thence by another wicket opposite they enter a lawny plot of ground, alike swept by stately oak trees. Here is the old timbered house which for centuries has been the parsonage of Shirlot. Within the porch Mr. Quatford waits, bare-headed, to welcome them; and then ooze out the little apologetic vanities of their sex, which have waned or slumbered, but are not dead.

"Never mind, ladies, superfine toilets for the occasion," smiles the chaplain, " they are those already of gentlewomen, and that is all sufficient. Mine is but a bachelor's home, and I have made no special preparation; for the honour and plea-sure of receiving you was but thought of an hour ago, when it occurred to me that if Miss Morfe were able to read her sweet story of 'Dora,' it could not be without exhaustion to both reader and listeners. Hence the hasty invitation. But expect only barren hospitality. Though to such as it is you are fully welcome, as well as to my roof —though it has no mistress to gracefully re-ceive you." As he speaks thus, the chaplain leads the way onward into a wainscoted hall, and into a noble room, used and furnished as a library. Here tea is set forth with a luxurious profusion, and an exquisite attention to grace and hyper-cleanliness that amazes the major part of Lady Herbert's gentlewomen. In their simple imaginations, a bachelor's home must necessarily be a scene of waste, ruin, and disorder—for to them it is unknown that with the most massive intellect is often combined as great capacity for small things as for larger. They have heard that the parson is a particular man, that Jenny, his maid, is the cleanest and quietest of old-fashioned servants, and that she has trained Peter to be as particular as herself; and now they witness that public rumour is not always at fault.

Mrs. Hutchinson makes tea. Mr. Quatford is the merriest of hosts, and when the hospitable meal is at an end and cleared away, Peter lights the great lamp. The chaplain then shows his photographs and old china, and when these treasures are exhausted, he would read some legend by Ingoldsby, or some poem by Hood, whilst the crochet and knitting needles go round. But the storm which has gathered and gathered now bursts forth. The rain pours down, the lightning flashes through the trees, the thunder shakes the hills, and amidst such grandeur of the warring elements, the lesser vanities of life can have no place. By-and-by, when the thunder dies amidst the hills, and the fading sun breaks lurid through the clouds, it is time for the Lady Herbert's gentlewomen to take their leave, which they do amidst the wafted scent of the new-washed flowers, and with careful steps towards their ancient home.

CHAPTER VI.

THE MATRON'S BIRTHDAY.

As Lady Herbert's gentlewomen emerge from the parsonage lawn to cross the highway leading to the belt of forest land this side the little river, Mrs. Hutchinson bids them good evening. Then ascending the road, she enters the village, and pushing open some gates set in a very ancient garden wall, she goes up a wide path to a well-sized modern house. The garden, the orchard, the dovecot, and a part of the outbuildings are all very old, but the original house, having fallen into decay some ten years before this date, has been rebuilt by its landlords—the trustees of Lady Herbert's charity.

The front door opening into the house-place or kitchen, the matron makes her greetings at once to the mistress of the farm, a tall, stout, hard-featured woman of between fifty and sixty, who, wearing a widow's cap, sits stiff and stern beside the fire. Her knitting needles go mechanically round and round a great stocking, whilst her ear and eye seem to be alike alive to all the sounds and movements of her household. At a distance across the great room, two younger women, much like the elder, sit before a little table, busy with some sort of gaudy millinery, but, more courteous than their mother, they rise and give the matron a seat beside them.

"I want to see Mr. Clayton," says Mrs. Hutchinson, after a few minutes' chat.

"Samuel's i' th' little parlour wi' old Morris o' Temeford, a-bargaining about a stack of oats. If thy business is about the farm, thou canst tell it me, for I be master and missis here." It seems so, for she looks hard and stern enough.

"No, I must see Mr. Clayton himself," is the concise reply.

"Fetch him then, Kissy, it 'll save that minx Molly being called off her work, and thou canst chat a bit wi' old Morris whilst Sam's here—for a bargain's a bargain, and the old man's money is safe and sure as the Queen's." Grumbling these last words in an under breath, the stern woman still plies her needles.

The young man comes in. He is tall, and better to look at than either his mother or sisters, but he is visibly in awe of the former, though his ordinarily wild and dissolute air is increased by the glasses of strong ale he has just been drinking with his customer and friend.

Making but concise reply to his greeting, Mrs. Hutchinson brings the little glass work-box from her pocket, and holds it forth. "Do you know this?" she asks.

Recognising it in a moment, the young man changes colour, but makes no reply.

"What is it?" asks the mother, rising and moving towards the table.

"This," says the matron, sternly, "that your son chooses to come where he has no business, to address my children, and force upon them trumpery presents such as this. It can be with no good intention, and I utterly forbid it henceforth."

"I only gave it to Rhoda as a little keepsake," replies the young man at length, and with more courage than his evident fear of his mother might lead a looker-on to expect.

"Oh, that girl," exclaims the mother, angrily, "the thing's just the t'other way—she's always running after Sam. Mary told us so when she stepped here awhile ago."

"It is untrue," replies Mrs. Hutchinson, " Rhoda is one of the most innocent girls I know. She is as incapable of a bold or forward action as she is lovely."

"What then? You don't want a young man of Sam's situation to come courting *her*, as if she was a lady, eh? Though if he looks after her a bit what harm's in it? As to a wife, he'd better not think of bringing one across *this* threshold in my lifetime! His father left me a two-third share in the farm, and I'll have no one put over me or my girls. Wives indeed!—that miss, your teacher, would like to be sitting in my chair, I know that well enough—but I'll ha' none of 'em. Neither a pauper brought up on a charity foundation, nor a miss that can do crochet and turn round globes, but wouldn't know one end of a milking-pail from another. No! such fine things won't do here, though we get talk enough about 'five hundred pounds when uncle dies.' But an old hen like me ain't taken with silly chickens' cackle."

Speaking thus, and laughing loudly at what she thinks is a humorous joke, the hard woman resumes her seat.

"Mrs. Clayton," says Mrs. Hutchinson, firmly, "understand one thing distinctly. No one at the hall wishes to interfere with your affairs. The teacher's incessant visits here are made wholly against my consent—indeed, without my approbation. But then, so far as regards me, she is her own mistress when the duties of the school are over. What I desire is, that your son will keep from hanging about the precincts of the hall. If he has business, let him come to me. For the rest, I utterly forbid his speaking to the children, be they the younger or the older ones."

"There, Sam," says his mother, "do you hear that? A young farmer like you, with two team of horses, and renting a hundred and fifty acres of land, is forbidden to speak to one of the *young ladies* fed by Lady Herbert's bounty! Come, if thou hast a spark o' my pride, thou'lt easily promise such a thing."

"I'll make no promise," he answers sullenly.

"I'm thwarted in-doors and I'm thwarted out, and I shall go the devil's way just now."

So saying, he strides to the door by which he entered, and, banging it after him, is gone.

"There," says his mother, as though addressing her daughters, "thou see'st what Sam is! Every bit like thy father, for when he sets his head on a thing there's no moving him. But he shall not bring rich or poor here; I've got my seat, and I'll keep it!"

With this determination, and reckless of what sin or woe may come of her pride and stubborn selfishness, she grinds herself down into her seat, as though she would sit there till the end of doom.

Saying little more, except to the sisters, as they sit coldly and intent on their task of covering some bonnet shapes with gaudy-coloured silk, the matron withdraws.

Henceforth, for days, things go onwards serenely at the hall. No forbidden feet trespass in its precincts, and little Rhoda being forgiven her sins, having received her good friend Miss Hazleburst's reproof with contrite gentleness, and being, moreover, most dutiful and circumspect, is once more as happy as she is fair. There are other maids as pretty—Selina, and Julia, and Nelly, and many more. They sing their hymns and say their lessons, and do neat hemming, and stitching, and knitting, and learn to brew and to bake, and to be neat housewives, under Tibb's rule; and all such holiday hours as they spare from play are industrially employed in the fabrication of needlebooks, pincushions, and other things for the expectant birth-day. The matron and teacher are supposed to know nothing of this work or purpose; and Miss Jones being in an unusually pacific humour, the children's happiest hours pass by undisturbed.

The spring has likewise broadened, and the weather is now divine. The casements of the seven-and-twenty gentlewomen's homes are ever open, their doors often so, and within you see many signs of days once brightened by prosperity, such pictures of dainty neatness, homely comfort, as may lead those to think—who view the world under its more solemn aspects—that there is something in charity after all. Draw the mean between the logic of Adam Smith and his illus-trious followers, and the enthusiasm of the phi-lanthropist, and we arrive, perhaps, at what *is* the truth in respect to the virtues of self-dependence, and the vices begot by ill-considered aid. In the battle of life some will fall, even through the treachery of others, or unforeseen accident, and to the staff which aids their rise who shall say nay? Not, surely, anyone who looks on these May-day mornings through the sunny doors of Shirlot !

Miss Hazlehurst is better, and comes down the great waggon-wide staircase for a sight of her little garden, where her peas are luxuriant, her mustard and cress and lettuces ready for a salad, and where her gooseberry bushes give great signs of abun-dance for the jam-pot. Occasionally she stops in the sunny cloister to chat with her neighbour,

Mrs. Eden, whose door stands wide, and opposite to which, twining up the pillars of the cloister, stand luxurious plants in bloom and leaf. The very door itself has a grand knocker—the mat and cloister floor around are scrupulously clean—and within you see what the gossips call the "show-room" of Shirlot. For it is charmingly furnished and adorned; its tables and chairs—its old china and knick-knacks—tell of better days; whilst taste in their disposal and dainty neatness betray the culture of race and blood. The old gentlewoman herself is still handsome and jauntily attired, but on her visage sits no smile. She is miserable, desolate, and alone; she is a mother, but, God help her! she never knew a mother's love for those she bore. But Miss Hazlehurst is a Samaritan—she speaks cheerfully, be the reply a smile or a frown, and leaving the county newspaper with her morbid friend, hobbles across the stone pathway of the quadrangle, and knocks at Miss Morfe's door. This is a pretty true sign that on days like these the happy and wise little gentlewoman is busy with her pen. True this proves, for, when the door is opened, there she sits at her writing-table, beside the sunny casement; whilst Nanny, moving quietly to and fro, prepares her mistress's dinner. There is abundance of books on bookshelves around the walls, and there are pictures and flowers; and old Tom, the cat, purrs at his mistress's elbow on the deep window-ledge, and Tott, the dog, is asleep in the great leather-covered chair—and thus the room and its mistress alike do honour to the noble goodness of the noble dead.

Laying down her pen, welcoming her cherished friend, whose second visit this is through these days of convalescence, insisting that she shall stay and share her humble dinner, which the other declines to do; for she well knows, if the little woman has a failing, it is too large a heart—though she will just stay a little while to chat and hear the news. So she sits down by her deaf friend, and the latter hints something about the tale of " Dora," she is busy with, and how it shall be read pro bono publico before it goes, and this will be soon, for one which is printing is much liked. To this she adds that she has had a charming letter from dear Amy this morning, who is counting of the summer holidays as only schoolgirls count. Then there is news of Mr. Quatford. He has had good tidings of his nephew Islip Austin, who will be at Shirlot in another week. There are rumours, too, of sad household quarrels between young Clayton and his mother; but on the threshold of these scandals the dear old ladies stay and drop the honey dew of pity and silence. Mrs. Boston has been poorly, Miss Simpkins has been almost invisible since the date of her parrot's injudicious revelation—and little Miss Thorne, wrapped up in the odour of her own sanctity, looks down in pity and immeasurable pride on all her sister gentlewomen. She could teach them, she could save them—for is not she, Elizabeth Thorne, one of the Lord's anointed?

So she thinks, poor soul, in her imbecility of bigotry, and prophesies a doom for all those of Shirlot who differ in opinion with herself.   None will be saved, except Mrs. Janet M'Phinn, an old Scotch gentlewoman, who lives secluded in the left gallery; and there are occasions when even this is doubtful, for Janet's notions on infant baptism are wide of the mark of orthodoxy.   So gossiping on these innocent things, enjoying the divine sun, conscious of the sweet spring odours which steal in through the open casements, gratitude and humility in their hearts towards God, and charity towards man—these wisest of Lady Herbert's gentlewomen pass a serene hour.

On her way home across the quadrangle, Miss Hazlehurst encounters Miss Thorne, though a stiff and patronizing "I'm glad to see you out again" is the only recognition the other deigns to make.   But, careless of this, Miss Hazlehurst hobbles her way up to her room, and to her dinner; whilst Miss Thorne, after having duly sunned herself in this, Mrs. Eden's cloister, and patronized all Shirlot by saying to old Harris, as he trims the lawn, "I'm glad my turf looks so well," and "I am pleased to see my orchard so full of bloom," departs to the wing where she lives. Here, up a staircase appropriated solely to the two rooms she occupies, she goes, and entering her sitting-room, takes her seat at a table; for this luncheon is spread—dainty linen, silver forks and spoons, two sorts of wine in decanters, preserves and marmalade in glass dishes.   Miss

Thorne's drink is water, her luncheon a biscuit, and when she has lunched, the wine and dainties go back into the cupboard, to come thence each day, the wine twice, during the solemn acting of this hollow farce of gentility. The depressed and shadowy-looking servant then retires, and Miss Thorne is left to her devotions and her solitude —till six o'clock, when dinner and dessert come on the table, the former announced by the tinkling of a bell.

After a silence of some weeks, George writes to his mother one of those plausible letters for which villains seem to have so great an aptitude. Mistrustful as bitter experience has taught her to be, exceeding love for her only child makes her in a measure blind; and hence, where in any other instance she would wholly disbelieve, she takes for truth, or at least partial truth, his glib assertions. He is well—he is steady—he works hard, indeed too hard—his home is most comfortable, though its rules are very strict—his master is kind, his associates gentlemanly. So, consoling herself with tidings such as these, her old cheerfulness in a degree returns, and she takes upon herself the heavy Temeford debts, with new resolves to pay them, and let bygones be bygones in her heart. True, she has days before this missed the valuable books from off her shelves, and is sure that only he could have taken them; but then she thinks he wished for them, and yet did not like to ask her—so even this dereliction of honesty she overlooks, and hides its shadow in her own heart.

Much to the joy of the twenty little mob-capped maids, the matron's birthday arrives at last, and all the mysteries of their needles are accomplished. According to old custom, they have a holiday, and the morning is spent in placing board and tressels, and making other preparations for a tea-party on a lawny plot beside the river. The woods are searched for flowers; old Harris, who is like a father to the children, calls upon garden and green-house for a further supply, and divers of the old gentlewomen contribute to the little festival. One gives a cake, another a bottle of her best cowslip or damson wine, another some pippins or pears of last year's growth from a choice tree—and these, with what Tibb allows from the kitchen, make quite a feast.

On the morning of her birthday, the matron is always duly invited by her two head scholars; and accordingly, as the afternoon now advances, she goes up-stairs to her room to dress. She needs some little brooch or ornament; so, going to the drawer, for the first time since the date when she drew it forth to give George the watch, she misses at once the valuable ring, as well as a pair of antique salt-spoons. She looks for these things elsewhere, but she cannot find them, and the conviction soon forces itself upon her mind that he on this occasion purloined them. His cunning must have been marvellous, his sleight and dexterity of hand still more so, to have effected this theft without any consciousness on her part, for she recollects that the moment she turned away was so brief a one. No one else since then has had access to the escritoire, or could by any possibility have had it, for the key is a peculiar one, and none but her son, as she well knows, had an idea that she possessed such a ring, for she had never worn it, but kept it by her as a reserve either for days which might be fraught with need, or as a wedding-gift to some good daughter-in-law, should George do well and marry. But all such dreams are at an end! For her can come no other days than—as relates to him—those of dread and infamy—and as the presentiment of all this woe dawns upon her for the first time, her despair is most touching. The things she has lost are worth some pounds; and this in itself is a trouble, for with such debts as hang over her, great shifts and poverty must necessarily come; but these are slight compared with the great dread of an evil name. For him she bore to be talked of and written of in newspapers as infamous, even though so young—and perhaps all this to end with a prison and a transport ship! The mere thought is almost death to her, for has she not striven to act so circumspectly through her days of widowhood, and to make her connection with Lady Herbert's noble charity one of staid repute and honour? "What will be said now?" she asks herself in her great bitterness, "when, perhaps, towards others he may act as worthlessly as he has done to me, and it is whispered he is a son of mine." Thus in her great dread she vexes her soul, and wishes, like Job, that she had never been born.

Time flies, and divers little taps upon the door at length remind her of the festival made in her honour, and that she is waited for. So she has to wash away her tears, hide, like the Spartan boy, her intense suffering under a smooth countenance, and go.

At a time of less tribulation, the scene when she reaches it would give her joy. The feast is spread in an open space beneath the trees, the carpet is one of smoothest turf, the pebbled river flows by with its eternal song, and beyond it, stretching to the distant hills, is the great sweep of unbroken forest land called Shirlot Forest, this crossed only by the highway leading from the ford. The tea-kettle boils in gipsy-fashion above a crackling fire of sticks, and old Tibb in her best gown sees that all is in due order.

So the meal progresses, and the little mob-capped maids wait dutifully upon their honoured guest. Miss Jones is in a mood of unusual suavity, and just as the meal closes some of the most kindly of the old ladies from the Hall come to see the little presents given, and to walk up and down upon their favourite terrace in the sun.

At last the gifts are brought — pincushions, needle-books, bags—enough to stock a bazaar; crochet-work collars, cuffs, and, crowning all, Rhoda's chief gift, a purse for the matron's son.

Evil as he is to her, this thought of him by one she loves so well as she loves Rhoda, touches her extremely, and her eyes grow dim with tears.

Prettily decked are the presents as they lie spread out in box and basket. They are nestled amidst leaves and many-hued flowers, and the perfume of the violets is so profuse as to hang like a cloud above them. No need of costly art and luxury here, for nature scatters her own incense above the little loving gifts. As the matron looks at them severally her attention is arrested by a small needle-book, covered with gaudy-coloured silk, such as weeks before she remembered to have seen in the hands of Kissy and Agnes Clayton. It is so peculiar that it is not to be mistaken; and as these young women are by no means generous, so as to be likely to give away fragments of the sort, she resolves to make some inquiry, that she may see if Rhoda has been again receiving gifts in a clandestine manner.

Presently, therefore, when the crowd around her begins to disperse, Mrs. Hutchinson asks Selina where the silk thus used came from?

"We don't know, ma'am," she replies; "it was put into our bag of pieces by some one—so we used it, though we've since seen that it is like that which covers the Misses Clayton's bonnets."

"You're sure that it has been no gift to Rhoda?"

"Dear, no, ma'am! Rhoda would take no presents from Mr. Clayton again. She promised you, and would not break her promise—for she cried very much that she had vexed you on that account, and would not be undutiful again, I know."

"You have never seen him about the place during play-hours?"

"He has been loitering at a distance several times, but Rhoda has never spoken to him, I am certain.   She would have told me if she had, for she has no secrets from me."   Thus innocently Selina speaks of her innocent friend.

Assured that the girl tells the truth, Mrs. Hutchinson interrogates Miss Jones, as the latter rises to leave the table.

"I know anything of the piece of silk?" she questions, in her accustomed flippant way, "how should I?   You must ask those to whom it was given.   Though you think Rhoda so very simple and childlike, she is not, as you may one day find; and the best thing, as many say, that you could do, would be to dismiss her from the school at once.   But I'll say no more, though I could tell and show you that that would soon change your opinion."

"Miss Jones, pray explain—"

The teacher affects not to hear, but, hurrying away with some of the younger children, makes as though she were at play, and in a moment is lost to sight.

Determining to question her ere the day has closed, the matron repairs to one of the terrace paths facing the little river, and watching the elder girls as they skip to and fro across the plashy stones, and into the shadows of the great oaks beyond, is soon lost in her own sad thoughts. A terrible agony oppresses her spirit, an agony all the greater that it may not be spoken of to others.

Running far into the shadows of the wood, hiding herself, or else finding her playfellows, and then coming quickly across the plashy stones once more, Rhoda thus plays till the evening fades fast. As she takes her last wild run round and round the great dusky bolls, she is suddenly caught up and borne some little way onward. She cannot struggle, for the arm around her is too powerful—she cannot cry, for her mouth is pressed close against the one who bears her; but her journey is but short, for in a few minutes, after a wild leap or two over what seems a boggy place, she is set down, and she sees in the semi-light that it is young Clayton who has thus so rudely separated her from her innocent little friends. Really terrified, and aware of the trouble which will arise if she is missed or discovered, she strives to free herself from the hands which detain her.

"You shall not go, Rhoda," is the fiercely spoken rejoinder, "till I've talked a bit with you. I have been hanging like a beaten dog for days about the hall to have speech with you—and I'll have it now, come what may."

"Please to let me go, Mr. Clayton," she says, as she weeps and strives still to free herself; "you have already got me into great trouble, and will do so again—let me go!"

"Listen! Come with me to Temeford to-night, and to-morrow, as God's my judge, I'll make you my wife. My horse is in the highway purposely. Come!"

"I cannot. You know well enough I am a poor girl—one whom your mother and sisters would only think of and treat as a servant. Let me go. Next Easter I am sixteen, and leave Shirlot to go to service, so please let me keep my promise to Mrs. Hutchinson, and to the end be good and dutiful."

"A promise!—what is that? Don't I love you better than all else in the whole world, and am I not going mad by reason of you? They say you shall not enter our house—I say you shall! We have strife enough already, matters can't be worse."

"Please, sir, forget me."

"Forget you? What does that mean from you? I thought when I last saw you, you said—"

"I said, sir, I was very sorry for you, that I pitied you for all the trouble you told me of—"

"Pity is akin to love, Rhoda," he interrupts again. "Now, tell me if you love me—if you even like me—it will be a comfort such as I haven't known this many a day."

"I don't dislike you. If you wouldn't be so fierce and rude, and will let me go, I will like you."

"Before I do that, you must say something kinder still. Sweet one, do! I am so wholly wretched and alone!"

"I am very sorry for you, I am indeed."

"That's not enough; say 'Sam, I love you,' and I'll let you go scot free, or almost."

She does not reply in words, but, raising up her pretty face—its outline just to be caught bewitchingly in the dim light of the wood—looks all its tender meaning into his. He interprets it rightly, but the interpretation only makes him wilder and fiercer than before.

"Come with me, Rhoda, do! Come to-night. When I first came looking at thy pretty face I had no honest meaning to set thee in the old woman's place. Now I have."

"Nay, please let me go. I like you a little, but I mustn't do wrong. I've promised my dear mistress I never will. Let me go."

So, struggling whilst he passionately kisses her, and would bear her more and more into the woods, she suddenly frees herself, and, dashing right across the intervening strip of swamp, is gone. He dare not pursue her, for he can hear the other children calling her by name; but he is maddened at her escape, and this all the more that she has so bewitchingly confessed that she likes him, even though so terrified to sin against her duty and her promises.

Muttering something to himself—for he is annoyed at her escape, though really deeply loving her—about "biding his time," and "taking his reckoning at a future day," he strides across the woodland to the highway, and thence into the village to the "Shirlot Arms."

Rhoda's short absence has caused no surprise to her companions—for it is so possible to be lost amidst the trees at that dull hour—nor is her breathless agitation observed; so when she and the other girls have assisted Tibb and old Harris to clear away the appurtenances of the little festival, they return to the hall. Here Miss Jones makes her appearance; prayers are read, and the little mob-capped maids retire to rest.

It is not long after when Miss Morfe and the matron wish each other good night in the left cloister. The latter has hinted, though not told, her great griefs to her true friend, and received some sterling advice, which it would be well if Mrs. Hutchinson would act upon, as well as listen to. Whilst, on the other hand, Lady Herbert's gentlewoman, having received divers messages that very afternoon, as to the audition of her new story, proposes to read it, or have it read, publicly in the hall one evening during the ensuing week. To this proposal the matron gladly assents; and it is finally arranged that each lady, irrespective of creeds, crotchets, or pets, shall be invited, and that coffee, provided jointly by Miss Morfe and Mrs. Hutchinson, shall be handed round, during such pause in the reading as may be, by Tibb and the four eldest little mob-capped maids.

Strongly impressed by Miss Jones's accusation against Rhoda, Mrs. Hutchinson seeks the teacher in a small room assigned to her private use. The visit is not very graciously received—for the young lady is supping off some delicacy that has been sent to her from the Claytons, and would willingly put off all explanation till the morrow.

"No! I wish to hear what it is without further loss of time. In a case such as this, there ought to be no delay."

"Well, it was only this—that when I went to the girl's work-box this morning, to look for a reel of cotton she had borrowed, I found a coral necklace."

"What of that! You know, Miss Jones, as well as I, that the children bring things from home—their poor possessions—which they make a mystery of, and hoard ; and which a kindly teacher wisely passes by. There can be no harm in this ? "

"Perhaps not. But you always take the children's part—so I'll say no more."

"On the contrary, I wish to hear this matter fully. If Rhoda is in error, be sure she shall be punished, and that severely. Who gave her the necklace, do you know ? "

"There's no doubt of who it was," is the ready answer, though the agitation which accompanies it shows what a personal interest the teacher has in the matter ; " it speaks for itself."

"In what way ? "

"There is a written paper there requesting the girl to meet young Clayton in the woods this very evening. Whether she did or not, is not my affair."

"It is. It is conniving at transgression. If you knew of this in the morning, you should have told me."

"Oh, I have ceased to make complaints as relates to Rhoda. They are not attended to. Things must take their course. She should be dismissed from the school now—the time may come when there may be a necessity for it."

"Miss Jones, I am astonished at your audacity. That there will be a need of *your* leaving here is quite certain, when you profess to know of evils beforehand, which you should, but which you do not, prevent. Fetch me the necklace and writing, and let me see them."

The unprincipled woman obeys with evident reluctance; and, coming back with poor Rhoda's work-box, shows in its most secret corner a single string of common red beads, attached to which is a strip of dirty paper. On this is written, in an evidently disguised handwriting, " Let me see you to-night, if you can."

" Rhoda may know nothing of this. Such a piece of writing and such a trumpery gift might have been put here by any one. I'll question her myself, and if she is guilty she shall not only be punished, but be never suffered to leave the precincts of the hall, except to go to church, till she quits it wholly next Easter. But till that time comes, I have no right to dismiss an orphan from the roof which shelters her." So saying, Mrs. Hutchinson takes the necklace and goes.

When all the keys of the hall have been, according to custom, brought to her, she goes upstairs, and entering the elder girls' chamber, approaches the bed where Rhoda and her friend Selina sleep. Both are buried in profound slumber,

and the face of the one is as sanctified by innocence as the other.

Regarding them with tender interest, the matron
presently awakens Rhoda, who, wondering, looks
about her.

"There is nothing the matter, Rhoda, only I
must speak to you. Put on a petticoat and come
into my room."

She obeys, and wonderingly follows the mistress.

"Do you know anything of this?" questions
Mrs. Hutchinson sternly, as she exhibits the
necklace.

"No, ma'am," is the wholly unembarrassed
reply; "I never saw it before."

"How did it come into your work-box?"

"In my work-box? Was it there? It was
not yesterday, when I went to take something
out. Indeed, I never saw it before."

"Nor this?" asks the matron, as she shows the
strip of paper.

"No, ma'am." But as Rhoda's eye falls on the
writing, and she reads it, her face becomes all
aglow.

"You saw this man—you met this man."

"The paper I know nothing of—indeed, indeed; but—" and the pretty maid, bending down
her face, and bursting into tears, makes full confession of all which has passed this evening—of
all—of everthing, except of the pretty upturned
gaze, which told so much of her pity, her liking,
her tender heart!

"You tell me the truth, Rhoda—you are sure?"

"I do—I do indeed, Mrs. Hutchinson. I told him I wished to be dutiful and truthful to you, and to be forgotten by him."

"That is right, Rhoda, and I believe you. For I never found you lie or prevaricate. Be a good girl, and I will take care to keep you out of this man's way. Next Easter you leave me, and I will find you some good place, where others shall regard you and take as much care of you as I wish to do. I have many troubles, child—many, and amidst them no comfort greater than to see my children worthy of their home."

So the matron kisses the pretty maid, who returns to bed, but not to sleep. She cries bitterly at having been wrongfully accused. And other tears are shed this night, when she is gone, and these are for a darker and a sterner woe.

CHAPTER VII.

SPIT, SPARK, AND TOM.—THE TALE OF DORA.

To each of Lady Herbert's gentlewomen it has been duly intimated that Miss Morfe's new tale, "The Tale of Dora," will be read, pro bono publico, in the hall this evening, Tuesday, June 30; hour, five o'clock; refreshment, tea and coffee.

Now, as some cannot or will not attend, it will be best to tabulate both those present and absent, with causes of absence.

ABSENT, OR NON-CONTENT.

Miss Thorne, reasons Calvinistic.

Miss Simpkins, illness of parrot.

Mrs. Mary Jones, mental incapacity.

Mrs. Miles, extreme age.

Mrs. Thelwell, bedridden.

Mrs. Janet M'Phinn, tender conscience.

Miss Holte, entirely deaf.

Miss Sullivan, best cap out of order.

Mrs. Hughes, gout and laudanum.

PRESENT—CONTENT.

Miss Morfe, in lady-like array
Mrs. Eden, in astonishing cap.
Miss Hazlehurst.
Miss Salway.
Miss Gregg, with dog Spark.
Mrs. Boston, with her little grandaughter.
Mrs. Smith, with humour satirical.
Mrs. Rutland.

Miss Leigh, without her cat.
Mrs. Quince.
Miss Stanier.
Miss Bodkin, with dog Spit.
Miss Penelope Pockle.
Mrs. Cranworth.
Mrs. Mynor.
Miss Hastings.
Miss Weld.
Miss Horatia Unity.

Eighteen gentlewomen in all, two pet dogs, the matron, the teacher; and it may be that, when tea is over, Mr. Quatford will come, for he has half promised his friend Miss Morfe that he will read her paper.   So, the ladies assembled, refreshment is handed round.

"I hope, ladies," says Miss Hazlehurst, when there *does* come a pause, "that the reading will not be interrupted.   Pets are sometimes troublesome."

"If you allude to *my* dear dog," replies Miss Gregg, tartly, "I, on his behalf, quite repudiate the insinuation.   Spark is a marvel of good behaviour; and he'll lie here, ma'am, in my gown, and listen with the gravity of his betters."

"Not if my poor cat Tom chances to peep round the open door," sighs Miss Leigh.   "Your dog, Miss Gregg, leads him a dreadful life.   Twice this very spring have I sewed up his ear."

"Indeed, ma'am !   Cats, then, should let dogs alone.   My Spark is not a philosopher."

"Ladies !" says Miss Salway, who sees a storm

is brewing, "we'll hope for peace. Pets, as Miss Hazlehurst says truly, are best in their proper places ; but if——"

"Miss !" exclaims Miss Bodkin, "pray understand that *my* tender and delicate Spit is in his proper place when by my side. Of late, too, his health has been a little delicate; so that were he left alone it might be most injurious."

"Pity," grumbles Mrs. Smith to Mrs. Rutland in an under-breath, "that the pair were not sent by general subscription to the water-cure. We should have two plagues the less then at Shirlot."

"Yes—yes," whispers Mrs. Rutland, *sotto roce,* "but Sally Bodkin doctors her pet at home. Homœopathic medicine, tincture twice a day, and globules at night. Light biscuits sopped in milk for breakfast, and beef-tea for dinner. It's a fact, I assure you."

"What's a fact, ma'am?" asks Miss Bodkin, who is a very stout lady with acute hearing, and whose large fat hand rests on her dog's collar as he lies in her lap, as though she was not quite sure of his pacific intentions.

"Why, Miss B., I just was telling Mrs. S. that you are doctoring your dog homœopathically."

"Yes, I am, and it's a great pity that some who are not dogs, but Christians, are not treated in the same way. It might cure them of the vice of saying what they should not."

"I beg you'll explain, Miss B."

But explanations, counter-explanations, and rejoinders are nipped in the bud by no less a cause than the slight disagreement of Spit and Spark in person. Mrs. Bolton drops a piece of cake, and Spark, who, as his mistress has hinted, is not a philosopher, but, on the contrary, very fond of the sweets of this life, jumps down to snatch it. Spit, who is a snarl, in spite of emulsive tinctures, envies it, and jumps down too—the result of which is warfare of a highly canine kind. The mistresses scream, the ladies laugh, and peace is not restored till either combatant is safe in his mistress's lap, with a piece of cake, and soothed by endearing words of "dear Spit," "sweet Spark," and "poor fellow."

Just as this tempest is over Mr. Quatford arrives. He takes his place in the midst of the ladies, has a kindly word for each, and tells them his deep joy. His nephew has arrived, and is greatly better. Then, prefacing his task with some complimentary words to Miss Morfe, he adds that the story is one of love and tenderness—such as might have been their own, long years before. He then begins and reads

THE TALE OF DORA.

"Tim," spoke the little old thin-faced tailor, as he removed his spectacles with his right hand, and laid his left gently on the sleeve-board across his knee, "just run to Martha Cadwallader's and get me two skeins of whitey-brown thread, for Bump the coachman said the squire wants these gaiters, and must have 'em.   Of course, of course, it being agin a law in nat'r for sich as squires to wait."

"Howsomever, don't say so to Martha, Tim," added a little old woman, who, fat and round as an October tun, was no other than the tailor's wife, "for she's a long, ay! and a taking tongue up at the hall!   And just too, beside the thread, bring half-a-pound of dips and a pound of moist sugar, which you mustn't put your finger in, nor break the candles."

Tim, a queer, shambling, nondescript lad of about sixteen, scrambled off the board at this bidding, not, however, without upsetting, as he did so, both shears and goose, and had received the necessary halfpence from his mistress, when the old tailor added, "Don't forget a note or two of the gamut as you run along. It's better than imitating Podd's cat or the doctor's dog. Do you hear?"

"And recollect about your finger in the sugar," chimed in the cheerful little round woman.

"Yes, sir—yes, mum," answered Tim in one breath as he latched the door.   But no sooner had he passed into the village street than—the old tailor's injunctions quite forgotten—he commenced his ordinary recreation by peeping over every blind and half-shuttered window, pinching every stray cat's tail, pulling the bright-rubbed handle of the doctor's gate bell, and by howling dismally through the spacious front door keyholes of such unmusical parishioners as waged war against his master in the matter of parochial psalmody. At length, after this full measure of disobedience against the solfa-ing injunction, he passed through Martha Cadwallader's garden-wicket into the half kitchen, half shop. After waiting a moment to ascertain the immediate state of Miss Cadwallader's domestic affairs, he rapped the pence intrusted to him pretty lustily on the top of the old counter; for this antique, red-nosed spinster, of supposed genteel connexions, and owner of known deposits in certain country banks, was cosily enjoying herself before the great wood fire in the kitchen grate, on the other side of the counter, a little round table being nicely spread before her. On this stood a suspicious dish, and on the warm hob something still more mysterious, and beside it a very comfortable mug of ale, just beginning to be richly white on the top.

Now, it was much whispered in the village that Miss Cadwallader enjoyed, through the agency of Bump the coachman, the monopoly of divers stray tid-bits from the squire's larder; that is to say, the fifth of a tongue, the tithe of a pheasant, or the third of a sponge-cake, or any other little delicacy in season. And the larger third of a very transparent red jelly, standing in a rich china plate, looked very suspicious on this occasion.

By the time the tailor's apprentice had chinked his halfpence once or twice upon the counter, Miss Cadwallader condescended to look round (she was perfectly aware who it was) and say, "Wait a moment;" and therefore whilst, behind the barricade of the large loaf, the drinking horn, and salt-cellar, she finished the remnants of a delicate little entremets warm upon the squire's plate that very afternoon, Tim had time to survey the counter and window.

Now, Miss Cadwallader, besides being the sole grocer, draper, druggist, flour-dealer, hatter, and bookseller of this remote western English village, was also post-mistress; and in this latter office ruled and made laws both parochially and extra-parochially, in the free-and-easy sort of way usually supposed to be peculiar only to kings ruling by the virtue of divine right. One law alone was fundamental and unabrogatable in this code of Cadwallader, namely, that "the squire must have *his* letters." Therefore, whilst the fragmentary tid-bit was being gobbled, Tim had time to survey both window and counter; to number the red-herrings, the balls of string, the papered-up hats, the eggs, and the brushes; to long for the liquorice and bulls'-eyes in the glass bottles; to mentally weigh the amount of cheese, butter, and bacon; to carry his eye along the geometrical lines of the crossed pipes; to speculate upon the contents of divers packets of tea, starch, and black-lead in the window, and of divers little paper funnels on the counter, containing halfpenny-worths of tobacco, half ounces of tea, quarters of sugar, and ounces of coffee, lately weighed by her own hand, and so delicately adjusted in price to the ignorance, necessity, or needs of her rustic customers, as to bring in about two hundred per cent., not to Her Majesty's exchequer, but to her own. At length Tim's eye arriving gradually at the low desk on the counter, it spied two or three letters, the superscriptions on which he was just mastering, when Miss Cadwallader, suspending her gastronomic delight over Mr. Bump's offering, approached the counter. Catching Tim's eye upon the superscription of the letters, she interrupted his curiosity by throwing down the half-pound of sugar before him, and demanding the money. But Tim had had other instruction from his master besides that of solfa-ing, and he now out with it, for he had no fear of the postmistress.

"Lord, mum, here's the blessed curate's letter! just the very one, I daresay, as Absalom Podd has often said Mr. Longnor has been looking out for this half year like."

"Parish boys," spoke Miss Cadwallader, with much wrath, "should mind their own business. As for the letter, the parson will get it soon enough in the morning, I daresay. The girl's sure to be in the village, for it's tea and coffee, candles and soap—and yet nothing but book, book. Four pounds eleven and tenpence three farthings down already, and no more sign of the money than of me riding in a coach and six—and giving such credit!"

"Well, missis," still outspoke Tim, with a courage that did his good and honest nature justice, "master always says the curate wouldn't wrong a cretur of a button or a needleful of thread; and as this may be the letter the poor gentleman has been expecting so long, just let me run down the lane wi' it. I'll come and give your sty a sweep, or the weeds a pull. You know I will."

But whether it was, or not, that Miss Cadwallader had not as yet tasted the creamed jug upon the hob, I know not, for she was inexorable, thrust forward the candles, sugar, and thread, counted the halfpence, said something of speaking to the squire about impudent apprentice-boys, and pointed to the door.

Tim reluctantly withdrew. Before, however, he had well passed out of the garden wicket, he was called back, the letter thrust into his hand, with strict injunctions as to its being delivered immediately; for having fallen once into serious difficulties with the post-office authorities, Miss Cadwallader (like the before-mentioned law-giver) was sufficiently politic to go as far as she dared in her self-constituted code, but yet to lay it aside the moment there was the smallest appearance of danger. Tim's only answer was as impudent as it well could be. " Yes, missus, I shall go as quick to the curate's as you'd carry it to the squire's;" and without further word, the tailor's apprentice ran up the street, wholly innocent this time of his peculiar twilight recreation of knocking, pinching, or peeping, and without pausing an instant, he burst into the tailor's kitchen, in such an unusual and wild way as to make master, mistress, and Leah, the little maid, look towards him with eager amazement; particularly when he held up the letter with a sort of triumphal wave above his head, and exclaimed, " Frightened Cad-

wallader a bit, I think, mum and sir, and got *this!*"
So saying, he gave the letter to his master, who,
having left the board during Tim's absence, was
now sitting in his arm-chair beside the fire. The
curiosity was intense; for the old dame, who was
knitting, and little Leah, who was laying the cloth
for supper, were soon peeping over the tailor's
shoulder to see the letter, and when they saw it
was large and had a great seal, and that now the
good old soul, the tailor, having duly examined
the superscription, rose to fetch his coat and hat,
in order to carry it himself, the curiosity of mistress, apprentice, and little maid had passed all
reasonable bounds.

Taking it carefully in his hand, and bidding
Tim put by work for the night, and get his supper
with Leah and his mistress, the old man set out
upon his walk, after adding that none were to sit
up for him beyond the ordinary time of retiring to
rest. Soon leaving the village-street, he entered
a green lane, which, slightly descending, was over-
hung with wide bushy hedge-rows, so garnished
here and there with old forest trees that, meeting
from either side, they formed one bosky canopy,
which quite shut out the rich soft twilight of this
summer's eve. In no great while these hedge-rows
merged into a tract of country which had once
formed a portion of a wide extent of wild forest
land, and the green sward of the hedge-rows into
the rich turf peculiar to sylvan and untrodden
solitudes. At a stone's throw from where this
lane terminated, and where began the ascent into

the more primeval forest land, ran a brook, crossed by a narrow ford. On this side of it lay, on either hand, a primitive church and church-yard, and a low, thatched, rambling cottage, called the " Parsonage," whose garden, rich in flowers and beehives, stretched far away beside the brawling brook. Little more than the forest-turf lay in front of the cottage, and knowing, by the sign of light in two of the casements, that Mr. Longnor was at home, the tailor gently rapped at the door, and at once lifting the latch, entered a room, half parlour, half kitchen—for it had the adornments of the one, and the homeliness of the other. Crossing to the glowing, cheerful fire-place (for in far-away country places such as this, where wood abounds, the nightly fire is rarely ever missed), and looking round the snugness of an old leather screen, drawn up to one corner of the fire-place, the good old tailor bowed thrice, as if before a potentate, and laid the letter in silence upon Mr. Longnor's old quaintly-carved desk. Thus aroused, the abstract curate looked up with a quiet smile, and whilst he said, " Well! this is kind, Northwood," broke the seal with hands as tremulous as if they had received a galvanic shock. And well they might, for there dropped from the letter, whilst he read, a £5 Bank of England note ; and the matter, though terse, was of such great meaning and interest as to make Mr. Longnor, the instant he had read it, rise, cross the kitchen, and tapping at a little door, say, " Dora, if yet awake, rise quickly and come here, as good old Northwood has brought us a letter, and there is news." He then came back to the fire-place, and grasped the tailor's honest hand : "It is not of my book," he said, with a weary sigh, which told painfully of months of expectancy and disappointment, "but news that is certainly flattering. The Society for the Advancement of British Science, requiring some geological verifications relative to a district in France, offer me, in this letter, the necessary mission, at a handsome remuneration."

"And just the very thing for you to accept, if I may be so bold as to give an opinion," spoke the good tailor, with his heart in his voice; "for such as care for you, Mr. Longnor, have noticed your pale face this many a week; and as for Miss Dora, not a rough wind of heaven shall blow on her, if I or my dame, or Tim, or Leah, our little maid, or the good souls at the 'Barley Mow,' can help it. So that mustn't be a hindrance, sir —indeed it mustn't."

The curate did not answer, for he had risen, as if impatient, and had already approached the door at which he had previously rapped, when it opened, and a young girl appeared. Her dress, though hastily put on, and loosely arranged, was exquisite in its becomingness; and as she stepped out, with naked feet, it fell round her in such folds as a statuary might have chiselled. Already aware that the good old tailor had brought a letter, she hastened with tearful earnestness to a hassock beside the fire, and listened whilst her father read ; and as she sat thus bending, her upturned face was such a one as comes not often to charm our innate sense of what is pure, and beautiful, and good; for it expressed childishness, love, hope, truth, and yet the grander qualities of intelligence and resolve. Hers was a small, frail, girlish figure, too; a bud rather than a flower; for whilst her small fair arms were finely rounded, her naked feet all plump and dimpled, her remarkable and glorious ebon-coloured hair so profuse as to fall far below the bodice of her little frock, yet her tiny hands, her little waist, her whole fragility, told of few, few years on this dear gentle mother-earth of ours. No wonder is it that sculpture is the grandest of artistic capabilities, when it has the attribute of representing forms like these; and freeing form from sense, and grace from mere mortality, so raises us, and lifts us yet a little nearer, and a little nearer heaven, by yielding to our sight what, we well fancy, may be some likeness to its angels!

The curate read, and when he had finished he dropped the letter from his hand, as if irresolute. But Dora, intuitively knowing the secret of this irresolution, came to his side and wound her little arms at once about his neck.

"If you love me, papa," she said earnestly, "you will go. It is the fullest summer-time, and every one will be good to me, I am sure; and isn't old Absalom Podd almost as tender to me as yourself, and isn't dear old Northwood here like a second father; and is there not, besides these, Tim, and

Ruth, and Leah, and Lucy Gray across Clun Forest, and Brindle, and Ned, and the bees and flowers! Think a minute of it, dearest papa, and you will find I shall be amused. You must go; indeed you must, if only for your health!"

So Dora talked, the old tailor persuaded, the curate listened, and at last consented. Upon again referring to the letter, it was found by its post-mark to have been a full day in the custody of Miss Cadwallader; the time given for preparation and reaching London being thus lessened to the following evening, when, if Mr. Longnor undertook the journey at all, he must reach the nearest highroad and travel by that night's western mail. This important step thus decided upon, and its otherwise great obstacle removed by the £5 Bank of England note enclosed within the letter, immediate preparations had to be commenced. Thus there was a long message to be delivered, the first thing in the morning, to Absalom Podd, the landlord of the village inn, the 'Barley Mow'; then a letter to write, for Northwood to send, by the special hand of Tim, to the curate of a neighbouring village, asking him to do duty once a fortnight during Mr. Longnor's absence; and lastly, this fine soul, stepping gently across the kitchen to the clock, brought from a peg beside it his sole black coat, and placed it in the tailor's hand.

"If you black the seams a bit, Northwood, and darn the cuffs, and put on new buttons, it'll do, I think, bravely," he said, with much cheerfulness;

"and when I come back there'll be a new coat, and what's more, a frock for baby Dora here" (in love he often called her so,) "for you see——."

"Yes, yes," quickly interrupted the old tailor, in a voice so tremulous, so quick, and yet so hearty, that one less abstracted than the curate would have noticed it; "the seams shall be quite black, sir, the cuffs all right, the buttons new, and the best shall be done with thread and needle, and all in time." Thus saying, and taking the old black coat upon his arm, the good tailor withdrew in much precipitation, under the sudden pretext that the hour was late.

Once alone, this fine noble soul, wasted and wan and ascetic, and past middle life, sunk into his old worn chair beside the fire, and Dora drew her little hassock to his feet. Thus father and child sat talking long and far into the night; talking in such a way as to make it, as it were, a pity for so much sense, persuasion, absence of self and self-consideration to die, unheard by other ears, upon the stillness of the night; for I believe, as fully as I believe in the great predominance of good over evil, that if communions such as these could be set down by recording pens at half their worth, the very words of man himself would testify to the divineness of my creed.

"I must have had some powerful friend in this business, my Dora," spoke this fine nature, wholly unconscious that his splendid acquirements, both as a geologist, especially in relation to this Silurian district, and as a scientific man, were well known;

"and I can think of no other than Mr. Riddle. His name does not appear, but his is the friendly hand."

"It is certainly no other, papa," replied Dora; "for we live in this far-away place, and can be known but to few."

"But when we have one grand, one large-souled friend, my dear one, like Walter Riddle, think how many small, narrow-minded ones he stands in place of! Yes, he has a splendid mind, and a noble soul to bear it company; and though I am the poorest curate amidst these far-away hills, I often think myself the very richest, simply in knowing a man so splendid and so just."

"And I, papa," said Dora, "fancy often I know as much about him as if I had seen him every day, though I have not since I was five years old, and now in three weeks I shall be fifteen. But we talk much about him, and this makes him familiar to me, though I remember little more than that he was tall and grave, and what now I should call stern."

"But he remembers you, Dora, well. As I have often told you, he talked repeatedly of you when I was at Broadlands last year; indeed, so often as to take an interest in you, like, as if you were his own child. He spoke admiringly of your simple, pure, child's life amidst these lonely hills, of my scholarly rearing of you, of your proficiency; and often asked if your beauty in any way fulfilled the promise of your babyhood. I said I scarcely knew, though you were good and kind, and eager to be taught; for the rest, I added, he himself shall paint the picture when he comes to see us, which he promised to do. And I count on your seeing him face to face, my dear one; for if you are yet too young to fully comprehend his genius, you will recollect that he has been my pupil, that his friendship is dear to me, and that you will regard him, reverence him, and, I may almost say, obey his scholarly advice, for my sake."

"I am sure I shall, papa; your words are always law."

As she thus answered the curate paused, for the church clock striking two hours past midnight, he, after a few further words about the morrow, embraced her tenderly, and dismissed her to her chamber. Thus separated, young Dora did not see the tears which fell, nor the chill sorrow which strangely crept over this dear father; nor, fortunately, did he see his child's assumed cheerfulness melt into bitterest grief as she crouched down at the foot of her little bed and thought of the morrow. But by-and-by, when the long wick of the candle had assumed the mushroom top it does when long unsnuffed, she trimmed it, gently rose (for by this time her father had entered his own chamber), and opened a little paper-covered box which stood in one corner of the room. Small as it was, it contained almost her whole wardrobe; and after due search therein, she brought, carefully folded up, from the bottom, a little white frock, which might have been worn by a child of four or five years old. It was a precious relic, for it was one her dead mother had arrayed her in newly, on the occasion of some little childish festival; and it had been laid by with tender reverence, only to serve some purpose as sacred as it was now to serve; for, reaching her work-bag, bringing the little round table to the bed's foot, and producing two or three poor tattered shirts from an old drawer, she dived the scissors deep, without hesitation, into the sacred garment, cut frills to make these poor rags more passable, and as the night wore on, as the candle burnt lower and lower, as the lonely church-clock tolled the hours, as the scattered forest boughs soughed gently to and fro, as the clear mountain brook rippled and rippled on, a sweet serenity soothed her guileless and most loving heart, and made the task as dear and light a one as any yet recorded of fair ministering spirits.

Another task of the same sort was proceeding elsewhere; for, as soon as he had latched the parsonage door, old Northwood tucked the coat under his arm, and hastened his pace into a run, till breathlessly he stood an instant beneath his cottage eaves. Unlatching this door (for in these primitive parts of England the house-door is rarely locked, even through the night), and entering with a gentle footfall, that would not have disturbed the lightest sleeper, he found, as he expected, that the whole of his little household had retired to rest, but the fire, carefully plied with fuel, burnt cheerfully in the wide old-fashioned grate. Rousing it into a still warmer glow, he lighted a candle, fetched a bit of supper from the pantry, and when eaten, replaced the plate by his well-worn bible, put on his spectacles, and sat reverently down. The book on this night, as if it had power to point out its own lesson, opened at the fifth chapter of St. Matthew, where the Divine Sermon on the Mount glorifies with its sublime morality the sacred page. And so he read, as it were, by intuition, " Blessed are the merciful, for they shall obtain mercy ;" and so having read, he resolved, whilst he paused a moment, to follow out the promptings of his heart. And so resolved, he read on ; and from this to a newer chapter and a newer verse, " When thou doest alms let not thy left hand know what thy right hand doeth, that thy alms may be in secret." Thus with this resolution, and the manner of its accomplishment, fixed in his mind, he reverently paused when he had ended, and prepared himself, his candle, his board for a night's work, took a quaint key from his pocket, and unlocking an old buffet, produced a small roll of cloth therefrom, though of the finest texture and the deepest black, took shears and cut a coat the pattern of the one he had brought to mend, and then mounting his well-worn board, plied with earnest, steady fingers, the swiftest needle which ever served in any honest worthy work. And thus the hours went on—work, work, work, work ; and yet no weariness, for it was holy service.

Beyond some few directions to honest Podd, the worthy landlord of the " Barley Mow," there was little for Mr. Longnor to do; for merely saying, "I place Dora in your charge, and all besides," was just the same as if the trust were minutely detailed in the lengthiest scroll of parchment, and sealed with the binding seal of priest or king.   But quite resolutely, and with womanly decision, Dora at once negatived Podd's proposition that she should take up her abode at the "Barley Mow;" and as the barest thought of quitting home—the dear household home—seemed to give her pain, her father soon consented.   But full allowance was given to Podd to come and work in the garden, for Tim to run errands and milk Brindle, and for Ruth to lay aside her service in the little bar of the "Barley Mow," every evening by nine o'clock, for the purpose of sleeping at the parsonage.   "Well, well," mumbled Podd, "I'm only to work in the garden, and see to the meadow and orchard, am I? But I'll make Dora, ne'ertheless, the best guarded flower in the country, for, a-dear! her beauty be a touching thing."   Thus mumbling, of which he had a great habit, Mr. Podd withdrew, promising to be at the church-yard gate with his old-fashioned gig at the very stroke of eight that eve.

Something like honest Northwood, Podd was full of weighty thought as he ascended to the village, and immediately saddling and mounting his old grey mare, he proceeded to an adjacent village, and finding an honest pedlar, who occasionally dwelt there, commissioned him to come and purchase the very best beaver hat in

Miss Cadwallader's shop, as if some far-away gentleman had given him the job, and after that to bring it up at once to the "Barley Mow." Then hastening homeward, he unlocked a ponderous oak bureau, took from thence four Holland shirts of curious fineness, only used on high days and holidays, and doing them carefully up in a silk pocket-handkerchief, laid the parcel ready in the bar, and then set about making his old-fashioned gig as trim and as snug as possible, providing it with a due number of warm caped coats for the journey.

This eventful day wore quickly away both with the curate and Dora; for the one had many papers to get ready and arrange, and the other a hundred labours of love to perform — to wash, and iron, and set in order the two poor shirts plied by such angel fingers.

After the evening's refreshment of tea, Mr. Longnor rose and said, "As neither Podd nor Northwood is yet come, my Dora, we will go a little walk;" and knowing what he meant, she followed him with reverend feet. They passed into the shadowed garden together; from thence across the mossied road-way, into the grey and still churchyard. The sun was sinking, and thus threw long strips of golden glory over many graves—making, in the splendour of their decking, no difference between moss and stone, poor peasant resting-place, and dust of wealth and birth; for in the embrace of beauty one law of pure equality alone is ruling potentate. So on the lowliest though sunniest grave, niched in the very quaintest and most ivied buttress of the old grey walls, they knelt together long in silence, for the hearts of both were over-full for words. At last, however, the curate said, " The sweetest spirit of thy mother watch over thee in my absence, Dora, and guard thee, dear one, and keep thee safe, as the most precious thing I hold in life ! "

" I shall be safe—I shall be safe," sobbed Dora; " nothing can harm me, nothing can change me ! God above, and my mother's dust so near, what harm can come ? " She said this with a light heart, and rose; for the welcome richness of the sinking sun, the trickling and the babbling of the water, the garniture of the forest boughs, the scent of the ferny woodlands, and the garden flowers, all served to calm their grief, and shed a balmy influence on their souls. As they passed through the mossied churchyard gate, the curate produced a key from his waistcoat pocket. " This must be yours, my Dora," he said, as he placed the key into the half-upraised, half-closed hands of the weeping girl, " for it belongs to the drawers so long kept locked. When I am gone, this night I wish you, as hallowing your lonely home with what is unperished of the beautiful, the pure, the good, to unlock these drawers, and look on what has remained untouched since the day she died. And seeing, take what is there and make them yours; her bridal gown and all, for her sweet sake." Thus speaking, they entered the house. Here they beheld Podd and the tailor, both so excessively happy and merry, that, though the cause was concealed, their cheerfulness gave Mr. Longnor spirits at once. And rightly they laughed, for Northwood had done so astonishing a job as to fully hide every white seam, make the cuffs glossy, and the buttons firm; and Podd had carefully strapped up the little portmanteau, and brought it to the door. How kind was this! The new hat could not so well escape detection; but the instant it was discovered by Dora, worthy Absalom made such a sudden grumbling about its being late, and that that night's mail would be certainly lost, that nothing more could be said or done than to put the little portmanteau into the gig, for this fine soul and good soul to bless and tear himself away from his passionately weeping child, and wave his hand with mute significance to the old tailor, whilst his bent and downward face left more to conjecture than to sight.

The young girl watched the gig till out of sight, and then returned to the solitary house, and closed the door. The old tailor respected her feelings too much to trespass on this desire for privacy, and so took his way home. But by-and-by Dora's passionate grief lessened, and remembering her father's last injunction, "as she loved him, to be cheerful," she closed the rustic shutters, put more wood on the fire, drew the comfortable chair and little green baize-covered table near, laved her face and hands, smoothed her beautiful and abundant tresses, and then brought the candle to the drawers so long untouched.

These stood in a recess beside the fire-place, and beneath a shelf consecrated by some of her father's rarest books—thus were the sacred things of the dead and living in close companionship. The locks were very full of dust; but after slight difficulty the first drawer was opened, and there lay, just covered and put as hands long perished had laid them—gown and scarf, petticoat and shawl. The first thing, almost, which attracted her attention, was a small white gown; a girlish, simple thing, almost fitted for herself. An irresistible impulse came over her to put it on, and so, coming and setting down the candle upon the little table before the fire, she unfastened her humble frock, and robed herself in its trim, simple nicety— short sleeves, low bodice, without one single ornament upon them. It was—and yet scarcely seemed too large. One half-hour's labour with the needle, a wash in the limpid running brook, ten minutes on the fullest rose-tree of the glorious June, and it would be fitted to serve again, what it had once served, a bridal. As she stood thus, it only fastened on in negligent disorder, never had the old distant mirror, on which the fire-light stole, reflected back a simpler, purer, more perfect little human creature, the whole wealth of whose passionately loving heart lived in those glad large eyes, as they travelled up from hem to sleeve, from bodice back to hem again! She stood as pure a thing as opening bud to its first morning sun!

Thus, as she stood, half mournfully, half gladly,

thinking of a hundred things which yet linked her to her dead mother, some hand knocked several times upon the porch door. It could not be Ruth, who could not come till ten on this night of Podd's absence—it could not be Northwood or Tim—it was, perhaps, some one of the distant parishioners, ignorant, as yet, of Mr. Longnor's departure, or a traveller asking the way. Without hesitation she crossed the kitchen, opened the door full wide, and a stranger, a tall, dark, stern-faced man, of middle age, stood before her. She stood, though thus in the doorway, in the full glow of the strong light which shone from the warm hearth, quite irresolute and speechless, looking up into his remarkable face. He was a stranger, but not a beggar or a traveller—she knew not what to say. At last he stooped down, and, in a low voice, said—his intense gaze never once removed from off her face, her girlish figure, her wonderfully becoming little gown—

"Dora Longnor?"

"Yes, sir;" and as she said so, she dropped a little curtsey; lowly, so very lowly, as if he were the greatest of the earth.

"And I, Walter Riddle;" and as he spoke he took her very little hand within his large one, and came into the kitchen and closed the door. As if expecting to see the curate, he went at once to the fire-place, and looked round the screen, "And your father?" he asked, in a voice of surprise.

"Gone, sir, this very evening. We thought

you knew." She spoke tremulously, for the intense gaze had never been removed.

He sat down at once in her father's old study chair, still looking upon her so fixedly, and said, "Tell me!"

In her own artless way, still standing, though shrouding her arms together as if to hide their roundness, she told Mr. Riddle of the whole circumstance of her father's absence.

He seemed surprised. "I mentioned him to the Association some months ago," he said, "as a capable person, in case the verifications respecting Auvergne and the Puy de Dome were needed. At that time they said they had a candidate of their own, if one were wanted. I had thus quite forgotten the circumstances, though seemingly so well remembered by themselves."

This inquiry ended, he began immediately to talk to Dora about herself; she still standing artlessly with her arms bent down before her.

"And why this gown, Dora—is it a holiday?"

"My mother's bridal gown, sir," and thinking of her, she burst into tears. Riddle drew her to his side ; and, as if at her father's knees, she sat down upon the little hassock. Presently she told him of the scene that evening by the grave, of the dusty locks, of the drawers, of this, her mother's bridal gown ; he listened intently, the whole tale was done, and her tears were dry.

"And you had never put it on before, only thus as I came?"

"I had never even seen it. An hour since,

and it lay where the dead had put it, and the very flowers and pins of my poor mother's marriage day still within." The large hand trembled; the small hand felt the vibration.

For many minutes the stern man sat silent; then he suddenly began to talk about her studies, bid her fetch her father's Schiller from its shelf, and taking a short, full-bowled little pipe from his pocket, which he called his " Churchwarden," lighted it, and bid her read to him. She brought the book, sat down again upon the hassock at his feet, he smoked, occasionally corrected her, or praised, but never once removed his gaze from off her face.

In this new relation of scholar and master, all other than a modest fear left the girl ; and sitting thus, all the unconscious purity of her nature outshone, and, for the full confidence between them, they might have been reading this immortal poetry together for an age !

And thus they sat together; Mr. Churchwarden having his old, black, smoky cavity replenished several times before this long lesson in Schiller was over. At length, some minutes after the book was closed, Mr. Riddle rose to go, which, as he did, a large shaggy hound crawled out from beneath one of the chairs, where it had been resting. Dora rose, too, from off the hassock, and brought the empty Churchwarden from the hob, on which it lay forgotten, and with it the candle, towards the door. As he took his little short thick Dutchman from her hand, and held that little hand within his own, he stooped a moment involuntarily, as if to kiss her; then, as if suddenly impelled by a more sacred and holy feeling, he merely pressed this little hand with kindly fervour, bowed low before her, as if in homage of her purity and unconscious trust, and saying that he should be there again in the morning, as he had already bespoken a lodging at the "Barley' Mow," he latched the door, and stepped out into the fresh and balmy night.

With a light, glad heart, proud of her master and the night's lesson, Dora went back to look anew at the Schiller, but it was gone. Yet scarcely she needed a book; there was so much on this night to think about, to wonder at, to reverence, that there she sat, still in the same posture, still in the long-past bridal dress, still as an early primrose opening to the sun, when Ruth, escorted by, and long lingering with, a village beau, rapped lightly at the door.

Till then, upon the broad, low, ancient church-yard wall, leaned a man; till then a shaggy hound lay silent at his feet; till then was innocence and goodness surely guarded, and only some half hour after did the "Barley Mow" receive its new-come guest.

Till it was far past midnight did Absalom Podd's new guest sit before the little parlour fire, filling and refilling his smoky Churchwarden more times than I can count; but the volume of Schiller, after twice reading over the lesson of the night, lay open and uncared for on his knee, for the fire seemed to be a book with endless pages, on which his gaze was fixed, and never altered.

With quite the early morrow—indeed, at an hour which, considering that it was past midnight when his guest retired, astonished worthy Absalom as he meditated, about this and other things, over his pipe in the little bar, Mr. Riddle strolled from the rustic inn. As this was one of the prettiest places in the world, with old timber gables, and jutting eaves of thatch, and with a sweet bowery garden, which almost rivalled that of the parsonage, no wonder that the stranger preferred to take his way along its flower-bordered walks towards the quiet fields which lay beyond. As he passed through the little wicket, on either side of which ran a long, shady, sweetbriar hedge, he met Ruth on her way from the parsonage; so, guessing from whence she came, he stopped to speak to her.

"Oh! dear, yes, sir," replied the rustic beauty, as she stood, with a basket on her arm, like Morland's country girl, "Miss Dora will be quite ready to see you, for I've righted everything up, as missis bid me; and dear old master was there by four o'clock, trimming the flower-borders and milking the cow, and old Northwood has been down to say that, as Leah roasts some fowls and makes a pudding to-day, the dear young lady mustn't be troubled about a dinner; so you'll find her, sir, in the curate's little book-room, sitting like the biggest lady in the land."

So saying, the maid of the inn dropped her

profoundest curtsey; for her master had announced in the kitchen, previous to her departure to the parsonage on the over night, that the new guest was some "great gentleman;" and passed on, leaving him to the sweet peacefulness of the solitary flower-decked fields. But he, ordinarily such a reveller in and reader of nature, was deaf to the low cadence of the wind as it lightly bent the grass and rustled the thick leaves of the bowery hedges—was deaf to the ripple of the brook as it sung its way amidst old gnarled roots and overhanging boughs—was deaf to throstles' and to blackbirds' notes, to the low call of kine upon the hills—was blind to flower and leaf, to field and wood, to earth and sky—saw nothing, heard nothing, and knew nothing, but that which lay before his rapid, eager steps. Calling back his hound, with a peremptory voice, if it chanced to go before, as if jealous that it should precede him by a hair's-breadth, he gained the sylvan parsonage; and, entering through its leafy porch, stood in the half-kitchen, half-parlour, which I have already described. Everything was still, and cool, and pleasant; the rich, warm morning sun fell in strips through the ivied casement panes upon the bright red floor; and through these casements and the open doors the brook breeze brought the garden treasures of the honeysuckle and the rose. One glance around, on oak buffet, quaint clock, old screen, wood fire, he uncovered, and, passing through the shadow of a niche-like doorway, found himself within Mr. Longnor's little study, and saw Dora seated on the wide old window-ledge. In an instant her work had fallen on the floor, for she had been sewing, and she bounded towards her father's friend with all the frankness with which a child seeks those it has been taught to love. But like was not met by like; so, awed by Mr. Riddle's somewhat cold and restrained greeting, Dora dropped a little curtsey, and stood downcast and abashed before him. Her guileless heart guessed not the secret and the truth, or the stern vow made over the fading embers of the rustic fire. But Hero, the hound, who had crept in unseen, taking as it were advantage of this pause, slouched forward, and was about to nestle his broad dewlap on her shoulder, when a peremptory "Down, sir! out, sir!" put an end to his kindly-demonstrative intention, and he slunk back to his place in the porch, quite downcast and subdued. Still more abashed, Dora was about to say something, such as, "good morning," instead of the impulsive, guileless, "I am so glad to see you, sir," when Mr. Riddle said abruptly,

"Come, Dora, put on your bonnet, and show me the woodlands; as your father is not at home, you must be my guide, as you probably would if he were here. Come, we can talk, for I have much to ask."

"Yes, sir; we will talk about dear papa, it pleases me so to speak of him."

"And about yourself, Dora. Now fetch your bonnet."

He said this in a way which prevented further

discussion; and, sitting down by the little door-way, so as there to have a full view of the kitchen, he lighted up Mr. Church-warden. Nor once, whilst Dora moved to and fro, plying the fire so as to last till her return, putting on her poor bonnet and childish tippet, did he remove his gaze, but watched her as a mariner a precious guiding-star. And well he might; for his heart was true in judging Dora, a precious little human creature. Already was the rare promise of her girlish beauty a thing of talk about that solitary country-side—already had her learning, and the rare pains taken in her educa-tion, been talked about by rustic folks over their winter's fire; on moorland and hill, in forest and by brook, had she been seen a companion of her father; and thus, with health, beauty, much knowledge, and extreme youth, and with a warm, affectionate, yet pure and guileless heart, she was one of those sweet spirits fitted by heaven to mingle with superior natures.

At last she came; her rich and ebon-coloured hair tucked up beneath her humble bonnet, her rounded arms scarcely shadowed by the little tip-pet, a small light basket in her ungloved hand. The porch door was locked, the key hidden in its accustomed place, and Dora led the way across the plashy stepping-stones of the rapid brawling brook.

They were soon amidst the wild primeval forest land of this sweet country. And in solitudes as deep—except here and there for a woodman busy in the bracken, or a charcoal-burner with his smouldering piles of faggots—as if on a western prairie, or an isle of the far Pacific. Sometimes on ferny uplands, sometimes by solitary oaks of giant growth, sometimes in deep glades, as still and shadowed as a Druidical grove (though such are rare, for much of this noble land is disforested), sometimes by mountain ridges, where the red sandstone yawned in picturesque declivities, and opened Nature's primal book for man to read; sometimes where earlier formations still cropped out, and showed the signs of long-passed surging oceans, monstrous and wild; sometimes by tarn and rivulet they wandered on, talking as Mr. Riddle wished the girl to talk, though not, perhaps, to that full measure which his soul required. For, light of foot, revisiting her father's haunts, and enthusiastic in that which had become to her, from the long and almost daily habit of her life, a second nature, she led Mr. Riddle to some of the places amidst the wildest recesses of the forest and the hills, where Longnor's most happy researches and verifications had been made, and naturally gave their several little histories, so interesting to the earnest student.

As the day wore on, the sun fell hot upon the forest-paths, though shadowed here and there by thick-leaved giant boughs; and as they had now walked far, since the old country church clock had struck nine, they sat down midway in a broad old glade, yet spared from the woodman's axe, and which evidently served the purposes of a road for

the charcoal-burners' wains, or for an occasional
horseman.   And here they rested on as rich a
carpet of flowery verdure as nature ever spread
for her weary-footed children ; the richness of the
golden sun crowning the dark holly-trees with
glory, and the fern and hare-bell, the bramble and
the feathery grass, timing their own faint melodies
to the rich diapason of the soughing forest boughs.
For a long way, till they thus sat down, Mr. Riddle
had been questioning Dora about her studies, and
so talking, and finding her knowledge on many
things even more accurate than he had anticipated,
he now, as he sat, relaxed from that stern, distant
manner which he had assumed; and Dora, thus
won from her timidity, opened the little basket
she had brought with her, and took out a small
flask of cowslip-wine, which was the very smallest
portion of what was held in an excessively fat
bottle, placed cunningly in the closet that very
morning by dear old Podd, and a slice of the nice
saffron-cake Mrs. Northwood and her little Leah
had concocted whilst the good old tailor had been
effecting his miracle upon the curate's coat. Breaking the cake within the leaves with which she had
covered it, she proffered it, and the flask, to Mr.
Riddle.   The first impulsive movement of his
hand betrayed how readily his heart accepted the
gentle offer; but the next instant he had repulsed
her with a cold " Not any, I thank you," which at
once paralysed the gentle and affectionate nature
of the girl.   She dropped the flask and cake, rose
quickly, and burst into tears.

"I will go home, sir, if you please; I am sorry if I have offended you; I hoped you would not recollect the difference between us; papa said that whenever you came you would not; that you were noble and kind; that—that—Sir—Mr. Riddle—if you came you would be like an uncle or a brother towards me. I will go home, sir—the charcoal-burners will tell you the way."

"Nonsense, Dora, nonsense! Come, sit down, and eat your luncheon. I want to be noble to you, Dora—noble as a god. This is why, perhaps, I am stern and cold. Now let us go back to last night's lesson—we may have to talk about this matter another day."

She had crouched down again upon the grass without replying, or without looking up, for her tears were yet undried, when the approach of some one on horseback struck her ear. She raised her face, and recognized in the old farmer-like rider, and his high-bred hackney, no other than Squire Fieldworth, whose letter-bag was so sedulously attended to by Miss Cadwallader, and whose coachman, Bump, angled so dexterously with jellies and cold tarts for the hand of the spinster and the strings of her purse. The squire was riding leisurely, and having nothing to think about beyond his dinner and his rents, he scrutinized Dora with much coolness, then her companion, whose bearing and appearance greatly excited his curiosity; and when he had ridden sufficiently out of sight amidst the trees, he gave a long, low whistle, of peculiar significance, and urged his horse into a quicker pace.

As this squire was at feud not simply with honest Podd, but with old Northwood, and half-a-dozen of the other parishioners, his only resource in the matter of satisfying his curiosity was Miss Cadwallader; and from her he learnt, not only that this stranger's name was Riddle, and that he had had letters that morning, re-directed from one of the great colleges of Cambridge, and from Broadlands Hall, in an adjoining county, but also all such particulars of Mr. Longnor's departure and business as Miss Martha had been able to ascertain through means good, bad, and indifferent.

Mightily full of all this village news, the squire would probably have delivered himself of it to his two eldest daughters the instant he arrived home, had he not smelt the savour of his favourite dish, and found the cloth already laid for dinner. As partaking of this meal was the most important duty of his life, he delayed imparting his own adventure, and such information as he had obtained from Miss Cadwallader, till his favourite pippins and his bottle were on the table, and his three daughters around him, the two eldest of whom were fair representatives of himself, and the third, some years younger (though by no means very youthful, and by a second wife), was the Cinderella of the household, for the sole reason that she had fallen in love with a member of a neighbouring family, not liked by the squire, because

their acres were fewer than his own.   As is usual
with Cinderellas, Anne was the bright light of the
Fieldworths.

The squire, having come to the end of his nar-
rative, poured out another glass of wine, and gave
another long and low whistle.   It meant much,
and was perfectly understood by Sophia and Jane.

"Of course," said Sophia, " my experience of
human nature teaches me that no good can come
of this matter.   And as for what any man can
see in such a low-bred girl, whose father pleases
her to consort with publican and tailor's wives, and
a miller's daughter, I cannot think.   But we shall
see!"   And this *sotto voce* parenthesis meant to
convey as much as the squire's whistle.

"Fie, fie," replied Anne, warmly, and with
much courage, considering her position in the
household; "why attach evil to what can only be
the purest and noblest friendship between such a
child and such a man?—for if you loved books, or
knew anything of literature, his very name would
tell you that Mr. Riddle is incapable, both from
position and character, of the evil you surmise;
and if this were not even so, I believe Dora Longnor to be——"

"There, there," interrupted the squire, "dunna
have any talk about her—I hate her and her father; and as for thy quarrels, go and settle 'em in
the still-room or garden; I want my nap, and that
more than all the Cambridge men or parsons'
daughters.   So be off till tea-time—though, I say,
Sophy, if thee think this man be decent enough

to eat off our family plate, write him a bit of an invitation, and send it by Bump to the 'Barley Mow'; and as on course he'll be rarely glad, he'll come, and we shall see what he's made on."

As the squire, before he finished this sentence, had lapsed into what might be called the first stage of his nap, and as both the elder spinsters had, for strong reasons of their own, already determined upon the simple squire's suggestion, they spitefully glanced at Anne, and withdrew, not only to write the note, and send it off immediately by Bump (a very convenient resolution in relation to a breast of the squire's spring duck, a few peas, and a rich cheese-cake), but to concoct such a plan of proceeding as might make Miss Cadwallader loquacious, without impairing their own dignity!—thus leaving Anne to take her after-dinner's saunter up and down the broad old western terrace, and none the worse for judging well and rightly of the pure, and beautiful, and youthful of her sex. Sweet Anne! None but the pure in heart see God!

Her tears were dry, her heart was light, her foot elastic, when Dora found the key and unlocked the parsonage door; for Mr. Riddle, though still cold in manner, had been less reserved upon their homeward path than hitherto throughout the morning. He had parted with her at the wicket, and entering the house alone, she found that the good Northwood's little Leah had been there, had replenished the fire, had placed the savoury little dinner so beside it that it kept hot, and had done such other small household offices as were needful.

So dining, Dora swung the kettle over the fire, set the hearth in order, smoothed her beautiful ebon tresses before the little oval mirror which hung beside the screen, and with hands as delicate and cool as the swift-running brook could make them, she took her work-bag, and the poor bridal gown of the past marriage-day, and went out and sat upon the turfed plot, so shadowed and so still, beside the trickling brook. It was a golden evening, and the bees still searched the flowers. She had not sat long before Tim, whose duty it was at this time of day to milk Brindle, came across the grass, bearing a little parcel and message from honest Podd, that she was to make some coffee for Mr. Riddle, who would be there by seven. The clock had already struck six, so she hastened to perform this new duty, and all was ready on the sweet cool turf just by the stroke of seven. The tall coffee-cups of purple hue (left by an ancient parishioner to Mr. Longnor), the golden-coloured cream in a small jug of crystal glass, the sugar in a little silver bowl of antique shape—all looked as if set out upon the shadowed sward to feed some dainty queen. Besides all this too was Mr. Churchwarden, who had been left in the little study that very morning.

The guest was punctual to his time; he surveyed everything at a glance, sat down upon the sward, bid her fill his pipe and pour out the coffee, and whilst she sewed he read the Schiller he had brought; now and then looking up from it to see those little fingers ply the needle, and by-and-by laying aside his book to smoke Mr. Churchwarden in silence. As the church clock again struck nine, and the shadows of evening fell around, he bid her good night, leaving her to fill up the time till Ruth should come in writing a long letter to her father.

As this day had passed, so did full ten others; and, accustomed now to his often cold and distant manner, Dora was Riddle's guide about that rich sylvan country of western Shropshire, and of an evening made his coffee and filled Mr. Churchwarden, and sat with him by that rippling brook till the shadows fell. And nothing could be purer than this communion; it was that of scholar and master, father and child, preacher and devotee. Old worthy Podd and Northwood were glad that Dora had such fine scholarly company, particularly as the curate had written to Dora a letter of delight and congratulation touching this matter.

As I have said, Dora Longnor had a little friend named Lucy Gray, whose father lived some seven miles across the forest, and kept a rustic mill, turned by a mountain stream, and hidden in old woods. Without this incident of Mr. Riddle's coming, five days would certainly have not elapsed, particularly on an occasion like this of the curate's absence, without Dora walking across the forest to the mill; and, therefore, the good miller, and his homely wife and little daughter, when they heard of Mr. Longnor's absence from a passing traveller, wondered much at being yet without a glimpse of Dora's face. So, at last impatient to see her little friend, the rustic beauty of sixteen put on her holiday frock, and new-trimmed bonnet, and little scarf, and taking advantage of her father riding across the forest that morning, mounted behind him on her pillion, to which was strapped a basket of country dainties for sweet Dora. As it strangely happened, Mr. Riddle was absent from the parsonage that morning, so Lucy, when she alighted at the gate, found her little friend ; and when the good miller had deposited his basket, pressed warmly and kindly his wife's invitation upon Dora, and promised to call again for Lucy in the evening, he left the girls together, and proceeded to the village on business. And now, arm-in-arm about the quaint old house and shadowy garden, the girls confided to one another their childish secrets —simple and girlish ones enough, but pure as the wind upon the mountain top, or the water from its hidden spring. In talk like this, of confidence and love, the day wore quickly by, till, in the shadows of the evening, they waited for the good miller on a rustic garden-seat, and again talked over what they had so much talked about throughout the day.

" I am sure," said Lucy, in reply to a question Dora had asked her twenty times that day, " that Mr. Riddle's coldness and sternness must be a manner put on. I am older than you, Dora, and fancy that men do these sort of things sometimes."

"Why?" asked Dora, with visible wonderment.

"Why?" said Lucy, almost harshly repeating her little friend's question as she drew herself away, and holding her by the waist at arm's length, looked sweetly into her half-tearful eyes and downcast face; "because you are so very beautiful, my darling, and he loves you!"

"Nay, nay," wept Dora, "this cannot be. I am such a child, and he so much older; besides being so high in station, and so splendid in his learning! It cannot be. Only it is a pity he is so cold and stern, and so peremptory, because I have that feeling in my heart as if I should like for ever to wait on him, ever be beside him, ever listen to him, ever be his little servant, and he my master, or like his sister or his daughter." And here she bent her head, and sobbed convulsively.

"Dora," said Lucy, as she folded the little weeping creature to her heart, "though you think it not, you are in love."

"Do not say so—do not tell anyone. Oh, no, it is not true!" cried the girl passionately, as she clung to her friend.

"Because it is so true, my darling," whispered Lucy, with a gentleness and grace which did her noble nature proudest justice, "depend upon it, I will be secret. Not even my mother, to whom I confide all secrets that are really mine, shall know it; and I am too proud of the confidence and attachment of one like yourself, so much better born and taught than I am, not to be sincere and truthful. So dry your tears, dear lady, and re-collect I am your friend in all things."

As Lucy thus dried Dora's tears with almost motherly affection, and Dora returned her friend's caresses, they heard the good miller's voice, and hastening to the house, they found him at the porch-door waiting for Lucy. As the evening was unusually dark for the time of year, and the way uneven across the forest, he did not dismount, but helping his pretty, much-loved little daughter to the pillion, as soon as she was ready, and repeating his warm and respectful invitation to Dora about expecting her at the mill, the girls leant their sweet faces together for a last farewell, and then the old steady horse was urged into a trot, and, once across the ford, was soon lost in the shadow of the woodlands.

The night, besides being overclouded, was un-usually damp and chill ; so, throwing more wood upon the broad old hearth, the girl sat down beside it, on the little hassock, as of old. Though full of thought, half hopeful and half sad, her ear was still alive to every sound which fell ; and when she heard the well-known hand open and close the door, and the now well-known foot come across the floor, the strange confession made to Lucy flitted again across her brain, and with all the feeling of one suddenly conscious of a monstrous crime, she was for the instant speechless and in-capable of motion.

" Dora !" at last was said, and looking up, Mr. Riddle was by her side, as she well knew, looking upon her fixedly; but this night there was a new and startling expression in his countenance. It bespoke hope, more than human admiration, and intensest joy, which, broadening into a smile of large significance, still beamed down upon her like some heavenly sun, as he passed, sat down in the curate's chair, and lighted Mr. Churchwarden. Trembling visibly, for she knew that earnest gaze was on her, as the tobacco smoke began to float in little spiral clouds, Dora did not dare to turn her face again. At length he repeated her name, and then looking up, she saw Mr. Riddle still smiled as he added—

"Well, are you willing to be obedient?"

"Yes, sir—in what? Shall I fetch you a book? —or——" She stopped here, and coloured violently, for she was now conscious that Mr. Riddle must have been near, and heard her half-sobbed confession to Lucy Gray.

"Yes, in the matter of a book, certainly—but a sacred one! For as you want to be my little minister, why——"

Burning with shame, and fancying that Mr. Riddle was satirising her presumption, Dora burst into passionate tears, and rose to leave the room with hurried feet; but Riddle, with one hand, restrained her, and made her sit down again upon the hassock.

"Now, Dora, I am not jesting, but speaking with that seriousness with which earnest men speak on matters of life and death. Now answer me as seriously as I am speaking; will you obey me in what I request?"

"Yes, sir,—I—I—will; papa said I was to obey you."

"Well, the matter is, that we, three mornings hence, go into an old church, not far from hence, and become man and wife! The little sacred ring on, my dear one, you will be the minister you ask to be, the one I require."

For some minutes Dora did not answer, did not look up, did not move; but at length, with inexpressible naïveté, as if silence made the fullest answer to the question, asked,

"But that is so very soon, sir; papa cannot know about it, and——"

The answer implied so eloquently, through silence, was paramount for the instant; and for the first time through all these days of acquaintanceship, and now only as a father to his child, he pressed his lips for the moment on her forehead, and bid heaven bless her worthy, genuine heart. Then almost immediately, again relapsing into his old stern manner, he added,

"No, one part of your obedience is, Dora, that no one must know it; but this only for a week. At the end of that time, I will write to your father, who, from some conversation we have already had, will be but little surprised; as also to my mother, whom my letters, since I have been here, will make a glad recipient of the truth. For this one week, however, let us be sacred from vulgar curiosity and vulgar talk; after that we will be on our way to meet your father on his return."

She placed her one hand out blindly towards Mr. Churchwarden, for her face was buried in the other, and when it was taken, asked,

"Not even Podd, sir, or dear Lucy?"

"Neither.   In this matter I sternly command; not from disrespect to either, my sweet wife in three days hence, but because love, in a stern and wayward nature like my own, is a jealous thing, a passionate, a secret thing; and after such long hoarding, after such stern resolve as I made the night I saw you first, unnecessary if your father had been here, but which I shall keep till the hour you are my wife, I want few to know how I first pour out my worship, my idolatry, my estimation.   In this matter my desire is to be free from vulgar curiosity.   For the rest all will be as your own dead mother could wish.   For my mother's home shall receive you; she who nursed me shall know from the first moment that you are my wife; and till the night before we are married, when I will come for a few moments to arrange about the morrow, I shall not see you again, as I must ride over to Broadlands, and make an old friend of mine ready for the office."

Dora made no reply, only her one hand rested near Mr. Churchwarden's black bowl and the clouds of smoke which now curled briskly from it. At length, she said, after a long pause, and with extreme and feminine naïveté, " Please, sir, what little gown shall I go to church in ? "

" Gown ? " and Riddle spoke as if the question surprised him, " why, of course, the one I saw you in ; wash it, alter it, do what you will with it, only, let it be put on somewhat as on the first night I saw you ; that is all I ask for, all I require ; and it will be much, Dora, much ! "

Then, as if remembering his stern resolve, he relapsed into silence ; though never once removing his gaze from off her drooping figure or buried face, or once taking his pipe from his lips. And when he withdrew that evening, much earlier than usual, his farewell was just as it had ever been ; and a stranger, who might have seen Dora light him to the porch, would have little guessed the sacred bond which was between them.

But though he quitted that warm fire-side, though the wind blew cold, and the night air was damp, he that loved so well lingered by the low mossied churchyard wall, not simply till Ruth was guardian of her little mistress, but till the taper's flame in Dora's chamber no longer twinkled out upon the eddies of the brook or on the sombre woodlands.

And if there are moments in the lives of all of us so exquisite in joy as to be worth the sorrows of a century to have known, the minutes of that night were of this character to this pure young child ; so believing, so unconscious of wrong, yet so immeasurably proud and glad of the worship of this exalted genius ; and if a doubt sometimes crossed her brain, as to error in not waiting for her father's sanction and return, she was (little heart) casuist enough to recollect that she had been told, and asked, to obey, on the one side by her father, on the other by him whose name had been a sacred household word since her cradle!

As soon as morning came, and, her household duties over, Ruth had departed, the little gown was brought from its drawer; and there was sewing, and washing, and ironing, till, as the sun fell on the morrow's eve, it lay ready like the folded flower within the greenness of the lily's bud.

That very same morning, the village urchin who usually bore the squire's letters between the hall and Miss Cadwallader's counter informed Miss Sophy's maid, as she peeped through the still room window, that "his missis had something to say to the ladies if they chanced to walk down the village that morning;" and Miss Sophy and Miss Jane, both fully understanding the purport of this message, equipped themselves and crossed the park to Miss Cadwallader's as soon after break- fast as the squire was safe in the stables.

Dismissing her few rustic customers as quickly as she could, Miss Cadwallader produced Mr. Riddle's letters of that morning, and amongst others one in which was plainly to be seen and felt a ring, a plain small thing without garniture of any sort or kind; and as it was much too small for any finger of manly size, it was, after being duly felt, wondered at, speculated upon, weighed, and so forth, fully settled as being a

WEDDING RING. And this conclusion arrived at, the spite of the spinsters was undisguised, particularly that of the two clothed in satin, whose polite, gilt-edged, hot-pressed note of invitation to dine off the squire's plate had had no other result than a cold and civil refusal from the lodger at the " Barley Mow."

" He can never surely be going to marry the girl," spoke Miss Jane, with much commiseration, " for though the man is a clown, and knows nothing of fashionable life, or what is due in respect to people like ourselves, he is surely too wise for a mistake of this sort."

Miss Cadwallader shook her head mysteriously, and then, much to the horror of the spinsters, entered fully into such particulars as she had been able to learn respecting the course of events at the parsonage. This was not much; but natures like that of Cadwallader bear an optical glass about with them of rare capacity in magnifying good into evil; especially in all which relates to the worth, the purity, or the truth of woman !

In all probability, at a gentle hint given, upon the spinisters' return, the squire in no great while would have been closeted with Miss Cadwallader, for he was particularly fond of a gossip, and the postmistress, as people in the village too well knew, had, on divers occasions, been zealous in gathering up little matters of scandal for his private ear; and the mysterious letter would have been touched, weighed, mentally assayed by this magisterial Solon, had not Podd at this instant, even as the ladies gossiped, walked in and asked for Mr. Riddle's letters.

"Pray, can you tell us, Podd," asked the antique Sophy, as the honest publican, gathering up the letters, was about to depart, "if it is true that the parson is absent?"

"Quite, mum," and Mr. Podd looked upon the ladies like a man who, though brim-full of news, was not desirous of imparting it.

"Indeed we heard so, but could not believe it, as we have seen a *man* walking with a *girl* several times across our park," said the ladies.

"*Girl*, if you please, mum," spoke Podd, his large old nose growing as white, for the minute, as Miss Cadwallader's best lump sugar, and then five shades redder than its natural hue; " but one that God made beautiful and good; and so it don't matter whether called lady, or girl, or child, if so blessed and blessing others. As for the *man*, mum (Podd's nose was strongly purple here), he's, folks say, the greatest learned gentleman in Cambridge, besides being a squire in the next county; and it's lucky that one who can talk so well and so informingly, and who looks on Mr. Longnor as a father, should be just here to cheer the poor child a bit in her own learned way! And there's his mother 'll be coming to see her, too, I reckon—which is making good, ladies, what Miss Anne said to me no longer than last night by the park gate, that she was glad I had got such a guest, and Dora Longnor an intelligent friend like Mr. Riddle. Now, good morning, ladies." So, finishing with this home-thrust, which quite brought the hue of his nose to its natural tone, Mr. Podd withdrew, leaving the spinsters to hasten home and duly impart these matters to the squire, as well as incite him to lecture the Cinderella of the household on the impropriety of any course of conduct saving contempt towards a "fellow" like Absalom Podd.

If Heaven's sweet stars be auguries of mortal fate, brightly they poured their splendour down upon this eve, on forest, mountain, and the purling streams!

And so the little marriage gown, being ready in its simple purity, and lying beneath the casement of her chamber, was hallowed by the descending radiance of these sweet stars, as angels, by the pressure of their sandaled feet, by every waving of their glorious wings, cast beauty on the earth, and deck it with the light of Paradise. Thus hallowed, and thus gloried, it lay when she who was to wear it stepped from the house, and trod the dewy lane. Scarcely had she come where the trees cast massive shadows, before the well-known step, the well-known pipe, were near, and then beside her. The first question was, why was she out in the dews of the night?

"I want to speak to you, sir," she said, with more decision than she had hitherto spoken.

"Well!" and there was haughtiness and conciseness in the rejoinder, as Walter led her from the shadows into the broad flooding light.

" Sir—please, sir—I hope you won't be angry —but I have been thinking how papa left me, as it were, in trust to Podd—it would not be well— our being—I mean, sir, our going to church to-morrow without Podd knowing—he is so good, sir."

" Your wish, my dear one, is gratified before it is expressed ; for Podd, who is even a grander creature than you imagine, he has been guarding you as many fathers do not guard their daughters : following in my footsteps, hearing much, nay, all I have said, and at last, this very afternoon, bringing me to full account, like the sturdiest old judge who ever wore a wig. Well, he is now fully in confidence, and after crying and laughing by turns, he commenced brushing his best suit, and laying out his Holland shirt, for he is to par-ticipate in to-morrow's ceremony! Are you happy now ? "

" So happy, sir——"

" Nonsense—not sir—I am always telling you about this matter."

" So happy, sir " (she made the mistake again, but this time without interruption), " that I do not seem to tread earth, for my conscience is happy about papa."

" Well, see here " (and he brought her still more into the flooding light, and showed her the ring), " this is the jewel for to-morrow."

She looked, but made no answer—though silence expressed more than words.

As if it pleased him to be taciturn, he led her to the porch, told her to be at the Edge-stone, two miles across the forest, by eight in the morning, where his servant would meet her with a gig, and then bid her the same self-resolved farewell as of old, and closed the house door upon her.

But till she was guarded safe and well by Ruth, till the taper from her casement twinkled no longer on the ripples of the brook, till the very forest boughs slept on the still night air, till even the ivy ceased to flap upon the casement panes, and the nightingale to tune her note, the husband of the morrow, leaning upon the mossied church-yard wall, guarded the young girl's rest.

*   *   *   *   *   *

The chaplain pauses here, and there is need.

The great door standing wide open, Miss Leigh's cat, Tom, has been for some time peeping round, reconnoitering the scene and eyeing his enemy Spark. But the black gentleman's mood is pacific ; he purrs and dresses his choice whiskers, and he would, were it not for Spark's evil eye, creep in and tuck himself up in his gentle mistress's gown— for Miss Leigh, though a little odd, is a charming lady. At last, hoping, perhaps, to make progress unobserved, he steals, cat-like, a few steps forward ; but his enemy is alert, and bouncing down seizes the miserable pet by the ear. Spit, hearing and seeing this, jumps down too, and a mêlée ensues.

"Oh, my poor dear Tom !" cries Miss Leigh ; "he'll be quite finished." "Come here, Spit," calls Miss Bodkin. "Spark, I'm ashamed of you," repeats Miss Gregg. But the canine tyrants, heedless of their mistresses' voices, worry the poor creature, and chase it up and down. Miss Leigh's grief and terror are excessive, and Miss Gregg and Miss Bodkin are ashamed of their favourites.

"Spark!" "Spit!" "Spark!" "Spit!" are words which resound through the hall. All the ladies have arisen in confusion, and the chaplain interferes; but the dogs, still worrying the favourite, are about to chase it through the partly open door, when a few blows from old Harris, who, returning from work, carries his garden tools in his hand, chastens with summary effect the spoilt tyrants, and they retreat howling to the protection of their respective mistresses' gowns. Poor Tom is then caught, and, with his ear all bleeding, is consigned to the care of two of the little mob-capped maids, who have been led to approach the great door by the hubbub made.

In spite of tartness of temper, Miss Gregg has great justice of heart. She condoles with Miss Leigh, apologizes and promises that Spark shall not offend again; whilst Miss Bodkin, a little less generous, says nothing, but resolving that Spit shall not be punished, even gives him a sly caress when all eyes are turned away. Peace is thus restored.

This the more readily that most of the kindly gentlewomen have been pleased with what they have listened to, and are glad when the reading is presently resumed.

* * * * * *

The stars, whose shining was so transcendent in its silver glory, were heralds of a morrow whose dawn upon the hoary mountain-tops lingered not long, but travelling on apace, over the craggy moorland and the thick-set forest-boughs, over the trickling brooklet and the closed-up cups of honey-laden flowers, shot through the leafy casement of the sleeping girl, and kissed her eyes with light.

She awoke, and soon was astir. As it was needless to awaken Ruth, who had been told by her master on the previous night that Miss Dora was going across the forest at an early hour, the young girl stole lightly about whilst making her few preparations, for it was needful to her heart to be alone in this strange hour. And these preparations were of the simplest and humblest kind. To put on her poor holiday frock, its little tippet, her humble bonnet; to tie the bridal gown within a handkerchief; to gather a few flowers for the hand she loved with such half reverence, half fear, and yet so well; these were humble things indeed, even for a peasant girl of many a mountain sheiling; but, in the gathering and confining of her splendid veil of hair, in the excelling beauty which was rich without adornment, in the grace, in the unconsciousness, in the faith and trust of soul, in the purity of heart, there was that which would have consecrated the bridal chamber of the rarest queen, and hallowed the holiest pathway ever trodden by human foot!

All ready—the flowers within her hand, her bundle on her arm, she took one last look of her father's sacred room, pressed down her lips upon the old worn desk, consecrated by the abstract gaze of many a studious meditation, and then going out, and closing the door softly behind her, she went upon her way across the silver trickling of the pebbled brook! She could not break her fast—her heart was much too full!

She was at the old Edge-stone some half hour before the time, but the sun had been there before her, and dried its thymy hollows; and on the grassy slope where she sat down, the tiny butterflies, with brown or azure wings, flitted to and fro, and the lark, heavenward and earthward, poured out its heart in joy!

For a mile across the open forest she breathlessly saw the gig speed towards her, and when it came up and stayed, an old servant, in a sober livery of grey, merely saying, "Miss Longnor, ma'am?" assisted her in, and drove back upon the path he had come. Nor did she want to talk—for as the old man assisted her into the gig, he placed a little slip of paper in her hand, on which was written as his credentials, "I am expecting you, my Dora," and this was quite enough.

After about two hours' ride, through sequestered lanes and woodlands of rich verdure, the gig stopped in the vicinity of a little secluded country church, and the servant led the way along a still and hidden path, to a sort of old vestry, or clerk's room, in the rear. As he lifted the quaint latch, and allowed her to pass in, she beheld Absalom Podd, seated by the sunny casement, with not only his Holland shirt and best suit on, but his spectacles also, for he was devoutly conning the marriage-service out of the clerk's book; it being full thirty years since he had studied that portion of the sacred volume. She went up to him timidly, laid her hand upon his arm, and said, "I hope you are not angry, Podd?"

"Why," replied Absalom very slowly, as he reverently closed the volume, and took her hand, "you see the thing is rather sudden, and might have been better left till your father came back; but as nothing of the sort would be listened to, I thought it best to come and see all was right; for I wouldn't trust my own father in such a thing. Nor, Dora, would I 'a consented in any other case but this, but that I know the curate 'll think it all right. But now, one thing, Dora—and recollect I'm just asking it as solemnly as the parson could himself—I mean, for you're such a child, do you love him?"

"Why, Podd," was the naïve answer, "if I didn't I should not come here."

"Ay! ay!" spoke Mr. Podd, assuming the air of one learned in casuistry; "many come, my dear, to sich places as these as have no more love in their hearts than a clock or a chest of drawers. But thee really do love, in the hearty way, I mean—eh?"

"I am very young, I know," replied Dora, as she laid her hand still more impressively upon the old man's arm, "but I am not so much a child but that I know the feeling of my own heart; and it is therefore in boundless truth and reverence I come here to-day."

"Well, well," replied Mr. Podd, his honest brain not fully understanding what Dora meant; "you mean by this to say, I suppose, that you love very much. So far, so right. Now, hast thee breakfasted?" Dora said she had not, nor did she need any.

But honest Absalom thought differently; so immediately unpacking a small basket he had brought with him, he displayed sundry refreshments, which, when he had set them out, he bid the young girl take, and then dress herself as speedily as she could, for "the folks were waiting in the church."

But her heart was far too full to think of fragrant cake or wine, or milk or fruit, set there; but hastily smoothing her rich gathered tresses, laving her hands in the clerk's old bowl set ready with the fairest water, she put on the little bridal gown, short sleeves, low bodice, little waist, and trembling in the loving sunlight shed upon her, stood there as if receiving invisible investiture by loving angels in her sweet office of a little wife. Yet, standing thus, only the smallest instant in the race of Time; for a hand she well knew knocked upon the door, then opened it, and Mr. Riddle stood before her, still stern, reserved, and self-restrained. With scarcely a greeting, and quite peremptorily and quickly, he pushed aside Podd's officious hand, and led her into the cool, the shadowed, and the quaint old church.

For, as if he wished the office to be quickly over, he allowed the venerable priest to make little more than the briefest greeting; and then placing Dora beside the time-worn cushion, the service was begun and said, without other incident more remarkable than that Mr. Podd hid his nose to a large extent in his best bandana pocket-handkerchief, after he was once fully assured that the sacred ring was on, and that the child of him he reverenced so well was the wife of Walter Riddle!

Yet, not even when the priest had closed his book with his mildest and his holiest blessing—for the extreme youth, and grace, and beauty of the girl touched well and finely his noble heart—did the stern husband relax his self-command, but raising the little weeping creature from the cushion, gently and tenderly though, as a mother her child, he hurried her into the vestry to sign the book (honest Podd, however, not a bit abashed —he would not have been had the husband been a lion or a griffin—putting on his spectacles, and not only standing by to see all this was properly done, but signing his own name in the largest round text), made her put on hastily her little tippet over the marriage gown, tie on her bonnet, swing the poor bundle on her arm, and then, scarcely allowing her to shake Podd, or the parson, by the hand (much less the clerk), he led her quickly from the vestry, across the still, quaint, rustic churchyard, and out from thence into a shadowed lane which wound upwards to the green acclivity of one of the loneliest mountains of this lovely land of Western Shropshire!

Nor did he stop, though this steep acclivity grew steeper to their steps; nor scarcely spoke a word, till on its grassy summit, open to the heavens, but neither looking west, nor north, nor south, nor east, but only on the splendid glory of the azure sky, he sought a little grassy seat of fairest turf, and raising her half-buried, weeping face, cast off her bonnet, so that her veil of beauty fell around her, and made her sit beside him. And now even she was startled, as, at his altered voice, she looked up into his face. For already she had guessed that his coldness, his sternness, his reserve were assumed; but not to the extent she now saw they had been, as changed, as altered, as her husband, as the friend her father loved, he poured out the passionate idolatry of his noble heart. All he had thought since the hour he had first seen her, all she had said and done and even thought — all aspects and all changes of her girlish beauty—all acts of faith and trust and naïve unconsciousness—all ministering offices, even to the uplifting of the old smoky, black-bowled Churchwarden, were chronicled, recounted, told, and told again, as if the Universe were listening, like a child, with full consciousness of its immortality, to the boundless wealth, and depth, and truth of HUMAN LOVE.

Nobler, more boundless, more exalted, and more purified was this expression too, for the faith

and stern reserve maintained beforehand.   He
had won this young and trusting creature by no
seductive words; no familiarity had lessened the
great respect between them; and now she was
his wife, now that she bore his name and held his
faith, now that the heavens were bright above
them, and the earth so fair around, this act of
noble and of sovereign justice was like a blessing
and a prayer whispered and answered in the temple
of the soul.

There was so much to talk about, of his mother,
of her father, of their home, of their future mode
of life, that some shadows had fallen on this still
and sun-lit spot before they rose, and crossed the
mountain towards the old hall of Broadlands,
about some five miles from thence.   So proceeding, they had perhaps left the grassy pathway of
the mountain two miles behind, and now were in
a green and shadowed lane which branched into
the woodlands, when they suddenly perceived a
traveller approaching them, who, by his dress,
and a small knapsack swung across his shoulders,
was evidently some gentleman making an excur-
sion across the country.   As he approached, and
passing them, cast a glance—half surprise, half
curiosity—upon the stern and haughty husband,
and the exquisite beauty of the childlike wife,
Dora looked up into her husband's face, and saw
such a stern expression on it, such a look of proud
defiance and dislike, as to make her, half trembling, stop abruptly and ask if he were ill.   But
her husband neither stayed nor answered, till a

bending in the lane fully secluded them from the traveller's view, when he said,

"No, my dear one ; but he, just passed, is the last man in the world I either expected or liked to meet on such a day as this, for I have much reason to believe that he is a mortal enemy of mine—perhaps the only one I have. His name is Horner, and he is Fellow of one of our Universities."

"Horner," and Dora stopped short and took her husband's hand, "he is surely the same that Anne Fieldworth should have married, and would, as papa has often said, if the old squire had not been so avaricious. Ay! it is a sad tale." And the little wife, sighing that there should be one human contrast to her own happiness on such a day, pressed closer to her husband.

"Well, my dear one," replied Riddle, as his sternness gave way to a milder and more gracious expression, and he looked down upon the pleading upturned face of his little wife, "we will not talk of these people. From what I observed, and from what Podd told me, I fear the Fieldworths are a bad, proud, narrow-minded race, a specimen of the worst form of English squirearchy."

"Ay, Walter," pleaded softly the little wife, "perhaps this is somewhat true, but not with regard to Anne ; she has, as papa has often said —and he knows many of her sorrows—one of the sweetest, truest natures human creature ever had ; and, as for the elder ones, so proud, and soured, and evil-tongued, perhaps it is disappointment which has made them so, for, since I have been so happy, Walter, so——well, I mean since you asked me to be obedient, I have thought that good and evil are nearer allied to happiness and misery than people think."

"Well, well," replied Walter, "no sinner but what you would find some plea for, my Dora; for mercy is more an attribute of your sex than of mine. But now cross this stile, my dear one, and you are *home;*" and as he said so, he lifted her from the lane on to the mossy sward of the woodland, and pressed her to his heart, as a sign of boundless welcome.

These old dim woods led fittingly to the broad secluded terrace of an ancient stone-built country-house; on the stained, buttressed windows of which the rays of the declining sun fell in burnished splendour. From this terrace, by a quaint, secluded postern door, he led her into a suite of fine old rooms, leading one from another ; one of which, a study, filled with books, in ancient presses, with carved reading-desks, with maps, and globes, and telescopes, scattered around the broad seats of the richly-tinted oriel windows, was prepared for their coming—for a meal, half tea, half dinner, was set ready; a fire of wood burnt brightly on the marble hearth, and the student's own richly embroidered chair, worked by a loving mother's hand, was set ready, with a footstool for the little wife.

Presently there came in to welcome her, Walter's nurse ; an aged, but still an active, cheerful woman; who, when she saw the rare loveliness of the girlish wife, coupled with what old John, her husband, had already told her, as witnessed by himself, and learnt from the proud garrulity of honest Podd, then and there, without restraint, without a minute's hesitation, folded the little trembling creature to her heart, and blessed her fervently, as though she were her child.

Then, with tenderness, and gentleness, and infinite respect, she led the sweet wife through this old, secluded suite of rooms, and showed the preparations made for her; then, after, as the descending shadows fell, the double meal was served, and shortly over; and as these evening shadows broadened into night, the oriel curtains were drawn, the rich lamp was set, and the sweet one—in the modest bridal gown, short sleeves, low bodice, little waist—her hair so gorgeous in its ebon hue, the sacred ring, so small, so round, so scintillating in the light—sat on the footstool at her husband's feet, old Mr. Churchwarden's little spiral clouds floating around her upturned, listening face!

She had been five days married, and the letters which were to tell the secret to her father, and to summon Walter's mother to his home, were already written. With that charming usefulness which was so much her characteristic, and so priceless to an abstracted man like Riddle, she had made her husband's breakfast, set it in the fashion which best pleased him, gathered new-opened flowers, yet beaded with the early dew, and set them by his cup, and welcomed him with loving smiles, when old Bridget, who always waited at this meal, brought in the morning's letters. The first he opened was from Auvergne, and full of hopeful news. The noble-hearted curate wrote that his health was wonderfully improved, that the needed verifications had not only been fully accomplished, but that important discoveries had also been made relative to the volcanic strata of the Puy de Dome, and that, commencing his return homeward in a few days, by way of Paris, whither some of the literati and savans had invited him, he hoped to find his Dora well and happy, and cheered by the visit of Mr. Riddle. And Walter smiled; smiled as he read aloud this letter, and gave it to his young wife, with an expression of such faith, and hope, and triumph, and proud and earnest love, as to make Dora kneel beside him as he took up the second letter. It had a large seal, bore an official look, and was brief; but scarcely had the proud, stern, ordinarily unimpassioned man read one line, before his faltering hands half dropped it, and his lips became so deadly white, though defiant as they grew more bloodless, as to paralyse the young and kneeling wife with terror.

"Why, Walter, husband, dear one—sir—" (for, as his proud lips grew prouder, her girlish fear and awe of him came back again)—"what is the matter?"

"Why—nothing." And he gasped, and

crushed the letter in his hand. "Why—why—only—that the chief Professor's chair in the University is suddenly become vacant, for ———— died yesterday of apoplexy, after an hour's illness."

"It is sad for the good and learned to die, because the earth can ill spare such," said Dora, quietly; "but why should it vex you thus, sir?" And she looked up into his face half fearfully.

"Why?" and he spoke so sternly as to make the young wife's very heart stand still. "Why?" (and he repeated his own interrogative with vehemence)—"why—why, because of this Horner—this man—this one who, through life, has beset every proud and honourable path of mine!"

"But still," asked the young wife, half fearfully, half tremblingly, "the Professorship is as much open to you as to him, is it not?"

"No," and he said this so sternly and peremptorily that she was tremulous with fear.

"Why, Walter, why? Papa has often said that you are one of the profoundest mathematicians and scientific men of the age."

He only seemed to hear her brief interrogatory, for, repeating it, and then hesitating for the instant, as if touched by shame even in the very blindness of bitter rivalry—he said softly,

"Because *I am married!*"

His young wife heard these words; rose very quietly, withdrew an arm's length from him, and then gently, yet with a deep and earnest pathos, never excelled by any human lips that ever spoke the words of grief and woe,

"And, Walter, do you repent it, then?"

He was touched to the very soul; all that was generous and noble and truthful in his nature at once accused him of meanness, and cruelty, and injustice; and he rose abashed and trembling, to fold her weeping in his arms, to kiss away her passionate tears, to plead guilty, to ask pardon, to love with more passionate idolatry, for the very question she had asked.

"Never, never, never!" he vehemently repeated, as his tears rained down upon her beautiful, and clasped, and trembling hands; "every hour only makes my worship of you more idolatrous, my wife, my Dora. Only, only—I am never coherent when this Horner comes within my way, for he has—hundreds of men say he has —crossed my path with every art and wile. No, no, Dora, by every vow I've made to you and sworn, believe that the very first night I saw you, as I meditated over Podd's parlour fire, I vowed myself religiously to the life I have undertaken; and judged finally how much nobler it would be to live with such a spirit as yourself than to lead the life of a cloistered monk; and to earn a future fame through the greatness of truth in written words, rather than be satisfied with the vain distinction of a professor's chair. There was both a present and a probable future in the one; simply a present in the other. Darling wife, I have erred;

and by your purer, and your nobler and more gentle nature, you must forgive!"

Need he have asked her? No! He knew not the deep generosity of the heart he loved.

"Walter," she said, after some minutes' silence, and when even the traces of a shadow had vanished from her guileless heart, and only somewhat of greater faith and earnestness was added to that already so profound and touching, "in such a case as this, and friends knowing not yet about the little wife you've taken, will they not gather and give suffrages towards your election? And thus showing your majority over that of Mr. Horner, give you all that thus to you is needful—the triumph of living noblest in men's minds. And will they not do this supposing that we keep our marriage secret another week; and cannot you, when this proud triumph comes, dear husband, calmly say that a little wife, just newly married, is a preventive to ambition of this character?" And sweetly she prayed him, with her arms around his neck, to think of this.

"And *you!*" he half incredulously asked, listening if only for the sake of a fresh week's secrecy, so dear to him.

"Why, Walter, in this case I must go home for a few days, say three or four; for there is Podd to pacify, and all the idle tales to silence by my presence, in order to keep the secret. But all will be well; for though to leave you will be so hard, there is dear papa to think of, and to make ready for his return; and then, the few needful days over, think how pleasant it will be for you to come and bring papa and your mother to see me in my lowly home!"

For awhile Riddle was deaf to his young wife's suggestion and entreaties; but intense ambition is often a co-equal with intense love, in stern natures like this of Dora's husband. But though most assuredly, if placed side by side, his worthy idolatry of this magnificent heart he loved so well would have outlived and been paramount above the other passions of his firm, resolved nature, still the desire of testing fame, the truth of friends, the approbation of the world, and the power thus gained of triumphing over the rival of years, joined to the increase of the personal sense of this rivalry, by the late strange encounter with Horner, made him consent at last, towards nightfall, to write to Podd and ask his secrecy for one more week, and settle that the morrow but one Dora should be driven as far as the moorland Edge-stone by the old servant, and returning home there for a few days, ostensibly for the purpose of preparing for her father's return, await the issue of such efforts as Riddle's friends might make, and his tacit triumph over Horner.

Though thus unworthily shadowing the truth of his pure and noble love for the little human creature he had made his wife, by one of those sophisms that ambition prompts, Walter with pain sent the letter to Podd, and prepared for Dora's departure. And in this newer, this golden birth of love, the hours passed on, and perished quickly like autumnal flowers, so that the morning of the parting came and found it sorrowed by the young bride's tears; but the far deeper ones of these she hid, and only talking of their happy meeting in a day or two, recollected and performed all the sweetest and most touching duties of a wife, by carefully placing the books her husband had to use, setting all things in the order which he loved, by removing much which might remind him of her absence, by filling old Mr. Churchwarden up to his very muzzle, and only weeping that she could not charge him fifty times, and, lastly, urging Bridget to be thoughtful of her master. But being unable to part with the smallest thing *he* had given her, she tied in her poor handkerchief the little silk gown Bridget had thoughtfully run together for her (Riddle would not part with the little sacred bridal gown), a rich shawl, and one or two other things procured for her; and sewing the gorgeous diamond ring, placed above her wedding-ring by Walter on the bridal night, in the waist of her dress, she tore herself from the embraces of her husband, and was helped weeping into the gig by the old servant, at the end of the wood she had so blithely entered on that day week, her sunny day of marriage!

So early had she started from Broadlands, that it was not much beyond noon when the gig stayed beside the old grey Edge-stone. After she had alighted, and old John had driven off, which he did reluctantly, and with promises to be back quickly, for it had been found necessary to take him and Bridget into confidence, Dora took up her bundle and proceeded on her way homewards. And now, as it seemed, almost for the first time, all the perils of her undertaking glanced across her mind; the inquiries, the gossip, the village scandal, and last, not least, old Absalom's stubborn indignation. But nothing was too much for Dora's faith and love!

She had proceeded about a mile from the Edge-stone, when, all at once, it crossed her mind and made her heart throb, that if her marriage were to be concealed, one of the first necessities was to remove her wedding-ring, as it would be sure to be immediately seen by eyes so quick as those of Ruth, and little Leah, and Tim, and yet it was the hardest sacrifice yet asked from the duty she had taken on her. Yet once to know this was a duty and a need was at once to do it. Just as this resolution was made within her soul, there came in sight across the forest way that honest pedlar who was so ably enlisted by Podd in the memorable matter concerning the curate's hat. So, as he carried simple wares about, tapes and ribbons, Dora stopped him as he said "Good day," and bought a yard of somewhat narrow ribbon, white and watered. As this pedlar, one of Wordsworth's noble kind, took the little coin in payment, he said, "Well, miss, God speed thee home; for there be that mad old woman, Martha Cadwallader, and the squire's two daughters (Miss Anne, bless her heart, isn't a wasp like the rest), and the old squire himself, and Bump, the coachman, a-going on about you, and say you've run off; but it's like 'em, nothing white but what they blacken."

"My heart and actions are pure, Ben," replied Dora, proudly, for she was, in so saying, vindicating her husband's honour as much as her own, "and so I care not; and for the rest, papa will be home in a few days."

"I'm glad of it, miss, for I come seven miles across the hills every Sunday to hear his fine sermons; as their good and hopeful words are a staff to me, and help me ably through the hard and struggling week. And so God bless him! And I say this truly, as you know, miss; for many a meal he gives me through the deep winter, when times are hard for such as toil like me. So good day, and bless you, miss, and don't mind Cadwallader." Thus saying, Ben proceeded onward, not without turning round every now and then, till distance hid her from his sight, to bless the beautiful and dear child of the curate!

As soon as profound solitude was around her, Dora sat down in a turfy spot, as still and sunny as that in which her husband had first poured out to her his passionate idolatry of soul, and taking off the sacred sign of marriage (the pitying angels know with what reluctance and what sorrow), hung it on the pedlar's ribbon, and putting this around her neck, hid thus her wedding-ring within her bosom! This safe, and with it all outer evidence of her secret, she hastened on her way.

Bathed in the golden splendour of the afternoon, her humble home to Dora never looked more beautiful; and all things had been so lovingly attended to by Ruth, and Absalom, and Tim, that as she set foot within its sweet old kitchen, its little, quaint, dim study, fragrant and breezy, for its casements were open to the sun—as she trod her little bedchamber dressed and trim, opened the cool dairy hatch, stepped round the bowery garden, and listened to the murmur of the silver brook—the sweet and low-voiced music of her cradle—went into the old byre to pat Brindle, lowing as she recognised the footfall of her little mistress, and into the stable to unloose old docile Ned, the pony, never was home more dear than now to this sweet creature!

She waited Podd's coming impatiently, as arranged by Riddle's letter; but it was fully eight before he came, and, as she expected he would be, in a very obstinate and irascible temper. For without greeting of any sort or kind he plumped himself down on a chair by the clock, pulled off his hat with a significant twitch, wiped his forehead with his pocket-handkerchief rolled up as tight as a cannon-ball, and began to growl like a bear with a sore ear.

"What's this thing wanted to be kept secret another week for, eh?—what good'll it do, what's the use on't, what'll come on't? The only thing I know is, I'll have it out to-night, and that I be determined on, if I die for it." And with this resolve he rubbed his head with his temporary cannon-ball till it was as red as a full-blown peony.

Dora endeavoured to pacify him, and to explain what the few and brief words of Walter's letter had failed to do; but at first he was very restless and unmanageable.

"I canna see it, I dunna understand it, and *I won't*" (and Podd folded his arms and looked defiant—that is to say, as much as he could); "and I must say plainly, child, that this husband of yours, with all his learning, is———"

"Hush—hu—sh—Podd," and the young wife pressed her hand upon old Absalom's pouting lips; "not one word against my husband—not even were papa himself the speaker—no, not one, for in this case the fault is mine." So saying, she knelt down and related the matter still more minutely to Absalom.

"Whew—whew!" whistled Podd, when the young wife came to the part about the letter Walter had written, and now somewhat pacified by her sweet pleading words; "the letter was sent off the night afore last, eh?—and should on course have reached me yesterday?" Receiving an answer in the affirmative, Podd whistled still more drily and significantly, and diving deep into one of his profound pockets, produced an old leathern pocket-book, with a strap and buckle which would have done for a portmanteau, and undoing this, produced the letter sent from Broadlands. A cursory glance showed that the seal had been tampered with, the letter opened, previously to its reaching the "Barley Mow,"

and the post-mark altered; and very rightly
judging that Miss Martha had been rather exceeding even the latitudinarian limits of the code
of Cadwallader, he whistled for some minutes to an
amazing extent, and then bursting into a huge fit
of laughter, which Dora well knew meant much,
at once consented, until the curate's return, to
keep the secret, provided old Northwood and his
dame shared it.   As he would listen to no compromise other than this, Dora at last reluctantly
consented; and Podd, now mighty full of some
great undertaking, presently withdrew, after
rousing the fire, laying the supper-cloth, and
producing from some hidden receptacle left outside in the porch, a considerable portion of cold
roast lamb, a currant tart, and a bottle of pale
ale, of his own peculiar brewing.

In the meanwhile, the woes and hopes of other
hearts were acting needed portions in this small
human drama; a small one, yet, as all human
dramas are, the fraction of a greater.   For
years it had been poor Anne Fieldworth's
sweetest consolation, whenever, through the pretext of distant charitable visits, she could well escape the rigid surveillance kept over her by her
step-sisters, to wander to those old fields and woods
once possessed by the family, whose youngest son,
William Horner, had been the object of her faithful attachment.   Though separated from him
through malignity and envy—though corrupt falsehood had served the purpose needed—though fifteen years were passed away and gone—yet, still

true to the moral excellence of her sweet and truthful nature, she had refused a dozen offers of wealth and rank, pertinaciously encouraged by her father, and now and then stole away to these old fields and woods, to strengthen, as it were, through retrospect, the faith she held, and meant to hold, to the end. Thus, on the very day of Dora's marriage, using the opportunity of her father's and sisters' absence at a neighbouring hall to dine, she had visited those old scenes with a freshness and interest which surprised even herself. For there is in psychology profounder interests and sympathies than men yet dream of, or science has yet revealed; as though she knew it not, a heart as faithful as her own, visiting these fields, no longer his, after his long absence of fifteen years, and drawn hither by the same memories as those which yet remained so pure in Anne Fieldworth's heart, had seen her seated under the self-same tree beneath which they had parted fifteen years before; and now would have made himself known, have again sat beside her, have again repeated what had been said so long ago, but for the bitter memory of a cruel and insulting letter sent as from her hand. But he had seen her, and that was enough; the visit to these old scenes, originally intended to be merely one of a few hours, had now been the lingering of a week at a little hostelry in a neighbouring village. But of this, or of his presence, Anne was still ignorant.

The evening following Dora's return from Broadlands, the squire, after his bottle, his pippins, and his nap, sauntered down to the village; and returning after a due interval, entered the parlour, where his two eldest daughters were engaged at their eternal worsted frames; for the one was working a hearth-rug and the other a monstrous cushion for the pew at church, which, when finished, was to astound, by its magnificence in heraldry, "the low vulgar curate and his plebeian flock."

"Come, girls," cried the squire, as he snapped his fingers and spoke with much glee, "ha' in th' toast an' th' urn; for whilst thee make tea I've a bit o' news for thee!" So saying, he sat down in his broad old chair, and commenced imparting sundry choice bits of news just fresh from the sweet lips of Miss Cadwallader. It happened, whilst he thus sat talking, that Anne, seated reading in one of the old broad window-seats of the adjoining room, with the intervening door partly open, was at last attracted by the often-repeated names of the curate and Dora; and in no great while startled by a disclosure still more significant, evidently imparted in the full belief that she herself was not in the immediate vicinity.

"Ha! ha!" laughed the squire, after imparting some of the news with which he was primed, and helping himself to a monstrous slice of hot tea-cake, "thee thought that was a wedding-ring in that letter, did thee, girls?"

"Indeed, papa," replied Sophy, with a show of virtuous contempt, "we care little about the matter." But this was a mere shallow pretext, seen through even by such obtuse penetration as the old squire's.

"But I do, and so do thee—for a woman's never at fault when a wedding-ring be in the case—and so I say my son Tom's curate shall be respectable; and this matter, say what ye will, of a girl disappearing, the Lord knows where, in'na so, and I'll see to the bottom on it, or my name is not Jonathan Fieldworth, Justice of the Peace for the county of Salop."

"Well, the truth is, papa," spoke Jane, by nature more garrulous than her sister Sophy, "we do know something of this matter, and might, perhaps, have mentioned it, did not Sophy and myself conceive this sort of topic unfit for gentlewomen like ourselves. But Cadwallader told us two days ago that she saw a letter in which this man Riddle implored Absalom Podd's silence as to that girl's absence for a week. What do you think of that?"

"Whew!" whistled the squire, "that is more than Cadwallader told me, as she knows I dunna side with her peeping into letters and things o' that sort. But this is how I think the matter stands—That there's been marriage talked on, and, perhaps, thought on—for every one in the village says as how the girl was courted, though in a rough, queer sort on way—but there's many a slip atwixt the cup and the lip; and so, the Professor o' —— dying in some sort of a fit, on course this man's looking sharp after the place,

and so, forgetting all about marriage, has sent the
girl back on old Podd's hands.   But I'll dive to
the bottom on't, you shall see."   Here the squire
paused a bit, and looked round the room with a
mysterious air, inquiring, as he did so, where Anne
was.   Being assured she was in her own room, or
else on the terrace, he continued, half angrily,
half mysteriously, for it really was tremendous
news both to the wrongdoers and to the unhappy
wronged, who, as the first little dreamt, listened
as a way-worn, thirsty traveller drinks of a refreshing spring.   "Ay, and this in'na all—for
Horner be in the next village, trying to buy some
on the old estate off Morris again—for he's been
making money, they say, in the University.   But
he shan'na have Anne, I know, nor she him; so
he may go and come again fifteen year hence, if
he like—eh! eh!"

"*He* here!" and both sisters spoke as if an
avenging angel stood at hand.   Presently, however, Sophy added, in a voice of consolatory triumph, "Well, it won't be for long; for everybody
knows that this Riddle and Horner are the bitterest rivals, and have been opposed on several occasions like the present, and will be so again, I
suppose, if this girl's disgraceful return be any
sign."

"Well, I dunna care," replied the squire, "so
that fellow be off; and as for the curate's mighty
pretty daughter, I'll know the whole truth, and
that afore long—so pour out another cup of tea,
and ring the bell for Anne."

But to meet her father or her persecutors at this moment was impossible, agitated, overwhelmed, full of contending emotion as Anne was; so passing out on to the broad old terrace, from thence into the wainscoted hall, and by the old polished oaken staircase, she gained her chamber, and there was found when summoned by Jane and Sophy's maid. By using the pretext of slight indisposition, she was suffered to remain there unmolested during the evening; and thus had time and opportunity to think over all which had been so unwittingly imparted to her. Her first surprise over concerning Horner's visit to the neighbourhood—her first intense joy sobered, of merely imagining that the same memories had led him back to these old scenes, after fifteen years' absence, as led her steps so often to them—her first passionate outburst of tears, though those of joy more than grief, dried by the secret and divine consciousness of faith and truth, her thoughts, with noble generosity and disregard of self, concentrated themselves upon Dora. Was she, so young, so beautiful, so pure—for Anne knew enough of Dora to answer for her with a fervent soul—was she about to enter on any ordeal more terrible than her own, for the mere sake of a rich and haughty man's ambition?—was the child to be thus sacrificed, and the father's heart broken?—was it because two men were rivals for such a bauble, that one of the most guileless and truthful of beings should be maligned and scorned?

"No, not if I can help it!" said Anne, fervently; "for I, a woman, have learnt, through suffering, the need my sex have of human sympathy." So reasoned and so argued noble Anne!

It was observable on the morrow that the squire mounted his hackney at an early hour, for a ride across the forest, for the purpose, if the truth be spoken, to find out if Dora Longnor had stayed at the mill, with her well-known friend Lucy Gray, during her week's absence; so, using this opportunity, Anne walked to the village and sought out Podd. But he, usually so communicative and friendly with her, was as impenetrable and mysterious as a Jesuit; and so full of humour and witticisms on the purport of the squire's ride that day, that Anne retreated and sought out Dame Northwood, fully assured that from her she should obtain enough of information to satisfy her anxious heart concerning Dora. But here she was more disappointed than even by Podd, for the good and honest dame would only say that though Miss Longnor had been away a week, as she supposed at the mill, she knew no particulars, except that Miss Cadwallader and some of the village folks had been very inquisitive about the matter. But for her part she loved Dora like her own child, and never troubled her head about what folks said, whilst her husband's heart was as light as it was; for it would be sad enough indeed if the least thing harmed Miss Dora!

Beginning to think that her own conjectures were, with the gossip which had engendered them, idle things, Anne returned homewards by the fields which skirted the parsonage garden, willing to see Dora if she could, without trespassing on her privacy. And this she did; for Dora was beside the porch, and, Anne speaking, Dora hastened to unlatch the wicket and lead her friend into the still and shadowy garden.

"I am sorry I cannot see more of you, Dora," spoke Anne gently, as she viewed with intense admiration (for she had a fine artistic eye) the splendid beauty of the little human creature at her side, and felt in her soul, with womanly intuition, that if the angels ever tread within the hallowed footsteps of natures like their own, they trod here now, on this very spot of earth, with sedulous and watchful ministry; "but you know too well the cause; though if our family visit the coast of Wales this autumn, and leave me housekeeper, I hope you will come and pass a day with me, as you did two years ago. But how well you are looking, and how beautiful you grow!" And as she spoke this, she smoothed back Dora's beautiful tresses with her hand, and pressed down her lips upon her forehead.

"I am glad you think so, Miss Anne," replied Dora, naïvely, "for papa is coming home, and that will be his first thought."

"A very natural one. But you must be very glad of his return, though you have had so kind a visitor, as I hear you have had."

She looked down, and saw that Dora was not only agitated but coloured violently.

"Yes—Mr. Riddle was—" And Dora, raising

her eyes, and seeing her friend's gaze fixed upon her, was too choked by some deep feeling to say more. But so far from interpreting this as a sign of guilt, Anne's own heart knew too well that deep affection has the tenderest of consciences; and now, doubly steadfast in her beautiful belief respecting Dora, and as assured of her affection for Riddle as if priestly confession had been made of it, she determined to follow the impulse of her own most genuine heart, and realize those dreams for this sweet child which might have been her own. She then changed the conversation, plucked a few flowers, and telling Dora she would see her soon again, hurried on her homeward path.

The squire returned home in a mighty ill humour to dinner, for his curiosity had been strangely rebuffed at the forest mill, not only by old John Grey in person, but by his beautiful warm-hearted little daughter, Lucy, who, suspecting the real truth, from what the pedlar had told her after his rencounter with Dora, so placed the matter before her honest father as to screen Dora, and yet balk the impertinent curiosity of such as might ask questions. But he had learnt sufficient, from other inquiries he had made, to convince him that Dora had not only crossed the forest on foot, but had been to and fro to Broadlands. And having ascertained this much, he determined to call at the parsonage the very next day, "and talk to the girl."

That same evening, Miss Cadwallader, being unable to "speak her mind," as she called it, in any other way "to the girl"—for Podd's dear old forethought had saved his darling child from the sorrow and need of a visit to the region of Cadwallader—put on her bonnet, after her shop was closed for the night, and went down to the parsonage, under the pretext of calling for her bill. She found Podd quietly smoking his pipe in the parson's chair, and Dora sitting on the old hassock at his feet, talking about her father's return.

"As I haven't seen you a good while, Dora Longnor," spoke Miss Martha, in a loud voice, as soon as her first rude salutation had been made, and she had sat down uninvited in the most conspicuous chair in the old roomy kitchen, "though, of course, taking into consideration the nice pleasant visit you've had lately, groceries was quite out of the question——"

"Especially sugar, in the Cadwallader line," interrupted Podd.

Miss Martha, pretending not to hear, continued —"So I must have my bill, as it's very likely the visit as has supplied you with groceries——"

"Or with a jelly," again commented Podd; "or the leg of a duck, or a pheasant with good bread sauce, or a nice bottle of bees-winged port."

"*My* respectability isn't easily insulted, sir," spoke Miss Martha, with much indignant wrath; "but I was saying, probably as that pleasant visit has supplied you with funds enough, and as I have a sum——"

"Yes, to make up another pretty little thousand in the county bank," again parenthesized the incorrigible Podd, though with a gravity that would have sat well upon a judge.

"A heavy sum to pay for goods people have had and never paid for, I shall be glad if you'll settle my bill without further ado; or else let me have something as a security—for——"

"Miss Cadwallader," began the sweet young wife, "I——"

"Hush—hush!" interrupted Podd, "you are too bad a cretur, Dora, to speak to a young, lovely, sweet-tempered, merciful woman like Martha Cadwallader, engaged to and just on the eve of being married to the squire's coachman. No; you're too bad, my dear. And now, Miss Cadwallader, as you have insulted this dear child as much as you dare, please depart to your choicest supper, provided from the squire's kitchen, and just be patient till to-morrow night but one, and you shall hear o' something to your advantages, I can tell you, as the blessed curate 'll be at home, and I can settle matters. So now be off—the squire's pretty little side-dish 'll be awaiting." So saying, he arose with much valour and dignity, and conducting Miss Cadwallader to the door, there not only wished her a further polite enjoyment of Mr. Bump's pantry gifts, but indulged in an immense fit of laughter before she was out of hearing.

Not quite so fortunate in his championship the next day, for he was detained by some important guests who had come to throw an angle in the lonely village stream, and to sojourn at the

"Barley Mow." Podd arrived in the afternoon, just as the squire was departing, after a two hours' reprimand, threatening, cross-questioning, and invective, more worthy of a Judge Jeffreys than of a plain tiller of acres. Unable to terrify her by threats—for her pure and holy conscience, tremulous as it was before a sister-spirit like her own, was nobly proof against the coarse and brutal questions of the squire—he at last had recourse to invective against her husband and her father. Here she was vulnerable, and though never once replying, yet her tears flowed forth; and old Podd found her, not only weeping bitterly, but pale and ill, as if stricken by the ague. Curbing his boundless passion at this sight for a more potent time of outbreak, Podd merely said, when he gained the porch and beheld the squire sneaking off, and Dora crouched upon a chair, with her head bent upon the lattice-sill, "I think, Squire Fieldworth, this matter would have been better left till the curate came home."

"Pray, who taught *you* to think?" roared the squire, insolently.

Though Podd's very blood boiled, he was too much a right-thinking and truthful man to hazard a quarrel at this juncture, so he merely added, in continuation of what he had already said, "Mr. Longnor will be home to-morrow night at seven, and he may be able to answer for his child."

"We shall see, we shall see!" roared the squire still louder, for Podd's coolness only made him still more irascible. "I'll take care to come and expose these doings—ay, and write to the Bishop the very next morning. My son Tom shan'na 'an a curate o' this sort—I'll come, you shall see, my fellow!"

He departed; happily, too, for Podd's wrath was on the verge of explosion.

It was beautiful to see with what tenderness and delicacy the old man soothed the weeping girl, and how he sought to dry her tears. "Oh, Absalom!" she said, as she wept upon the old man's shoulder, "I did not care what he said of me, because you know how false it is; but when he called papa bad names, when he said Walter was a villain (and I scarcely know how he had offended the squire, except it was by refusing his daughters' invitation to dinner), I could not help weeping bitterly; for papa is so good, and my husband so dear to me!"

"Ay, ay," sobbed Podd, mingling his rough tears with those of the beautiful young creature by his side, "he may be very dear, but he should not have laid such a cross upon thee, dear child."

"*I* took it, *I* took it," wept Dora; "not one word against him, Podd—the fault is mine."

But she was worn and ill; so in no great while Podd started off, and putting his old horse in the gig, drove Mrs. Northwood to the parsonage, she being rather lame, and soon was the sweet wife hushed upon her pillow by one who loved her well and knew her secret.

This night was an important one in the life of Squire Fieldworth. For, as was his custom when terribly chagrined, he took a bottle before dinner, another after, and in this condition, scarcely knowing truth from falsehood, he poured out, to the astonished ears of Anne, his threats against Longnor, and magnified his evil suspicions into certain and proven truths. Hatred, fear, terror, disgust, seized, by turns, the heart of his long ill-used and unhappy daughter. Was it true, then, that Dora had been led away from home, and was now to be deserted, for the mere sake of ambitious rivalry? She asked herself this question till her heart grew sick; and now urged to that point when we brave the worst for a sacred duty, she retired to her chamber as quickly as she could, and, putting on a large cloak and bonnet, and descending by a back staircase into the garden, she commenced her old walk of seven miles through woods and lanes. It was a dark, wet night, too, for the time of year; but for this she cared nothing; and so, whilst the sweet wife nestled to her pillow, Anne Fieldworth braved the rough night for her sake!

It was nine o'clock when she reached the village, where she still hoped to find Horner, and anxiously sought the little inn. Almost as one whose fate hangs upon a negative or an affirmative, she asked for Mr. Horner, and found, to her joy, that he was still there, though preparing to leave at an early hour on the following morning. Desiring not to be announced, she tapped at the little parlour door, and, entering, closed it, and saw before her, at a table reading, the old friend of her youth. Gazing at her, wet and travel-worn as she was, Horner sat speechless; but Anne soon gave signs of her being no apparition, by sitting down and explaining in as few words as she could the object of her visit, and the sacrifice she asked to save Dora.

"I have reason to think, Mr. Horner," she concluded, "that rivalry has more to do in this matter than ambition, as respects Mr. Riddle; and as for Dora, for whom I plead, she is too noble, too pure, too much a child to be thus sacrificed—to be thus condemned to lingering years and broken hopes."

"Of the cause of this feeling of rivalry on the part of Mr. Riddle," said Horner, gravely, "I know not, nor can conceive, for I have always, by every action and by every word of my life, placed him, as he is, both in position and transcendent ability, pre-eminently above myself; unless it be, as I have had much reason to think lately, the work of designing and pretended friends, to serve purposes of their own. Of the youth and beauty of her you plead for I can speak, for I have seen both with my own eyes. And now it is yourself, Anne, who must, as it were, answer your own question."

As he spoke he looked gravely and mournfully into Anne's face.

"I answer it?" asked Anne, trembling and turning deadly pale.

"Yes; for though you sent me such a letter as you did fifteen years ago, still have I never altered

in my first feeling for you; and learning that you
were still unmarried, I came down to these old
scenes some ten days since, in the hope that we
might meet, and, emboldened by some sign from
yourself, might proffer to you again the same,
though now more wealthy, hand I did fifteen years
ago. But not having met with such opportunity
—and this silence, if you knew I was here, con-
firming what I had been so long reluctant to believe—and urged, too, by the letters of many
friends, to return and oppose Riddle in the forthcoming professorial election, I had prepared to
depart and undertake a contest which, if success-
ful, would be a bar to any future change in my
position."

Not waiting to reprove or to explain, Anne
knelt by Horner's side, and poured out, in scarcely
lucid words, all the insult, the indignity, the persecution, she had suffered in his behalf; and how,
whilst she had never swerved in her love and faith
for him, she was equally guileless of a cruel letter
or a cruel thought.

Horner listened amazed and dumb, as this gra-
dual disclosure of the baseness and the treachery
which had thus so long divided her faithful heart
from his, developed the sordid nature of the father,
and the vicious dispositions of her two step-sisters,
and before she rose again all possibility of rivalry
was at an end, for poor Anne, so long unhappy,
had, in happy words, consented to be his wife.

"And now," said Anne, "never will I return to
that miscalled home again; but whilst you, this

very night, or early in the morning, dear William, seek Mr. Riddle at Broadlands, and place before him the injustice of feeling hatred or rivalry against you who know it not—whilst in telling him of our reconciliation, or rather reunion, and, through it, of your impossibility to contest this honour with him—whilst you tell him of sweet Dora's love, and the risk her life and reputation are running in this false conflict between affection and ambition, I will hasten to Dora's side and there await your return." And the happy lady, renewed, as it were, by youth again, thus sought to serve the fortunes of her little friend.

No sooner was this plan talked over than it was acted on. A covered gig was procured, which the landlord of the little inn undertook himself to drive, and in one hour from this time Anne alighted at the parsonage-gate, whilst Horner proceeded on his way to Broadlands.

Anne found Dame Northwood sitting knitting by the fire, and waiting till her patient awoke out of the deep and refreshing sleep into which she had fallen, and so to her at once (for she had known her from a child) Anne poured out her heart, both as to herself and Dora. No sooner had the lady ended, than Dame Northwood, taking up the candle quite mysteriously, led the way into Dora's chamber, where she lay in profound and balmy sleep, and, shading the light as she approached the bed, turned slightly back the coverlet, and exposed to the wondering gaze of Anne, as it lay amidst unfastened tresses, still hung to the pedlar's ribbon, on the matchless bosom of the girl—THE HIDDEN RING!

Surprised, overcome, almost wild with joy, Anne's convulsive, though smothered, sobs awoke Dora, who, finding in an instant that her secret was known—for Anne held the sacred ring within her fingers and pressed her lips upon it—all was confessed and owned, and Anne now knew that Dora was a wife.

And now Anne related all which her fears for Dora had led her to undertake; and, in so undertaking an act of pure and holy friendship, what happiness for herself had sprung up!—and how the morrow, which would bring Dora's husband, would also bring a friend to her own heart.

"Sweet Anne, what priceless news this is!" wept Dora.

"Yes, for fifteen years," spoke Anne, still kneeling and still cherishing within her hands the hidden ring, "this is the first minute that I have known happiness. But, oh, dear friend, for ever through your future life believe in the purity of the zeal with which I wished to serve you—for *I* had a crushed and broken heart, and wished to spare *your* youth and beauty such an ordeal of long suffering; and if I now ask a reward for my humble service, let us make the sign of our sisterly friendship and affection this one—that, under all circumstances and all changes, we have faith and trust in the virtue of our sex."

"We will," said Dora; "and our husbands will have faith with us, I am sure."

Whilst the night thus passed, and the homely parsonage thus sheltered Anne, Horner proceeded on to Broadlands; and reaching its outskirts at an early hour, he procured some breakfast at a little rustic inn, and, after it, went on foot to the Hall. Amazed at this visit of the man he had been led to believe his worst enemy, Riddle received Horner with haughty coldness; but when Horner, stating the object of his visit, spoke of Dora's cruel persecution by the squire and Miss Cadwallader, of Anne's generous interference in her behalf, of his own probable change in life, of any absence of rivalry or evil-doing on his own side, and how he wished to be considered a friend rather than an enemy, and at last pleaded Dora's love as a hope that Mr. Riddle would be true to her, all that was noble in Walter's character ruled supremely, and taking Horner's hand as he led him to an adjoining room, he said, firmly,

" As we have hitherto strangely misunderstood one another, Mr. Horner, we shall henceforth be the truest of friends—for as you, in rescuing Anne Fieldworth from her miserable home, can be no longer, even in semblance, an enemy, I could, by no possibility, be yours, for Dora Longnor has been my wife since the day I met you on the mountain side. But here is her father—returned well and happy, as you see; and here my mother, both longing, as I do, to behold one so pure, and true, and beautiful."

Thus, as Riddle spoke, he led Mr. Horner into the breakfast-room, where sat Dora's father and his own mother, to whom he related all these strange circumstances; and whilst thus, happy to praise Horner's noble generosity, he blamed himself for having suffered Dora to quit his side, even for an hour, for a motive so childish and unworthy, he added emphatically,

"But I will repair the wrong with noble penitence, and with the worship and duty of a life."

And, in conclusion, he explained that Dora was scarcely from his sight before he repented, and would have brought her back but for the anticipated pleasure of sharing with her her father's return and his mother's visit, to both of whom he had despatched the written letters on the very day of Dora's departure.

No time was lost after breakfast in their departure for the parsonage, which they reached in the early part of the pleasant afternoon, just when the sun is most golden and most beautiful. But they could in no way anticipate the love and care of Dora, who was there all ready to meet them, and to be folded in a loving father's and loving husband's arms, and by turns to be caressed by Walter's mother.

" You should have let *me* know somewhat about this matter, sweet child," chided Walter's mother, " if only for the sake of fittingly preparing your home. But on your return you will find it more worthy of you as Walter's wife."

But scarcely had the curate warmed his hands before the blazing fire (for he loved a fire at all times), scarcely had the young wife and her husband strolled round the sweet sequestered garden, scarcely had Anne and William sat down in the quaint little study, or Podd arrived, or Leah and Mrs. Northwood commenced preparing tea (for the company had dined early on the road), before the squire burst in unannounced, and with him his two daughters; for Anne's disaffection and retreat to the parsonage were now known, though nothing, as yet, of her interview with Horner.

In a moment he approached the curate and commenced his angry inquiries about Anne, in a way which brought in, not only Podd, but Dora and Walter from the garden.

"You won't say, will you?" again repeated the half drunken squire, "that my daughter's here, will you?"

"Mr. Fieldworth," replied Longnor, quietly, "this conduct is most unseemly! I am but just home from a long journey, and wish for a few hours of quiet repose with my child and friends."

"Child!" ejaculated the squire, foaming with wrath; "pretty child for any un to be proud on. Dunna thee know she been across the forest, the lord knows where, and for a whole week? Dunna thee know my daughters here shall never speak to her? Dunna thee know that I shall write to the Bishop in the morning, and that my son Tom is already looking out for a new curate——"

"Mr. Fieldworth!" spoke the haughty and self-collected husband of Dora, "Mr. Longnor is perfectly aware his daughter went across the forest; Mr. Longnor is perfectly aware your daughters will never again address his child; Mr. Longnor is perfectly aware that you, sir, will need a new curate: but it is because his daughter went across the forest to become *my wife;* because your daughters are too unworthy for speech with one who bears *my* name; and because Mr. Longnor is inducted into the living on my estate, that your son will need a curate. And now, sir——"

Maddened by every word he heard, the squire would not outlisten to what Mr. Riddle had to say, but now recommenced the subject about Anne; and had just burst out into a fresh invective against her, and into new threats of searching for her, when Horner, opening the study-door, came in leading Anne.

The sight was too much for the patience of either the squire, or Miss Sophy, or Jane, and they all three darted forward and tried to separate Anne from Horner. But the man was nerved against their spiteful impotence. "For fifteen years," he loudly said, "you have separated us, but you shall no longer; your rage is as powerless as your threats."

"But she shall come home!" said the squire. "You had better come, Anne; and that this minute."

"I will not, papa!" replied Anne; "for fifteen years you and your daughters have served me as you pleased; henceforth my course is my own."

"Then not a shilling of my money shall you have!" swore the squire; "and my doors shall be closed against you!"

"So be it," replied Horner; "before the week is out she will be *my wife*, and need neither home nor friends."

"But if she thinks to have her clothes, she is mistaken," threatened Sophy; "*I*'ll take care of that."

"Or any plate, or linen, or jewellery," added Jane.

"Keep it all, keep it all!" spoke Anne; "I shall be rich enough in having a worthy husband."

These words were too much to bear, and the exasperated spinsters would possibly have proceeded to extremities with Anne, had not Riddle, using the extraordinary self-command so much his characteristic, peremptorily closed the conversation by ushering the squire and his daughters to the door, and here, relieved by Podd, closed it upon them; for all three, in utter hate, and spite, and malignity, were too contemptible for manly argument.

The squire might have been more restive, or his daughters have attempted a vicious assault upon Anne, had not Mr. Podd said gently, " You recollect, Squire Fieldworth, when you so wantonly and so maliciously insulted the dear curate's child yesterday, that I left a little matter to settle with you, which shall be settled now upon this very spot, if you do not go through this gate quietly and quickly."

The squire glanced up into the resolute face of the lusty yeoman, and seeing there an expression not pleasant to his cowardly feelings, he muttered something about "a warrant next morning," and his daughters some such words as " wretch," and " vagabond," and then walked off at a quick pace.

And now the door was closed upon them, happiness began. Dame Northwood got the tea-table ready, and brought out the world of dainties contributed by Podd ; and whilst Anne made tea, and the curate and Horner chatted, and the old lady listened, Dora found, and filled, and lighted Mr. Churchwarden, and sat by her husband's side.

By-and-by all the dear and loving neighbours came in one by one—old Northwood, and Mrs. Podd, and twenty others, to see the " dear curate," and congratulate " Miss Dora " on her marriage, for the news had spread.

Tea over, the curate adjourned to the garden, and there, walking up and down, related his journey to his parishioners. As he did so, and no one stood in the kitchen but Podd and Mrs. Northwood, some one knocked at the porch door, and honest Absalom, opening it, beheld Miss Cadwallader, true to her appointment.

" Ay, quite punctual I see," he said, as he came out into the porch, and closed the door mysteriously behind him. " Now this is the bill I have to talk to you about;" so saying, Absalom produced his ponderous pocket-book, which undoing, he brought forth the letter which had been tampered with ; " for I have two witnesses who were watching you whilst you opened it ; and so, if you do not now depart, and not only give the curate a reasonable time to pay what he owes you, as well as deliver other folk's letters besides those of the squire, and try to keep a peaceful and truthful tongue, as true as I was christened Absalom Podd I'll report you, and the matter of this letter, to the Postmaster-General. Now, go home and recollect two things—*my* advice and *your* future words about my darling child, dear Dora."

Miss Cadwallader sneaked away more abjectly than the squire.

As the evening shades descended, Horner and Anne returned with Mrs. Riddle to Broadlands, for such few days as would pass till they were married; and thus once more the old home consecrated by stillness, Dora sat between a noble husband and a noble father on the little hassock before the blazing fire, the happiest of young wives and children.

"And now, papa," asked Dora, hiding her blushing face within her loving husband's hand, "do you think, if you had been at home, you would have consented to what Walter asked?"

"I hardly know; but so that you are happy, so that you are Walter's wife, I ought to be rejoiced."

"I am, I am most happy," said Dora; "and I would hide my ring a hundred times rather than not be Walter's wife."

So saying, she untied the hidden ring from round her neck, and her husband placed it on again, and with a father's blessing.

*   *   *   *   *   *   *

As I write, the fiddle sounds merrily from the

distant hall, for it is Christmas night, and full eight years since my tale was done. And round this Christmas fire, heaped up with glowing logs on this the widest hearth in Broadlands Hall, sit the curate, and Walter's mother, and Horner, and Anne, and Lucy Gray and her husband, a neighbouring gentleman, and Dora and her husband, and they talk of old times and things; that is, as much as the fiddle, and the children's voices, and Absalom Podd's merriment will let them, for a grand game is proceeding in the hall, as Dora has a troop of little children, and Podd is their merriest friend.

Anne has been asking a question, and Dora answers:—" Why, Miss Cadwallader married the squire's coachman, as you know, and in less than a year he had run through her entire savings; he then deserted her, and she is now in a neighbouring workhouse. Now, let me ask you where Jane and Sophy are?"

" Why, since papa's death, and brother Tom has come to the Hall, they have been living at Bath, and there, it is said, Sophy takes something stronger than mineral waters; whilst Jane goes much to church, and flirts when not so occupied. But we hold no intercourse; they have never forgiven my taking a husband, or loving Walter and you."

At this moment little feet patter into the room, and little voices exclaim, " Papa, mamma, dear old Podd has been telling us such a beautiful story, at which old Northwood has been crying.   It is about your wedding ring, and about how much papa loved you, and how beautiful you looked the day you married."   And as she is so still, and they think her more beautiful than all the world besides, they cling around her, and kiss her for this sweet story's sake.

When the tale is done, the ladies look round to thank Miss Morfe, but this truest and best of Lady Herbert's gentlewomen has modestly withdrawn.

CHAPTER VIII.

AN ERA IN TWO LIVES.

IT now being holiday-time at Whitelands, Amy Morfe the younger travels down by speedy train to Temeford, where a kindly neighbour living hard by Shirlot gives her a place in his gig homewards. She is expected. Days before the preparations for her coming have been begun—are only now ended, just as on this sunny July evening the sun begins to fade upon the gilded vanes of Shirlot.

Amy is fifteen, and very lovely in her way. That loveliness of auburn hair, and fair skin, and large grey eyes; that loveliness of a gentle yet at the same time thoughtful and energetic character. Very unobtrusive, yet warm-hearted and generous is Amy; and when she does win a place in a human heart she is sure to keep it.

Her aunt, to whom Amy is all the world, thinks her grown and fairer than ever. She lays her hand upon the young girl's hair, and kisses the soft braids, and then the kindly face, and assents to Nanny's opinion that her "young missis is grown quite a woman." When the garden has been visited, the ripe gooseberries tasted, the pets caressed again and again, the newly-tuned piano just tried, and all the changes in the humble home noticed and commented on, Amy sits down by her aunt's side, and they gossip through the pleasant tea hour. Amy has much to tell about her school, its scholars, teachers, and the prizes given; this subject exhausted, she in her turn asks questions.

"Miss Hazlehurst has gone to see her nieces, who have each a government-inspected school in adjacent villages in Yorkshire. It was a long journey for the dear old lady to take, but her lameness has of late been a little better, and Mr. Weston, the doctor, thought change of air and scene would do her good. So Mrs. Hutchinson, with her usual goodness, saw her as far as Temeford; and half way on the journey, where there is a change of carriages, her nieces met her. Since her arrival I have had several letters from her, and they all tell of her better health and her great enjoyment. Still she will be happy to return. Shirlot is very dear to her, and her quiet fireside the best of havens. She hopes to be home again, my dear one, before you leave."

"That is six weeks hence, deary, six long happy weeks."

"Yes, darling, but they'll only fly too soon. Well, as to further news, poor old Mrs. Jones is gone at last. Her mental imbecility, and at times her extreme violence, could come under no sort of management here, unless a person accustomed to the insane were specially engaged; so her friends have removed her to an asylum, and her pension is to be allowed her, though absent, during the rest of her life. Her room—next Mrs. Eden's—is therefore empty, except for an old sofa and table, which were left unsold when the rest of her things were parted with. It is a dismal looking place now that all signs of life are gone."

"I should think so, though it used to look so pleasant, with its glowing fire. But Shirlot is a place of change."

" It is indeed—and of surprise, too, sometimes. Only think, Mrs. Eden's daughter is coming at last to see her mother. They haven't met for seventeen years, and the old lady is in great spirits—for a time. For a time—for the good spirits will not last—no more than any show of tenderness. It is an infinite pity, for, by her confession to me and many more, this, her only daughter, is the sole one of her children who in any way aided her before she came to Shirlot."

" Then I should think she is good as well as clever, for though a young woman, she is like you, aunt, a writer of books. The name of Lucy Eden is well known amongst us at school, for three of our usual prize-books are by her. I hope she will come whilst I am here, for one of these books is such an especial favourite with us, that I shall like to see her."

"There are many here, Amy, who have the same curiosity, though the motive is so different. The real one is whether she is, or is not, like her mother. They dread the latter, and if so, the briefer her stay is the better."

"It is impossible, aunt. If you yourself think for a moment, the thing is impossible. No one *could* write such books as the one we girls love so well, and be at the same time vindictive, remorselessly cruel, proud, and penurious."

"You are perhaps right, dear one, as the event may prove. As to other news, Miss Sophia is still greatly incognito, and Mrs. Quince has had her daughter here, setting her to rights again, but without avail. A dozen hours after, the old gentlewoman's room was in its habitual state of muddle, untidiness, and uproar. As soon as this was the case, she declared to Mrs. Eden that she was "again comfortable." To prove this state of serenity, she has invited some dozen old ladies, myself and you included, to tea early next week. Her friend, Mrs. Boston, has been sending to London for some account of a great Cooking School in which a lady distantly related to the latter is much interested; so it is to be read, and tea given; for Mrs. Quince declares she doesn't like so much love and nonsense as in the stories we have had read, but good matter of fact things. So we are to have the Romance of Cookery, if such there be."

"Perhaps so, deary. There is more poetry in prosaic things than we imagine. Now, let me ask after Mr. Quatford, my good, best friend, as I have reason to say."

"You have, indeed, Amy. We have seen little of him lately, except on those days his duties bring him to the Hall. He is much occupied with his nephew, who is a shy, grave, studious man, whom scarcely a dozen persons have yet seen, though he has now been here some weeks. Twice he has called upon me, and once each on Miss Hazlehurst and Mrs. Hutchinson. This is all. But now he has gained greater strength, I am told that he makes his way from the rectory garden, and is often to be found in the adjacent fields or woodland, stretched on the grass or withered leaves, and utterly lost to all around, in some book he is studying. The country people pass him by, and he seems to heed them not, for he neither looks nor speaks, nor seems conscious of their presence."

"And you like him, aunt?"

"Very much; though so different to his uncle. He is too stern and concise for ordinary people's liking; but under this somewhat austere bearing I am sure he hides a generous heart and a simple nature."

"Your idea of character, auntie, is usually so just, that I suppose you are right here. Now, tell me how poor Mrs Hutchinson is, and whether her son is making his way in London as he ought?"

"If silence is any proof of well-doing, he is; for it is now some weeks since his mother heard from him. I can see that she is uneasy and wretched, though she tries to hide both. Her dread is not without reason, for when he came to bid her good-bye, he behaved scandalously to her, though in what way she never distinctly told me. Even thus much is to be kept secret; though where so much is hidden, and what is known is so bad, the worst may be suspected. Poor thing! I only fear that in her case, and with respect to her son, she is doomed to drain the bitter cup of woe to its dregs."

Young Amy is very sorry, for Mrs. Hutchinson is so kind to her aunt, and so much a favourite with herself. As they talk on thus confidentially, the teacher is reverted to.

"To the surprise of everybody," says Miss Morfe, "old Mrs. Clayton is becoming quite tolerant of Mary Jones's incessant visits. She even asks her herself, places her a chair by the fire, and seems as though she would in time think of her as a daughter-in-law. Perhaps this has been brought about by sundry visits the old lady has been paying to Mary's uncle—a farmer living a few miles this side Temeford, and by her son's unsteady course. She may think, by permitting him to marry, he would keep more at home, and neglect less than he has lately done the interests of the farm. Be this as it may, the Claytons' home is a most wretched one, where plenty and wealth neither give nor bring peace."

"Mary's presence there as mistress—if she ever should be—will not improve it, I think, aunt. She always appeared to me to be not only ignorant and commonplace, but malicious as well, and wholly unfit to be a guide or companion to children."

"So it seems from some things which have come to my knowledge with respect to her conduct towards Rhoda. But she is to leave Shirlot next Easter, I understand, though she hints that the notice to leave is quite convenient, as she intends to be something better than a teacher after that."

"Really. Well, aunt, as tea is now over, I will run out and see the children, for I can hear them at play, and give the little presents I have brought them."

With this, the happy school-girl kisses her dear old aunt, and collecting her little gifts, bounds with them across the cloister, and the sunny lawn, to the playground beyond, where the little maids drop their curtseys, and welcome the dear young lady.

From this evening, and for several successive days, Amy Morfe has enough to do to pay visits. There are most of the old gentlewomen to see, to stop an hour here, an hour there, to drink tea with Miss Hazlehurst, and Miss Salway, and Mrs. Boston; she spends half a day with Mrs. Hutchinson, and discovers young friends in the farms and country-houses around, for she is a favourite. These little festivities over, she falls into her habitual quiet life of studies of various kinds. Then for amusement she sits in the sunny window, or steals into the shadowed orchard, and reads Walter Scott's novels; that pure and exquisite delight which can come, in all, its intensity, but once in a human life.

Never idle, her aunt is busy with her needle or her pen; Miss Cramp, the village dressmaker, who goes out sewing at so much per day, is called in to make Amy's frocks, newly purchased at Temeford, out of the proceeds of Miss Morfe's two last tales; and so the time glides by. One afternoon Miss Cramp needs ribbon or sewing-silk, which the village shop will not afford; so Amy, in order to obtain it, sets off to a village about four miles distant, the way to which lies by pleasant fields and a wild moorland tract of picturesque beauty.

The dog is her companion. After passing down some little way the hilly road to Temeford, she crosses a stile into deep-hedged fields, across which lies a path that shortens the way considerably. She has pursued this nearly to the end, and is approaching the last stile, when the dog bounds forward to the hedgerow, and, frisking round and round some object in its shadow, testifies to its joy and recognition by little barks and whines. As soon as she is near enough, Amy sees that the object which attracts him is some one lying on the grass, who, with his wide-awake pulled over his brow, rests his face on his upraised hand. There is a book before him on the mossy bank, but, disturbed by the dog's recognition, he is looking round as Amy advances. She calls the little animal, but he only frisks the more round and round, so she has to approach and catch him in her arms; she then perceives, what she has already surmised, that this is Mr. Austen, the chaplain's nephew. She has never seen him before except at a distance, but the various descriptions given of him tally precisely with the aspect of the gentleman who regards her. He has an austere, penetrating look; his complexion is bronzed, apparently by exposure to the sun; and his age seems more than what it probably is. His unceasing gaze embarrasses her; so, taking up the dog, averting her face, and saying, half inarticulately, "she is sorry for Totty's rudeness," she hurries towards the stile. She is scarcely over it before some one speaks to her; so looking round she perceives that the gentleman has risen and followed her. He is tall and very dark, and when he speaks his manner is concise and austere.

"What is your name?" he asks as he stays by the stile.

"Amy Morfe, sir."

"Miss Morfe's niece?"

"Yes, sir."

"Why is it that I have not seen you there when I called?"

"I do not live at Shirlot, sir; I am a pupil in a training college near London; I am but here for my holidays, and came but a few days since."

"Indeed! Take the dog up again, as I am coming over the stile." Thus he crosses, and walking slowly onwards, renews his conversation.

"Where are you going to?"

Amy says where, and on some little errand to a shop.

"Well, I'll walk beside you till the lane opens on the moor. Do you return the same way—and how long shall you be gone?"

She says she shall, and her absence will not be more than an hour.

To this he makes no reply, but walks on with her along the turfy lane—sometimes silent, sometimes regarding her, sometimes asking her questions about her college and its methods.

It has been a very hot day, and as the lane widens out towards the common, there are more trees, and therefore more shadow, but the air is very close and sultry. Taking off his wide-awake, the gentleman bids her take off her hat too.

"Aunt doesn't like me to get sunburnt, sir," says Amy, wondering at the question, for she thinks it a rude one.

"Young ladies should always be obedient. Take it off till you get to the common, not fifty yards hence—you can put it on again then, for I go no farther."

She obeys him, for there is that in his manner and tone of voice which makes disobedience impossible—especially to him who, as she well knows, is Mr. Quatford's nephew.

When the hat is off he says nothing, only so regards her that she is glad to step on in haste and bring the walk to a close. Then she says

"Good day," without scarcely a look, so abashed is she; and, walking forwards, ties on her hat as she goes.

She crosses the moor, reaches the village, finds what she needs in the village shop, and returns. To her infinite surprise, as she approaches the lane again, she sees the strange gentleman on the grass—not studying from any open book, but watching her return, as it seems. When she has approached him within a few yards, he rises, and making no comment on his stay, accompanies her on her return, though his mood seems silent, for he says but little. Occasionally he goes on before; and when they reach the opening from the fields into the highway, he bids her an abrupt " good afternoon," and goes rapidly forwards towards Shirlot.

The deaf gentlewoman is looking out for her darling—for tea waits—and she is always uneasy when Amy is absent. Presently the latter tells her aunt of meeting with the shy, absent man— or the " fil-los-fer," as the wiseacres of Shirlot call Mr. Austen—but as Miss Cramp is present, little is said thereon, and the matter passes by and is not again reverted to.

The next morning, whilst the young girl sits beside her aunt, intent upon some of her studies, there is a knock at the door, and Nanny opening it, Mr. Austen enters. Miss Morfe is surprised to see him, for Mr. Quatford has told her that Islip always spends his mornings in abstract study, but he makes the excuse of bringing a paper from his uncle; and when he has sat and talked a time he goes.   He seems to take little heed of Amy— he says nothing of his walk the previous afternoon—and any one would think that he was the most indifferent man in the whole universe to outward things.   But he is not.   His keen glance, his quick ear, draw inferences from a look or a word in which another would see or hear nothing.

From this date Mr. Austen pays Miss Morfe an occasional visit, and Amy is almost sure to encounter him in her walks.

CHAPTER IX.

THE QUINCE TEA-PARTY, AND THE STORY OF THE SOUTHWARK INN.

TUESDAY morning's letter-bag brings Mrs. Boston the paper from her friend, and Mrs. Quince, being duly informed thereof, invites her friends for the following day.

"You'll expect plain fare and plain usage," are the words appended to her verbal invitation, and everybody at Shirlot knows what this means. Indeed, to tell the truth, precise, highly-bred ladies like Miss Morfe, Miss Salway, and Miss Hazlehurst, would rather be absent than present; but, then, the strange old woman has many kindly traits of character, and they do not like to give her offence. At a hint from Miss Hazlehurst, they all determine to take their tea beforehand, and thus be armed against any casualty in the matter of the tea-kettle or viands.

The day has come, and the hour of invitation approaches — but could Mrs. Quince's good daughter—who lives about twenty miles away, the orderly companion, housekeeper, and friend of some aged cousins—see the state of affairs, she would be horrified. The carpet is rolled up in a corner of the room, the sofa heaped with litters, the ornaments belonging to the mantelshelf stored away in some unknown drawer—there is a water-jug here, a broom there. A dozen coarse blue cups are, without a tray, placed on a rickety deal table—there is a bottle set to hold milk, and some sugar in a jam-pot. Thick lumps of bread adorn a pewter plate, and a huge plumcake, all spread away and shapeless, is still in the tin in which it was baked. Mrs. Quince has tea-things somewhere—china plates enough for the service of a feast somewhere—a paper tea-tray somewhere—but she is muddle-headed, and cannot tell. Her whole life has been a muddle, and will end in a muddle, for to her it is a state of comfort and happiness. Born the daughter of a country gentleman, she brought her husband a dowry of twenty thousand pounds; but he, through ignorance in farming, and she by waste and bad management in her house, soon muddled it away. Sirloins and rounds of beef stood in the great kitchen to be cut at will—the beer-taps were ever on the run—wine and spirits were poured out for every guest. In the abstract, she was not dirty or extravagant, but she was a muddler—and thus her fortune was wasted like snow in a torrid sun, and from worse to worse things went with her and her husband. Each

R 2

farm they took was smaller and poorer, and when old age approached she was husbandless and homeless, except for such a one as her daughter could afford her. Pitying friends stepped in, her case was represented to the Trustees of the great Charity, and though it was not so worthy as many a one placed before their scrutiny, it was told in truth that her family had farmed on the estate, even in Lady Catherine's time, for at least two hundred years; and so they appointed her, and she brought to Shirlot her muddling economics. Here her good daughter comes over occasionally to "put her right"; the matron, in her monthly visitations drops hints, or even sternly reproves—but all to no purpose. In a few days things drop into their wonted course; and as it was in the beginning so will it be to the end—muddle—all muddle!

In pleasant conclave, as Mrs. Boston, Mrs. Hutchinson, Miss Salway, and Miss Morfe walked up and down the cloister the previous day, the paper was read, and judging that its contents can in no possibility do Mrs. Quince any harm, on the contrary, good—if the philosopher's axiom be taken at its worth, that 'no effort is lost,' they are rather glad that Mrs. Dumple's niceties should have voice in such precincts. It occurring also to Mrs. Hutchinson's mind that her twenty little maids may listen with profit, it is arranged on this, the day of the party, that Mrs. Quince's door shall stand wide open during the time of reading, and that, a form being placed in the gallery, the little maids shall sit thereon, with good old Tibb as their companion. Mrs. Thelwall's door, which is next to that of Mrs. Quince, is also to stand wide open, so that she, poor bed-ridden lady, may listen to the recital of some of the good deeds that are taking place in a world lying far beyond her own.

Well, four o'clock comes, and with it the ladies —for so early does Mrs. Quince drink tea. As they come slowly up the waggon-wide staircase and enter the great quaint gallery, with its six large, sunny, lattice windows, and a greenhouse of bloom on every ledge—many think with grateful hearts that Shirlot is a lovely place, and bless in reverence the dead whose bounty so long ago made it theirs. They stay at Miss Hazlehurst's door, and that dear gentlewoman coming forth, they pace up and down the gallery a few times, and two or three more kindly than the rest step into Mrs. Thelwall's room to speak to the poor bed-ridden lady who now for five years, night and day, has never left her bed, and who, but for Mrs. Wiskit her attendant, and Robin her cat, is very lonely. Her temper is not very amiable, her gratitude for any kindness shown her not very warm, but she has good friends, nevertheless, amongst her sister gentlewomen—women who, having themselves suffered, know what the evils of suffering are. So Miss Morfe makes it her religion to see the poor lady three or four times a-week, and chat with her, and tell her all the news she has read in the newspapers. Young Amy carries her flowers, and, patronising Robin, has won thereby a warm place in the poor, weary, morbid, but kindly heart; and other good gentlewomen, such as Mrs. Cranworth, Miss Salway, and Mrs. Weld, do as many charities as scanty means allow. Thus there is a heaven's bounty even here, in this sad room.

Mrs. Quince receives her friends with hospitable greetings.

"Glad to see you, ladies, and hope you'll be comfortable and at home. I've not much holiday array for you; but you'll excuse it—some of my things are put away, and I couldn't find 'em."

When her friends are seated, Mrs. Quince proceeds forthwith to make tea. But her habitual string of disasters pursues her. The kettle has boiled so long that nearly all the water has evaporated, the key of the tea-caddy cannot be found, and milk is forgotten. But Mrs. Hutchinson, who is present, and who has foreseen, from long experience of Mrs. Quince, that all these disasters would arise, summons one of the elder children, and soon the hall-kitchen supplies all that is needed. Tea thus progresses, is soon over, for the guests are moderate, as may be foreseen; and then Mrs. Quince, sweeping the things into her closet, only breaking a cup or two and the tea-pot in so doing, plumps down into her great chair, and declares she enjoys having a party better than anything. The door is now put open;

Tibb and the twenty little maids are seen to be assembled, the divine evening light still lies in golden length along the gallery, the hush of peace broods round and through and over these olden walls of Shirlot; Miss Hazlehurst adjusts her spectacles, shakes her snowy pocket-handkerchief, looks round to see that there is attention due, and then begins this reading of

THE SOUTHWARK INN.

Of all the dolphins that ever swam a league in the great deep, that were ever chiseled in stone, or carved in wood, or tricked by a learned herald, or set forth on a sign-board by a painter of lively imagination, or fashioned in gilt gingerbread, none ever approached, either in spread or might of tail, in roundness or largeness of ,eyes, in depths of yellow, blue, red, and green, on back or fins, to the mighty "Dolphin" in Southwark; which, carved in wood, and adorned by a bygone painter's brush, was the sign of a large old-fashioned inn, ruled for a long generation by the line of Dumple; and now by Margery Dumple, widow, and sole executrix of Jonathan Dumple. It is true that its rainbow tints were somewhat faded, as any dolphin's would be that had been perpetually swimming through the rain, the snow, the sunshine of some forty years; yet, nevertheless, if half the happiness, if half the smiles of sunny human faces, if half the fruits of nature, which in that time had passed beneath its spreading tail, could have been gathered into one, and cast as sunshine on it, every old faded fin and scale would have rivalled those of the dolphins of southern seas, that, sporting on the mazy surface of lightly curling waves, throw myriad rainbow tints upon the front of day.

Beneath this mighty Dolphin was a wide old gateway, with heavy wooden gates, chained back to either wall; and this opened into a very large yard or court, on two sides of which, in addition to the one facing the street, was built the inn itself; whilst the fourth was occupied by lofty waggon sheds, immense ranges of stables, granaries, and store-chambers. The yard, partly paved and partly flagged, was ornamented by a pump in the middle, from which led towards one side of the stables a range of quaint and massive old stone watering-troughs, now partly filled with earth and dust, and such stunted fungi and lichens as thrive in places of this kind; though there had been a time when thirsty teams just off the road, and freed from bit and collar, had slaked their thirst in the clear and brimming waters which then filled them. On the paved side of the yard, nearest the inn windows, some bushy laurel, myrtle, and arbor-vitæ shrubs grew in punchy wooden tubs, painted green, whilst here and there, round a spare bit of wall, the jutting gables of the twisted chimneys, and the thick posts which supported the great wooden gallery, ivy, of many years' growth, climbed and twisted.

The " Dolphin " in its day of highest glory was the largest inn, and one of the most noted, on the south side of the Thames; for it was not only that country squires, their wives and daughters, and substantial farmers and yeomen, rested here on their way to London—but, also, where were put up, and from whence were dispersed, the rich treasures of those loaded wains which had toiled a monstrously slow way from the homesteads of the weald of Kent, from Surrey, and from Sussex. Here, in autumn, as orchards were stripped, filbert bushes and hazel copses rifled, harvests garnered, and the laden wains came in, might be seen a continuous fair of buyers and sellers; the ruddy apples piled in sacks, and the fresh-gathered russet-coloured nuts thrown in heaps upon the granary floors, filling the whole place with the mingled scent of the orchard and woodland. Other seasons brought wains as profusely, if not so richly laden, for there was the cherry season amongst the rest—not to speak of a continuous consignment of butter, poultry, and eggs to the metropolis—whilst travellers always to and fro, the going and return of the four postchaises, the horsing of two rumbling old coaches which travelled southward, and the custom of a respectable class of tradesmen, gave to the " Dolphin " that mighty air of business, of which by fame, and from honest dealing, it was well worthy.

But this was in the " Dolphin's " meridian days —those days when it had brewed mighty hogsheads of ale, baked weekly many sacks of flour, and roasted half-a-dozen sirloins and huge ribs of beef

at a time ; and when, all day long, bells were ringing, chambermaids and waiters running to and fro
along the gallery, waggons and horsemen passing
in and out beneath the archway, and stablemen,
waggoners, and helpers toiling and moiling in the
great yard and sheds.

Most surely somewhat of the "Dolphin's" glory
had faded, even when about 1805 Jonathan Dumple
brought home his pretty Margery, then eighteen,
from her father's old grange in the weald of Kent,
where, with five sisters and six brothers, she had
been well and lovingly nurtured in the sweet virtues of chastity, charity, thrift, and admirable
housewifery. Her love story had been touched
by no sorrow ; its simile might be found in an early
violet, plucked just as it began to peep, all scent
and beauty, from the leaves, and then and there
set for ever in some place of shelter where no rude
hand could take it, and from whence its odour
might be richly shed around : for, returning from
a great holiday visit to London with her father,
young Jonathan, looking from the bar window,
had caught a glimpse of her sweet face as it was
nestled beneath the huge hood of her father's chaise,
and admiring it, and learning the possessor's name,
he went the very next May down into the weald,
and courted her in her father's blossoming orchard;
and when the apples grew red and golden in the
autumn time, he went again and married her, in
the quaint old rustic church near at hand, in the
presence of her father and mother and a host of
her relatives. Thence he at once brought her home

to his widowed mother, who received her as Noah
the dove into the ark, and without one pang or
jealous stipulation resigned every household duty,
and trust, and possession into the young wife's
hands; and the latter was not a mean one, for the
Dumples had been for generations a thrifty race,
and had much substantial wealth in beautiful old
plate, fine linen, rich antique china and glass, and
other household goods. I shall open Mrs. Dumple's
linen chest by-and-bye, and possibly peep at her
plate, and into the china closet; but this is to
come.

This trust was worthily bestowed. For ten
years Margery and Jonathan lived together in the
holiest concord, the "Dolphin" flourishing to a
great extent, and then death stepped in and made
her husbandless and childless in the space of six
weeks. For a time these losses bowed her to the
earth; but by degrees her spirit rose again, though
tempered by a sweet gravity that added a new
charm to the touching faith and charity implanted
by her birth, and by her parents' rule. The "Dolphin" continued to flourish, till several changes
removed the great lines of traffic, till farming and
orchard produce were forwarded more expeditiously
than by team and wain, till farmers found markets
nearer home, and the owners of country halls and
landed wealth set up their modern equipages at
the more fashionable hotels of the west end.

Still the "Dolphin" thrived when no other inn
in the like position and under the like circumstances
would or could have done; for its well known name,

its cleanliness, its comfort, its able management, brought many a visitor, and many a traveller out of his road; and haughty country squires and great landowners, who, boasting old and hereditary Saxon names, would not have bared their heads to the titled aristocrats of modern date, rarely came to town without a deferential and personal inquiry concerning Margery Dumple.

Nevertheless, by imperceptible degrees the business waned away; room after room, stable after stable, became disused, two kitchen fires served instead of five or six, the old servants, as they from time to time dropped off, were not replaced, and here and there about the courtway, the waggon sheds, or the stable doors, where yet a scrap of hay or straw lay, it was rotted and long trodden down. But good Margery had so husbanded her widow's store as to be well-to-do in spite of all these changes time brought about, and still, with one man and four women servants, kept up much state and hospitable comfort round her; and she could have afforded to do this, though no guest or traveller, or country wain, ever passed again beneath the faded grandeur of the "Dolphin."

A few years ago, and on a January evening, about the hour of five, strong candlelight shone clear from two chamber windows out on to the court, as far as the great stone drinking-troughs. This appeared to be a sign of some importance, as a man with a quaint, odd-fashioned face, after first peeping round a half-closed stable door, was next seen fully, and presently beside the pump itself, where, dipping his head in a fresh-pumped bucket of water, up and down like a duck, he next buried it in a great jack-towel he had brought from the stable. Whilst this process was going forward a woman's voice called out from no great distance, whereupon the hearer, resting his face on the towel, as a horse his neck on a gate, hallooed in answer, "Ye—es, ye—es."

"Tummus, Tummus—the dear missis is gone up to dress—and so get ready—and then come in and have a cup of tea in the bar; missis says so."

"Tea," muttered Tummus, in a voice which tried hard to express a grumble, but couldn't; "that's all the vimen think about—jist as if a young man like me was all sure to be the same vay o' thinking—but it ain't so; for ven I take a family coat o' arms, it shall be a pipe, and not a tea-kittle." Then aloud and in a voice no more like grumbling than a cheerful tone is to a dirge, "Thank ye, thank ye. I'll come as soon as I've got vaistkit and coat on."

So saying, and to show his attention, Mrs. Dumple's renowned Tummus, concluding his bath, bolted back into the stable, there to complete his toilet, it being one of the well-known peculiarities of this young man to consider the stable the only habitable place, and the corn-chest or bin therein the only wardrobe in which one in his line could, with due regard to personal dignity, stow away articles of his toilet, or other miscellaneous property.

The room from whence the light so strongly shone was Mrs. Dumple's own bedchamber, wherein, assisted by two of her servants, she was now fittingly dressing for an appointed friendly tea-taking with a very old and highly-honoured friend of hers, Alderman Rudberry, the great city silk-merchant, to whose house, in the neighbourhood of Cornhill, Tummus was presently to escort her; for so great was her horror of cabs, omnibuses, and hackney coaches, as to cause her never to travel in any vehicle except the "Dolphin" chaise. As she thus sat in an ample chair covered by rich brocaded silk, one servant arranging her simple cap of costly though old-fashioned lace, and the other placing on the toilet-covers, as she brought them forth from well-filled drawers and quaint jewel-box, a filmy cambric pocket-handkerchief, ruffles, and a large gold brooch set with divers coloured hair, it was plain to see what sort of woman Margery Dumple was, by the serene yet firm expression of her somewhat wrinkled face, and by the exquisite cleanliness and order of everything around her. These conspicuously shone forth in her own person, for though her old-fashioned satin gown was on, and Becky, her most confidential servant, was now pinning over it a small lace shawl of the same richness and fineness as her cap, there could yet be seen, coyly peeping forth, nice cambric frill and edge of snowy lavendered linen —both being silent evidence of Mrs. Dumple's great word "*thorough*," which, well understood and acted upon through a long life, had brought fortune to the saucer-eyed "Dolphin." All else was stamped by the same sign : the fine toilet-cloth, the laced pincushion, the quaint china and lacquered toilet-boxes, the massive silver candlesticks, the large bed, the neat carpet, the bright fire-place, the drawers half opened here and there with their oozing perfume of lavender and rose leaves, and, lastly, the dress and appearance of the two old servants themselves, betokened what were the results of Mrs. Dumple's text.

As soon as her toilet was completed, and the old lady had taken such a view in the mirror as to satisfy herself that all was correctly as it should be, she took two keys from her pocket, and delivering them to Becky, there soon stood upon the table an old-fashioned tin box, which unlocked, Mrs. Dumple took therefrom sundry parchments and papers tied together with red tape, and then relocking, not however without some tears trickling down the furrows of her face, and a sympathising "Don't take on, dear missis," from both Becky and Doll, the box was carefully replaced, and Mrs. Dumple, preceded by her two servants, descended down-stairs to her own parlour, where one cup and saucer, a small silver tea-pot, a cream-ewer of the like metal, and divers light refreshments, such as cake, bread and butter, and thin slices of tongue, were neatly set forth; as Mrs. Dumple, though most frugal in her diet, always prepared herself for a "visiting tea" by a "home tea," in order to duly meet such possible contingencies as an unboiled tea-kettle, or pekoe without a dust of her favourite green in it. Becky made the tea, poured it out, fashioned a delicate sandwich of the thin-cut tongue and bread and butter, roused up the merry little fire to a still merrier glow by a gentle poke, and then retired to the bar to do honour to the pekoe there, for unholy bohea was in no wise permitted to throw a discredit on Mrs. Dumple's word " thorough," meaning thereby justice even inside a tea-pot. The old gentlewoman, thus left alone, fell into deep thought; and so sat, evidently oblivious of her " visiting tea" with Alderman Rudberry, till, after divers taps on the door, it was opened, and there respectfully advanced to the little tea-table a procession, consisting not only of the four maids headed by Tummus, but of an owl and a large goat, likewise old, and with an extent of beard that was prodigious. Tummus, who bore the owl on his arm, was now habited in dark blue plush " vaiskit," with shiny sleeves, in top-boots, cor- duroy smalls, and in a shirt the bosom of which was an amazing hieroglyphic of minute stitchery. Perhaps for the instant Mrs. Dumple was sur- prised, for her many years' servants looked grave, and even the goat rested his bearded chin upon the edge of the table in mute solemnity.

" Missis," began the " Dolphin's" hostler, in a voice of infinite respect, " the vimmen here can't make up their minds to say what they have to say ; and so I've made bold to come in and say it for 'em, and jist add a vord or so o' my own. Now, we all on us know, mum, that you're going

to the Alderman's, and that, von vay or t'other,
there 'll be a settlement o' this here Dolfin
kvestion, and, of course, it'll be adwerse to the
Dolfin.   The Alderman 'll say, what's the use,
Mrs. Dumple, o' rooms vithout travellers in 'em,
fires as are never needed to varm, or roast, or
bile, beds vithout sleepers, varming-pans vithout
use, rummers vithout cold or hot in 'em, and
stables vithout 'osses, truffs (troughs) vithout
drinkers, vhips vith no vipping, chists as vont no
corn in 'em, and post-shayses as never go a mile;
so he'll say—and wery nattarally, mum, for them
as ain't bin reared in Dolfin vays can't have
Dolfin feelins—'Sell the old inn, Mrs. Dumple,
it'll fetch a good price, for the ground it stands
on is wal'able for many things; dismiss yer maids
and that old Tummus, as have got sich a little
to do, and go into the country, and have a cottage, and a shay, and a cow, and perhaps a pig or
two, and you'll be happy.'   But we, mum, as
know what Dolfin feelins be, and a-judging by
vot ve feel vithin ourselves, say, and ve know
it too, that you'll pine and droop at the loss o'
everything you've seen and known so long,
vether the thing be one o' feelin or not.   The old
staircase as dear master and the little uns trod,
your old rooms, your old fire-place, even the
pump, and the Dolfin hisself, are nat'ral things,
as you vont know how to be able to do vithout; and
such, mum, are 'pinions ve'd kiss the Book on.
Now this is the 'rithmetic o' the thing, Becky
having jist scored it up on the bar-slate:—Becky

herself forty-vun years, Doll thirty-five, Cis and
Lettice ten and fifteen years each, and me, mum,
Tummus, twenty-eight years the wery next third
o' March, that being the day (it's bin reg'larly
scored on the lid o' the biggest corn-chist) in which
I fust see'd the tail o' the Dolfin, it being then,
mum, as bright as a brass varming-pan. And to
this there is twenty years to set down for Billy,
and twelve for the howl, vich, as newspapers say,
ven they hadd up, makes a sum total o' vun
hundred and sixty-vun years. Sich being the
case, and the sum 'd be wery obvious if a man had
to pull it from his pus, there can't be a parting o'
none on us; so, mum, the wery Dolfin 'd say it
hisself, if he vos given to conwersation. And
now, mum, vot I respectfully recommend is this,
that as rails have taken avay 'osses, and new
roads travellers, that I do a little gratis rubbing
to a few cab 'osses veekly to keep my hand in,
jist as I polished my own boots tvice this wery
morning, and vos so far oblivious as to fancy 'em
those of a squire in parlour fourteen, and of a
voman vith a red nose in number six. Then,
mum, ve could now and then jist take in a few
respectable people, and give 'em bed, breakfast,
and clean boots, telling 'em ven they ask, that
the Dolfin's forgot his writing and don't make
bills now-a-days. Hearing o' this they'd sure to
come again, so as to make a sort o' bustle now
and then, jist by vay o' keeping your heart up,
mum, and our hands in—for on course, if ve can't
git travellers von vay ve must another, jist as the

bird-catcher said ven he took both a salt-box and a net into the fields vith him; and so, mum, there might surwive and git abroad such accounts o' your melted butter, your Irish stews, your roasts, your gravies, as might be put in practice, and not die out vith the Dolfin; for even Job hisself, mum, vos he in this land o' Huz, might had a few tears to the lot, he vos so uncommonly given to veep, if sich a thing as your Irish stew vos gone like the gilt off the Dolfin's tail. So, mum, this is our conwiction, and to vich I, Tummus, hostler at the Dolfin, put my hand."

Though this address, delivered as it was with profound gravity, and with such visible illustration as might be used throughout the before-mentioned eleemosynary treatment of cab-horses, would have raised the good- humoured merriment of an audience less interested than the one which listened, Margery Dumple only benevolently smiled as she said—"Your advice, Thomas, would I fear be found, if put in practice, a worse thing than empty rooms and no customers; but one thing be you all assured of, that whether I keep on, or leave the 'Dolphin,' nothing parts us till you yourselves like to take a new mistress and a new home."

"And that'll *never* be, mum," spoke Tummus and the four maids in a breath.

"Well, keep your hearts up then, for you have no worthier or kinder friend than Alderman Rudberry; and to tell you the truth, I think he has got some benevolent plot or another hatching in his mind, which will not only keep us here, but make us useful; and God grant it be so, for though I am nearly fifty-nine, and not so light of step or quick of sight as you remember me, still there's some service in these old hands still."

"Ay! ay! mum," responded Tummus, "and in yer good heart, too; and so, as you don't think much o' my adwice concerning the cab 'osses and gratis travellers, only teach some dozen tidy girls how to make mutton-broth, bile a potato, and knock up an Irish stew, wash a shirt, sweep a hearth, and have a bit o' a smile for a husband as comes in vith th'burthen o' a day's vork on his back, and you'll preach a sermon, mum, as may have a woice through many ginerations."

"We shall see, Thomas. Now, take this will and packet of papers, and button them carefully under your waistcoat, for they are——"

"I know, mum, they wouldn't be safer under the munniment."

"The lease of the 'Dolphin' and my husband's will," continued Mrs. Dumple; "and now get the lantern, and you, Becky, help me with my cloak and hood,"—for Mrs. Dumple, despising such things as cap-boxes and baskets, always went forth to "visiting teas" already dressed in her best cap. Tummus soon re-appeared with a huge lantern—unlighted, however, and which was about as much needed through the quiet thoroughfares of London as an umbrella on a frosty night—and wishing her four maids good evening, and patting the goat, now stretched full-length upon the hearth, with its head upon the fender, and coaxing the blinking owl, now transferred to the shoulder of Cis, Mrs. Dumple, with the light active step of a woman of thirty, had soon passed from beneath the time-honoured shadow of the "Dolphin," on her way to Alderman Rudberry's.

Though Tummus well knew that his duty was to walk respectfully behind his mistress, yet the liveliness of his imagination kept him in such a perpetual state of hot-water, by inducing him to fancy every passer-by a porter with a load, or a footman with a prodigious width of shoulders, and every lamp-post a prize-fighter or a grenadier, that he was continually either at her side, or on a yard or two before, to receive, like a wall, the first shock of such battering-rams as this imagination of his conjured up.

However, without accident, and in due time, Tummus knocked for his mistress a double-knock on Alderman Rudberry's door, and soon after she had duly arranged her cap, kerchief, ruffles, brooch, and mittens in the best bedroom, and by the aid of two wax candles, the little old gentlewoman of the "Dolphin," in Southwark, shook the Alderman by the hand, and was placed by him in an arm-chair, extraordinary for softness and comfort, beside the tea-table.

The silver urn, as if it knew what was required of it, not simply boiled, but hissed and made steam to an amazing extent; and the pekoe, with a dash of green, was of absorbing excellence, so that the tea passed off charmingly ; and when cleared away, and the chairs drawn near the fire, and a little screen just put behind Mrs. Dumple's back, and her feet on a velvet-covered doss, and the will and papers on the table, and the Alderman with a pen in his hand and his spectacles on, not to mention two huge cats on the hearth, the room looked the snuggest place in wide London.

Thus comfortable, for a long time the two friends sat and talked over many matters of business relative to the "Dolphin," as might be gathered from what Mrs. Dumple replied, when, after some half-hour's argument, the Alderman paused.

"It is so good, so very good of you, Mr. Rudberry, thus to lean to my old whims and fancies; for in truth I do not think I could tear myself away from the old place all at once."

"Not good, or kind, or anything of the sort, Margery, only dutiful," went on the Alderman; "for you it was—God bless you, woman, for your Christian heart, as men do bless *all* women thus gifted angel-wise — that took me shoeless and friendless from the straw of a country wain, that fed me and housed me, and was a mother to me, and led me to be what I am, an honest and prosperous man; and therefore duty—duty is the word;" and as he spoke, Mr. Rudberry rose in reverence to his guest, and stood till bidden to sit down again. "And so," he presently went on, "my idea is, that we turn the old stables into a Cooking School, wherein you can teach some of the most needed lessons of our daily life—not thereby, Margery Dumple, as we have just said, to raise up cooks

for hotels, or mansions, or palaces, but to make
the probable wives of labourers, journeymen, and
little shopkeepers sufficiently skilful to turn a
scrag of mutton or a few bones, with the addition
of potatoes, onions, salt and pepper, into a dish
glorious enough for a king. Ay! ay! Margery
Dolphin, live to teach but one hundred English
girls to make Irish stew, boil a potato, and place
the meal upon the three-legged table as it ought
to be, and you'll have done more for the social
life of England than half the laws trumpeted in
Parliament, and set down pompously on parchment. And that there may be eating as well as
cooking, we'll contract to supply a mid-day meal
to certain Ragged Schools with which I am connected; and when it is a higher dish, such as
oyster sauce, it shall be for my own table."

So saying, the Alderman rang for wine, and a
glass a-piece helping them onward with their
further business, concerning the lease of the
" Dolphin," and Jonathan's will, it soon became
supper-time. When this was announced they
adjourned to the dining-room, where a supper
was set forth, so cooked and ordered as to fully
justify the " thorough " maxims of the "Dolphin's"
mistress. In due time after this, the old gentlewoman again retired to the best bedchamber and
the brilliancy of the two wax candles, and, when
duly hooded and cloaked, was led down-stairs by
the Alderman; Tummus, fresh from the kitchen
(for " visiting tea and supper" were synonymous
with Mrs. Dumple and Tummus), adjusted his

mistress's clogs; and the old gentlewoman so
standing, and happening to turn her eyes to a
half-opened wareroom-door, a rich glow of silver-
coloured satin flashed across her sight; so, stepping with the Alderman to admire it, they thus,
as they both stood, little dreamt that one hundred
and fifty-four yards of its like in beauty and
richness lay on the forthcoming road of dripping-
pans, potatoes, and Irish stew.

By twelve o'clock the hospitable shadow of
the "Dolphin" again protected Mrs. Dumple.

Having once broached the idea of cooking
schools, and enlisted in their behalf the warm
sympathies and admirable knowledge of Margery
Dumple, Alderman Rudberry lost no time in
debate as to their utility, or the possibility of
their being brought into existence like any other
of the forms of industrial education. He therefore sought out the promoters of such ragged
schools as lay within a reasonable distance of the
" Dolphin," and which, conducted on the industrial principle, retained the majority of their
scholars through the mid-day hours. From
these he learnt, as if by one assent, how valuable
would be a supply of plain, wholesome, well-
cooked food to their several schools; the two
main difficulties against supplying destitute children with a *self-earned* mid-day meal having
hitherto been rather the expense of cooking, and
the want of needful premises, than the prime cost
of the food itself; for there were scores of honest
citizens, wealthy salesmen, and butchers of the

great markets, and dock merchants, down to the thrifty shopkeepers of the surrounding streets, who would willingly give kindly gifts of meat, rice, and vegetables; what was further wanting was a capable and willing hand to superintend, and to teach the change of these materials into savoury soups, Irish stews, and good plain puddings, and, through such teaching, rear the hard-working mechanic a thrifty wife, and bless the citizen with a household treasure, that besides setting on her cap jauntily, and having a silk gown and a parasol in her box for Sundays, could roast a leg of mutton brown and with gravy, and boil a dish of potatoes with a reasonable hope that, when arrived at table, they should neither be mistaken for roasted chestnuts nor for stones. It was therefore arranged in the first instance with two schools, that at sixpence a head for a week of five days, such sixpence to be strictly the product of the children's own earnings, there should be supplied a daily meal of such savoury but plain dishes as in honest Margery Dumple's judgment were advisable as well as practicable.

Next came the scholars—for, as Mrs. Dumple justly reasoned, it would not, in the first instance at least, do to take girls thoroughly untrained. Alderman Rudberry therefore made the city charity schools his chief places of selection, where girls in blue, or green, or brown gowns, white tippets, mob caps, and bare arms, had been duly taught their samplers and their catechisms by a prim mistress, and their curtseys and their walking order by a cocked-hat beadle, full of reverence for the parson, but of contempt for the clerk and his psalmody. As well he might make choice within such rigid bounds of irrefragable orthodoxy, for none gave so many Easter buns, or so much Christmas pudding, or begged Mayday holidays, or went so far as to bribe with a silk gown the rigid protestantism of strict mistresses to go beyond the facts of Jonah's whale, or Aaron's rod, to some little matters of geography and history, as did Alderman Rudberry; and, therefore, as he went up and down the several schools, selecting eight towards the first twelve scholars Mrs. Dumple was to undertake, he little knew what mingled hope and fear quickened the ruddy current of many a heart hidden beneath the trim quaintness of bygone days. For the selection too which he made, the Alderman, bachelor as he was, might have been taking lessons, for a fair portion of his life, from portraits of a Sir Joshua of the past, or a Watson Gordon of the present, so inimitably did he pick out the sweet faces from the multiplicity of prim caps that passed in review before him: but there I think Alderman Rudberry was exactly of my opinion, that beauty has usually a connection with truth, let people say what they will. Be this as it may, most certain it is that when the eight stood forth in their first interview with Mrs. Dumple, in the alderman's parlour, never since pious citizens first made pious bequests for the furtherance of parish learning, did eight sweeter faces glance from their quaint

framing of band and frill. Their names were as
follows :—

Anna Hillman.	Mary Aston.
Grace Lawrence.	Alice Taylor.
Julia Bunyan.	Barbara Longmark.
Rose Clarkvoice.	Jessie Hayler.

And when to these were added the two daughters of two of the Alderman's Spitalfield weavers,
and the little god-daughter of a poor brother of
the Charter-house, there were three more, thus
named :—

Henriette Boncœur.   Ursula Penn.
Nelly Chester.

Making eleven scholars, and leaving to Mrs.
Dumple's choice one vacancy; which for the present was all she desired.

The third, and hardest thing of all, was the
" Dolphin " itself, for not only were there his
spreading tail and his once-gilded fins to take
into consideration, but the four maid-servants,
and Tummus into the bargain. However, most
things went on pretty smoothly till the appointed
morning, when the worthy Alderman arrived with
a surveyor, in order to look over the " Dolphin "
premises, with a view to such alterations as were
needful; it being one of Margery's provisos that
her own immediate dwelling should remain the
same, and that the cooking kitchen, or kitchens,
should be formed out of Tummus's particular
region—the stables. He there found those of the
" Dolphin " in great consternation, for Tummus,

having been taken ill the over-night, with what Becky gave her opinion was "quinsy, as he couldn't speak," was now confined to his chamber; whilst Margery, and Cis, her cook, were gravely closeted in the before-mentioned little parlour, in deep discussion as to a series of domestic remedies. However, when the worthy Alderman had somewhat consoled Mrs. Dumple, she consented to put on her hood and clogs, and step with him and the surveyor across the yard, to the great range of stables, the largest of which, according to one of Tummus's mighty boasts, heard often and far beyond the "Dolphin's" bounds, "had held two hundred 'osses, with only the inconvenience o' th' fat man in the crowd, ven he vos a lee-tle hot," but which when reached was locked, and no key could be found. As it was natural to suppose that Tummus held it in possession, Becky was dispatched to his domicile above one of the stables, but soon returned without it—"Poor Tummus, shaking his head, missis," said Becky, "to say of course there isn't one." But the good Alderman, a little more versed in Tummus's whimsicalities than Becky or Mrs. Dumple, repaired in person to an adjoining stable of somewhat reasonable dimensions, mounted a sort of ladder, and entered the chamber, which, time out of mind, had been dedicated to the especial service of the head hostler of the "Dolphin." It having now been so long the peculiar domicile of Tummus, and a place wherein his innocent eccentricities had had full play, Alderman Rudberry was not at all surprised to find it what it was, or that Tummus, among other things, having long ago dismissed a stump bedstead, had formed himself a nightly couch within the body of a roomy post-chaise, which, somewhere about the days of Goldsmith, had been the pride and glory of the Southwark inn. Its front had been removed, and the wide old inside-seat lengthened out so as to hold a comfortable bed formed of stage-coach cushions, whilst the clumsy doors, with their glass bull's-eye windows still hanging on either side, and the roof (as was the case with the sedans and coaches of a hundred or more years ago) still letting up and down, the whole formed, in the estimation of the " Dolphin's " hostler, " an uncommon convenient bed, which none o' the ' Dolfin's ' four-posters, though clad in dimity or chintz, came anigh." Equally too in keeping were the ancient saddles, bridles, bits, whips, and other riding and coaching gear, which hung around the walls in a mode that would have warmed the heart of an antiquary of the turf. But let the rustiest bit and snaffle hang there in peace; for there are coming oyster sauce, and Dumple Irish stew, whilst human nature shall show its tears and smiles!

"Tummus," spoke Alderman Rudberry, gently, as he rapped his finger upon the top of the chaise, as if it were a snuff-box, " I'm sorry you're ill, and I will come and talk to you presently, but your mistress wants the key of the large stable."

At this the top of the chaise was slightly

heaved up, a nightcap was seen, and its tassel shook negatively.

"Well, well," spoke the Alderman, quite coolly, "I'm sorry for it, we must resort to the kitchen-poker, that's all." So saying, the Alderman moved as if to retrace his steps. At this the chaise-top was deliberately raised up, more of the tassel, and then the night-cap itself was seen, —then the most melancholy face of Tummus himself, as if in full reality he had now taken the decadence of the "Dolphin" to heart—then a large, old, rusty key was thrust forth, and then once more the tassel shaking negatively, down plumped the top of the chaise, and a groan declared pathetically from within that the key of the "Dolphin's" citadel thus delivered up into the hands of the Moabites and Philistines, nothing was left for the ancient hostler to do but to shut himself up for ever in the post-chaise, and set out with it, then and there, on its journey of oblivion.

Alderman Rudberry made no reply, but descending with the key to where Mrs. Dumple and the surveyor waited, it was put into the lock, with difficulty turned in its rusty wards (for the stable had not been open for at least two years), and the door pushed open, when a scene presented itself which fully astonished both the old landlady and her friends. Every stall in this vast stable was a mushroom bed, and though it was evident that, since the stable had been shut, crop after crop had sprung up and perished, still were the floor, the rotten litter, even the disused stalls, white as a sheet with what had sprung and grown like a gourd in the night. Nor was this vegetation the mere coarse fungi common to damp and confined places, but the edible, flesh-coloured champignon of the mushroom tribe, which is raised in hotbeds for the London markets.*   When their astonishment was somewhat abated, and Becky and Cis had been called to view the prodigy, the Alderman and the surveyor crossed to the further end, and thrusting back a rude wooden shutter, found that it looked out on to a large plot of ground, totally disused, and only covered with the rubbish of fallen bricks, rusty iron, and old wood, whilst a few docks and nettles grew rankly here and there as in a city grave-yard.

"What place is this?" asked the Alderman, turning round to the hooded old landlady.

"Why, belonging to the 'Dolphin;' it was, in my poor Jonathan's days, used as an extra yard for country carts and waggons when the inn was over-full.   But now it has not been used for many years; I thought, however, that trade might thrive again, and so I've never liked to let

* A fact; many of the great stables on the northern roads, that in the days of coaching glory accommodated a daily average of from two to three hundred horses, were, when first disused at the opening of the lines of railways, thus converted by a process of nature into vast mushroom beds, which, with little or no care or cost, supplied for a considerable time this coveted luxury to the London markets.

or sell it, though often offered large sums of money. We are all given to hope, Mr. Rudberry."

"Yes, of those things that have the seeds of vitality in them, but not of those which are utterly perished. And to hope to keep this old inn to its old use, is to attempt to rock a full grown man in the cradle of his babyhood. No, no, my dear Margery—nor is there any cause for sorrow that it is not so, for on the graves of the men of yesterday rise the homes of the generations of to-day. That it is so, is nature's greatest law, and therefore it is for us to sow, and tend, and harvest in accordance. But," he continued, thoughtfully, in a few minutes, and still with his arm resting on the dusty, rotten shutter-ledge, "you must let me buy or hire this bit of land, Margery, for, if the cooking school prosper, I may make an important use of it." As he said this, Alderman Rudberry smiled, and then turned to business with his friend.

The premises were found to be of enormous extent, and covering a space of ground which, for London, was marvellous. Stables, one after another, coach-houses, granaries, waggon-sheds, all of which, at a comparatively trifling cost, were convertible into kitchens, store-rooms, sculleries, and bedchambers above. After this thorough survey, the Alderman and his friend adjourned to one of the "Dolphin's" fairest rooms, and there, after a savoury luncheon, presided over by the dear old landlady, proceeded again to business, which was not finished till a late hour.

That evening, somewhere about nine, as Margery was thoughtfully sipping her accustomed glass of negus, Becky bore in a message that Tummus, having risen and crossed to the kitchen, respectfully begged to talk to her for a minute or two.

"By all means," said Mrs. Dumple, kindly; "let him come in, and make him a glass of negus, Becky, nicely hot, and with sugar and nutmeg."

In a minute the renowned hostler came respectfully in, looking with a more woful visage than the "Dolphin" had ever seen, and with such disregard to his ordinary attire as to be enveloped in a coachman's old great-coat, to which was added the warmth of a large scarlet comfortable.

"I am sorry you're ill, Thomas," said his mistress kindly, with difficulty making him take the seat Becky had set, "but you must have the doctor, you'll soon get better then."

"I should, mum, if doctors could cure 'arts, but as they can't, I must be contented to go off slowly with wexation. For on course, missis, fil-lo-si-fer as I may be in some things, I can't see the Dolfin a-going to pieces in the fashion it will be without coming to a stand-still."

"But, my good Thomas," reasoned the surprised old gentlewoman, "you yourself told me how beneficial it would be if poor girls were taught to cook. Why, yourself spoke of the Irish stew as if it were worth being remembered."

"Yes, mum, it's wery true, and I meaned what

I said; but it vos cooking taught in the Dolfin kitchen, and in grates as has always bin grates, and not in stables turned into other things. I do regard you, missis, and the dear old place—ay, that I do; but ven I shall see bilers and saucepans instead o' 'osses, and hear a hissing and a frying instead o' them sounds as are come nataral to me from long use, my 'art'll go clean out o' me, missis, I know it."

"Well, Thomas Brownsmith," began Mrs. Dumple, gravely.

"No, mum, my name's Dol-fin, if you please—Tummus Dol-fin—"

"I have humoured your whimsicalities," went on Mrs. Dumple, not appearing to heed this interruption, though scarce able to restrain her smiles; "I have done my honest duty by you as a mistress; if, therefore, you cannot be contented with circumstances which I in my old age cheerfully and willingly submit to—"

"But, mum," interrupted and argued Tummus, "*you'll* have the Dolfin rooms, the Dolfin stairs, and all the Dolfin things jist about you as you've bin used to for so long; vhilst, as is nataral, the minnit von old stable goes there'll be another, and the place has as bin so long mine, the chist-lid vere I've scored my reckonings, the chist itself vere my best vaistcoats and shirts are, that old precious Dolfin chaise, in vich I'd hoped by-and-bye to shut down the vinders, and go my last journey in; the bits, the vhips, the snaffles, and dear master's old saddle, all must go, missis—all must go; and so, missis, though I *can* bear a deal, I shan't be able ven it comes to *that*."

"Dear me, dear me," said Mrs. Dumple, energetically, as she rose and hastened quickly round the table towards her honest servant, "I mean no such thing—indeed I don't, my good Thomas, Cis and Becky know it; indeed they do. For it was only this very morning that I said over and over again, to our good friend, Mr. Rudberry, 'Whatever else is changed or altered, Thomas *must* have his old room and the stable beneath left untouched. For, besides that he has gathered about him many things of the old inn's better days, poor Mope the owl is used to the old cage beside the window, and the old goat Billy would miss the rack and manger he has been so long used to.' No, Thomas, this *is* what I said, and this is the first time Margery Dumple's servants have done her honest care for them an injustice."

So saying, the old gentlewoman settled down into the nearest chair, and sobbed in the wounded tenderness of her pitying soul. It was not often she shed tears, but these were real ones.

"Mrs. Dumple, mum, missis, dear missis," began the contrite and repentant hostler, "jist lift your head and take your face out o' your han-ker-cher, or those tears'll quite finish me off, and I shall be doing sum-fen desperate with a razor. I am unfeelin', I am a monster, I am unjust, I know it, mum, I know it, for the Dolfin lives in the very middle o' my 'art, and I can't help bein' tender on these here pints. But all's right now, mum, and a little o' yer gruel'll set me straight agin; for ouly leave me jist enough o' th' old place as may give me at times a wision o' th' old Dolfin in its pride, and I'll peel taters and onions, stir saucepans, and turn roasts, and even put on an apron if you vish it; anything, mum, so the Dolfin don't quite svim away and be heard of no more by them as has known him so long."

So restraining her tears, wiping her eyes, and forgiving her honest servant, Mrs. Dumple rang for the nicely sugared and nutmegged negus, and harmony was restored, Tummus declaring, as he made his departing bow, "that the morning's sun 'd shine on him a renowated cretur."

As the Alderman was a thorough man of business, and, like a good chronometer, never lost a fraction of time, the great "Dolphin" yard in Southwark was soon filled with bricklayers and carpenters, and at the end of two months from the day of commencement, the great stable was turned into an admirable kitchen, duly fitted with steam-boilers and ovens for cooking on a large scale; and an adjacent stable, of smaller dimensions, into another kitchen, neatly fitted up with tables and dressers, and with twelve small kitchen ranges, fixed separately at intervals in one long wall. One large waggon-shed was turned into a larder, another into a store-house for vegetables, whilst, formed out of other portions of the buildings, were pantries, closets, and a scullery; above these, one of the ancient granaries was converted into a dormitory. The area of the yard itself was turned up, rolled, and gravelled, the pump and old watering-troughs removed, and in place of these a plot of turf laid down.

During this time Mrs. Dumple had not been idle. In the first place, divers sorts of spices had been pounded, as were also certain herbs, such as mint, thyme, sage, and sweet savoury. Then an old city warehouse had been visited, and rolls of blue and purple print for gowns, linen for cooking-aprons, and towels, and muslin for caps bought and sent in; and when Becky had been duly to the several schools, to the miserable homes in Spitalfields, and to the quaint room of the poor brother of the Charter-house, with whom the little god-daughter took tea that afternoon, and had made sure of the measure of the eleven coming scholars, Mrs. Dumple and her maids set to work, cut out and sewed, and neatly marked and numbered small caps, frocks, and aprons, in which, seeing that order and propriety are an absolute and necessary portion of all social lessons, due instruction in the civilizing art of cookery was to be taken.

On the appointed evening, therefore, when, as Tummus said, "the Dolfin had fairly put on his white apron," the eleven scholars came, and were duly received by Mrs. Dumple, in her own private parlour close to the bar, where, after each had received a welcoming glass of the " Dolphin " ginger-wine (which, according to Tummus, " was fit to put life in a dead man "), and a slice of Cis's plum-cake, Mrs. Dumple folded her cambric handkerchief on her knee, and made the following little speech, Tummus and the four maids being permitted to be auditors :—

"My dear Girls,

"You are come hither to learn of me, who have had much experience in these matters, one of the most useful, yet, strange to say, most neglected things in domestic life—PLAIN COOKERY ('Hear hear,' from Tummus, and 'hush' from Mrs. Dumple). I want to instruct you in nicely roasting a small joint of meat, so as not to serve it with a spoonful of hot water in the dish, but with a nice proportion of good, thick, rich, savoury gravy; I also shall teach you how to boil potatoes, so that they be mealy and well done; also to make mutton broth, Irish stew, good melted butter, and plain rice-pudding; and perhaps to these I shall add some general information on domestic economy and management. I therefore hope, my good girls, that you will be attentive, steady, cleanly, honest, frugal, and industrious. In that case you will not only reap much advantage, but, when fully competent, be able to take good places of all-work, or return to bless your parents' homes. But my exertions, or those of Alderman Rudberry, will depend entirely upon your individual conduct."

After this address, and the scholars' dutiful promises, they retired to the "Dolphin's" ancient kitchen, supped, and then Mrs. Dumple went in and read prayers, after which they departed to the new dormitory, where in due time the fine old lady followed, pressed the head of each upon its pillow, and audibly prayed God to bless her honest though humble labours, as He will—dear Margery Dumple,—for any form or approximation to truth is His. The infinitesimal point obeys the same laws as the sun which moves in majesty and splendour through the universe.

For the first fortnight the eleven scholars were duly instructed by the four old women-servants in household duties—such as bed-making, chamber-sweeping, grate-polishing, and washing, ironing, and the care of furniture and linen. At the end of that time, the great kitchen being entirely ready, Mrs. Dumple gave her first lesson. It was Monday morning, ten o'clock precisely, the steam flowed round the great stew-pan, the onions and the potatoes were peeled, when Mrs. Dumple, in a plain chintz gown of lilac colour, a neat unadorned cap, and a Holland apron, the hue of snow, crossed to the new kitchen. There, seated in an easy-chair, a little table before her, and a wide dresser round her, so as to form three sides of a square, and the girls duly standing in their neat attire, five on one side and six on the other, she thus began :—

Irish Stew.

" Remove the potatoes to one side of the dresser, and the onions to the other, and then six of you slice the potatoes and five the onions, into nice even slices—(a potato on a plate was brought to Mrs. Dumple, and she showed how). Now remove the sliced potatoes by degrees to the largest cullender, and nicely rince, after them the onions—(this was done).   Now five or six girls go to the larder, and fetch the twelve necks and six breasts of mutton, with which Mr. Whiteman, of Newgate Market, has so kindly furnished us, and then, attending to the mode in which Cicely, my cook, will remove the superfluous fat, and nicely cut up one breast and one neck, follow her example.   Whilst four or five are doing thus, let two attend to the stew-pan.   (Mrs. Dumple was obeyed, and this preparation of the meat being duly in progress, she turned her attention to the two girls now at the stew-pans.)   Now, Rose Clarkvoice and Jessie Hayler, pour into the bottom of the pan half a pint of water; now place nicely in a close layer of the fattest meat, now sprinkle over the tin measure, marked number two, full of salt, and number four, full of pepper; now a close layer of the sliced potatoes, next an equal one of the sliced onions ; now half the same quantity of pepper and salt, and again meat, seasoning, potatoes and onions."   With a little of Cis's superintendence this was all accurately and nicely accomplished, and the immense stew-pan being full, one pint of water was poured over all, the lid of the stew-pan pressed tightly down, and Tummus, who had taken upon himself this portion of the duty, was called in to turn on the steam, which he did with as immense an amount of hissing force as if he were rubbing down the mighty steed of an Alexander, or of a Nimrod of Brobdingnag.

"And now, girls," spoke Mrs. Dumple, as she

produced her ancient pinchbecked watch from her side-pocket, without which (the gift of Jonathan on her wedding day) she would not have risked the accurate roasting of a sparrow, " it is just precisely a quarter to eleven—at half-past twelve the stew will be done—and will not require to be touched till the lid is permanently raised ; though, if the stew were in a saucepan over an ordinary fire, two things would have to be particularly observed—it must be stewed slowly, and on no account allowed to boil, whilst it might want an occasional stir ; though the great art of cooking this excellent dish is that by close covering the savoury aroma is kept in.   And so, girls, as there is leisure, clear neatly away, and put some plates into the steam-closet to warm, as Alderman Rudberry, Mr. Whiteman, and the parish officers are coming to taste the stew at half-past twelve o'clock precisely."

And certainly half an hour before that time, such a splendid, savoury, life-giving aroma began to flow up, and down, and around the ancient " Dolphin " at the gateway, that passers-by stopped to ask what it was ; for, as Tummus said, " it operated like galwanism."

In fact, so extremely savorous was the great Irish stew, and so finely compounded into one perfect aroma were the pepper, the gravy, and the flavorous onion, as to make Alderman Rudberry smell it before he alighted from his carriage, the poor brother of the Charter-house as he stepped in at the gateway, and the six or seven gentlemen of the vestry, even though, as they came along, they were much abstracted by a grave discussion on parish rates.

But when they entered the kitchen and severally smelt it in perfection, when they saw the simple apparatus, the nice order, the comely and neat appearance of the girls, and lastly tasted the stew itself, their admiration was still more self-evident; whilst it might be remarked, in particular, that Alderman Rudberry, after the first spoonful, set down his plate, gazed with a bland smile upon the scholars, and then going to the window before-mentioned, looked out through its now glazed cavity, with a dreamy, abstract sort of benevolence strongly written on his face, as if he had mentally travelled onward into a future full of pleasant, homely, cheerful scenes; just as, after rough ploughing, and the winter time, we live to see the flitting lark amidst the greenness of the springing corn, or, later, hear the rustle of the harvest's ripeness.

In the meanwhile, Mrs. Dumple having retired to change her dress, now returned nicely habited in her shawl and bonnet, for it had been arranged that she should accompany this sort of deputation to the adjacent Ragged School, the great Irish stew, still sacred in its stewpan, going before in the " Dolphin's " largest hand-barrow, and in the especial care of Tummus and his " second-best vaistcoat;" for Margery's favourite servant was decidedly of opinion that the making public *such* a dish as the " Dolphin's " Irish stew was an event of vast significance, and worthy of due honour.

"And now, gentlemen," said excellent Margery, as she led the Alderman and his friends down the great kitchen towards the lower one, vastly pleased that her admirable dish had elicited such earnest praise, "you see how by a little method all this has been done, and how easy, by the same attention to order and cleanliness, a large number of Ragged Schools might be supplied with cheap, wholesome, and well-cooked food, whilst, at the same time, practical means would be at hand for training successive classes of female children."

"Yes, yes, I understand so far as to the training up useful servants and good wives," somewhat impatiently interrupted one of the churchwardens, who, though a schoolmaster, was by no means eminently gifted, "but I don't see how this food could be conveyed to any distance—it is, in fact, an impossibility——"

"No more, my dear sir," replied Mr. Rudberry, with a smile, "than that a pieman or a hot potato man should carry his bright-rubbed tin and its little charcoal fire from St. Giles's to Mile End, and find when he got there that his pies or potatoes were 'all hot.' This point has been taken into consideration, and when we once find that Mrs. Dumple's Cooking School does well in all other respects, depend upon it we shall not lack means of transport, either as to celerity or to keeping 'all hot.' The one thing will be achieved by a luggage cart and a good-paced horse, the other by setting stewpans over a portable brazier. Not a point has been forgotten, sir; the renowned Tummus may yet in some sense be the 'Dolphin's' hostler."

"And there is another thing to be considered whilst looking at the possibility of these cooking schools," said Mr. Whiteman, the benevolent salesman before spoken of, "and that is, the probability of the increased supply and low price of meat; two things tending to this more than others are—cheaper transit by railways as new lines are opened, and the increased power which knowledge is conferring on the agriculturist and stock-feeder, of converting the produce of the land more cheaply and speedily into the best descriptions of animal food; for till our lower class of population be better fed and better housed, the schoolmaster is comparatively useless."

"Well, gentlemen," said Mrs. Dumple, "if food is to be good and plentiful, as God pray it may be, never was there a better time than now to teach the rising population how to use it with advantage and economy—and so step here with me, if you please, for my good children are not to be made simply cooks for hospitals, taverns, or schools, but also for humble firesides and narrow households." Thus saying, the worthy old landlady of the Southwark "Dolphin" stepped into the lesser kitchen, and showed its twelve small fire-places, its separate dressers and closets, and her own chair, wherein she would preside over the nicely-roasting small joints of meat, the nicely baking small puddings, the well-boiling of potatoes, and even an occasional ascent into the higher regions of melted butter and oyster sauce.

"That will be whenever I have a dinner-party, my good Margery," spoke the Alderman, "for if there be anything in the whole art of cooking which comes like vanity and vexation of spirit from a common hand it is—oyster sauce."

Mrs. Dumple smiled while she added, "Ay, Mr. Rudberry, that is only because, like my Thomas, you are too partial to what he calls 'Dol-fin vays;' but I shall strive to add some other things to these lessons, which I am sure even you will say, would, if known and practised, add largely to the worth of better cooking; amongst which will be the setting each one of these twelve small fireplaces in order, as if children had to sit beside it, and that those who toil to bring home the daily bread were expected."

So, adding this little piece of morality to her practical text, Mrs. Dumple showed the beautiful arrangement of this novel school-room; and presently, it being fully time, she took the Alderman's arm, and proceeded with him and the little party to the Ragged School in the neighbouring street, whither Tummus had already conveyed the Irish stew, and assisted the mistress to distribute it amongst the children. These were in full enjoyment of their savoury meal as Mrs. Dumple entered the boys' schoolroom, and so intent were all on the business in hand, saving those who had finished their share, that scarcely a look of curiosity was raised.

"Do they like it, do you think?" asked Mrs. Dumple, softly, of her favourite servant, who, leaning against the wall beside the empty stew-pan, was contemplating with a philosophic air the scene before him.

"I think so, mum," replied Tummus, as in a moment he resumed his wonted attitude of respectful deference, "for you see they don't look as if they vos doing much in the vay o' study jist at present, or unless they be like the Emp'ror of Cha-ne I once read on, who couldn't make his dinner vithout birds' nests and nightingales' tongues. No, they say they never tasted sich a dish afore, a matter I think uncommon likely, as depend upon it, mum, not one on 'em ever put up his 'os at the Dolfin, or called a vaiter in to order sich a dish."

Mrs. Dumple smiled as she listened to her servant, and then turned away, for the Alderman had bidden every lad that had enjoyed his dinner lift up his spoon, which being done by the entire school without a single exception, it clearly convinced him that the savoury dish had been fully and worthily appreciated.

"As this is the case, my lads," he said, "that you have enjoyed a meal worthy of a king's palate, it is as well to let you know the condition on which one like it may be daily eaten. *That condition is work.* Each one who works steadily in his industrial class through the morning or previous evening, as the case may be, will be reckoned to have earned at least the necessary penny for this daily meal; thus it will be his own, and not a charitable gift—a needful distinction to make, my lads, as you must learn to understand. But he who does not work will not be permitted to eat. It is God's law, and he who would be well thought of by his fellow-men must obey it. Therefore, let the savour of this Irish stew teach you the most needful lesson you have to learn, which is, that if you work, be honest, be frugal, be sober and care-taking, a meal as good as this may bless your lips each day of your life; but if you be idle, drunken, dishonest, and wasteful, nothing of the kind can be permanently yours, for the riotous profusion of crime and profligacy wastes like ice in the sun!"

Though not a word was spoken in reply, the look of earnest intelligence which might be seen on many of the laddish, eager faces, convinced the worthy Alderman (who, by the way, was always dropping a little economical seed into untilled land of this sort), that the lesson was for the most part understood; so, taking worthy Margery's arm, he proceeded onward into the girls' schoolroom. As these had been served first, they had wholly finished their meal, and now, under the care of their mistress, were washing up the tins and spoons with which, through Mr. Rudberry's bounty, they had been supplied. One little tin only remained as it had been served, and this stood at the end of the long writing-table, and before one of the younger girls, who was leaning forward with her face hidden, and resting on her arms. This sight of untouched food amongst children who rarely tasted a comfortable meal excited the good landlady's curiosity, and she inquired of the mistress if the child were ill.

"I scarcely think so," replied the mistress, in a voice only sufficiently audible for the landlady's ear, "but the poor child, though young, has much sensibility; and if I mistake not, the thought of her mother's destitution and death makes her heart too full to eat. I think this is so, for though perfectly destitute and friendless since her mother's death some short time ago, she is too good a child to feign or make believe;" and as she spoke, the kindly mistress bent down and touched the child's face. It was raised, and though her eyes, as the mistress had conjectured, were dim with tears, Mrs. Dumple saw in them a vision of her youth, her father's sunny orchard, and the reborn face of her favourite playfellow, a neighbour's child.

"My dear," asked Margery, quite nervously, "was your mother or grandmother's name Lockly?"

"I do not know, ma'am," spoke the child, with the voice and manner of a better life than that around—"mother was always very secret about her history, it was the thing she most tried to hide."

"Ay," replied Mrs. Dumple, "we are some-times mistaken in faces, as I may be with yours, but as the mistress speaks well of you, and you are so friendless, my servant Becky shall step round and inquire more about you, for it may be in my power to be your friend."

The child did not even say "thank ye" to this promise of Mrs. Dumple's friendship, but with a sort of vacant apathy rose from the form, and with the mistress's permission putting aside the food to take home with her, was presently lost to sight in the crowd of other children.

It happened, however, that though this child's face was constantly in Mrs. Dumple's thoughts, the business of the school delayed Becky's intended visit for several weeks; for, the plan of the school succeeding, people began to be interested in its method of management, and to come to and fro "in a vay," as Tummus argued, "to make the Dolfin feel hisself young again." For at first people had laughed at the absurdity of such a thing as a Cooking School—some on the grounds of bad economical policy, and others at the folly of supposing that any of the thousand points of education rested in a saucepan; but those who had had, for any length of time, dealings with degraded, ignorant, and helpless portions of the population saw the matter in another light. The great difficulty, hitherto, in introducing the industrial principle into Ragged Schools, had been the need of bodily refreshment, appropriate and close at hand, during the short time which necessarily intervened between the hours set apart for different processes of mental and industrial instruction. For in these hours of leisure where were children to go who had no homes; or if so, only places which desecrated that name?   Of whom were they to ask a meal in either instance; or how possess it at all, unless it were stolen in the streets through which they prowled; and when out on an errand of the kind, like famished dogs, what learnt lesson, what moral rule, might limit the lust of crime, or what schoolmaster reasonably expect the child back to his restraining hand?   What schoolmaster moreover could gain the attention of hungry children, or engraft upon a mind worn by the morning's labour the moral lessons of the afternoon?   Either thing was an impossibility! There was, therefore, policy in the plan which brought this needed meal to the schoolhouse door, provided the child were made to feel that it was his only on the condition that it was purchased by so much labour, and so much self-denial implied in this labour.   This was the coin, just as if it were in the shape of a penny, a shilling, a guinea, he *must* give before it were his; the only philanthropy in the whole case being that those who had time, opportunity, and knowledge were willing, like kindly parents, to order that that which was thus earned should be brought to the possessor in the shape most beneficial both to his moral and physical nature.

Before, therefore, Becky had made those inquiries which Mrs. Dumple had so long intended, the three great Ragged Schools in the neighbourhood of the "Dolphin," which mainly owed their existence to the exertions and charity of Alderman Rudberry, were supplied by the Cooking School with a daily meal.

Thus, in the course of a few weeks, Margery's eleven pupils had, in addition to the several times repeated Irish stew, assisted at the making of mutton broth, pea soup, rice milk, and a marvellous sort of cheap haricot, made out of fragments of cold beef, and greatly enriched by spice, fried onions, and stewed carrots, and were therefore now supposed to be in a fitting state to receive their first lesson in the lesser kitchen, in the more sacred duties of home and homely life.

It was a lesson as to roasting meat—a great primary lesson, as it were, concerning brownness and gravy—and this was it. Cicely having closed the door and retired, Mrs. Dumple, in her neat morning dress, walked leisurely down the kitchen, and saw that in eleven out of the twelve little fireplaces the fires burnt clear and brightly, and where they did not she took the poker, cleared the bottoms from black coals and cinders, and gave that little electric stir which permits the flame to go upwards, and puts a soul even into a fire-place. Next, she had the cinders swept up, and then the very clean little dripping pans being put on their respective stands in front of each fire, some plates and dishes in every little hastener, a basting spoon, a dredging-box, and a clean preserve jar set on every girl's table, as were the several small-sized joints of meat from the respective pantries, Mrs. Dumple retired to her presiding chair, and spoke in this loving way to her scholars :—

"My dear children,

"A well-roasted joint of meat is such a rare thing as to make me hope you will well attend to this lesson, for scarcely one other I can give you equals this in value. The usual way of roasting, for instance, a fine leg of mutton, is to tie it on a string or to hook it on a bottle jack, and set it down before any sort of fire, black or bright, as chance may be, and to leave it to its fate, without dredging, without a sprinkle of salt, without basting. And when it is supposed to be done enough, it is pulled up, like a trout out of the water, thrown on a dish, and (my girls, I never have patience when I speak of this thing) a little hot water poured over it, and (Heaven help my indignation!) called gravy. It should be called liquid make-believe, not gravy. And all this without reference to what is in the dripping pan; the delicious gravy, the excellent dripping, into which, if a few large red hot cinders drop, it is all one, as the cook, with sublime indifference, thrusts the whole into her grease pot. Well, this pale, sickly-looking, half-cooked, graviless joint, being called roasted, is sent to table, to fill half those whose misfortune it is to partake of it, with scarce repressed disgust, and make many a man sigh, as the ill-conditional morsels choke him, over the folly of his wedding-day. But learn from me the despised art of roasting and making gravy, and in houses where you may be servants no sigh of this kind will ever be. One golden rule in all roasting is, my dears, not to be afraid of a dredging-box. In many middle-class houses, and especially in those innumerable regions of hot-water gravy, London lodging-houses, where unhappy people are taken in, and themselves and their meat "done for," maids and mistresses look upon dredging-boxes as if they were rattle-snakes, for of course brownness and gravy are no help to the grease pot. But, now put down your eleven joints, and let us see in what way the dredging-box is serviceable."

ROASTING MEAT.

"Now, the joints being put nicely before the fire, let them twirl some five or six minutes, so as to warm (this was done); now sprinkle a pinch of salt over each, and lightly, though entirely, dredge with flour, and so that some be lightly spread over the dripping-pan. (This was all nicely achieved, except by the two girls from Spitalfields, who from the first had been the dullest pupils, whilst Nelly Chester was the brightest, and therefore Mrs. Dumple arose and assisted them.) Now that the flour has adhered somewhat to the meat, baste gently with the fat which has dropped. (This was done.) Now, the meat being about half roasted, ladle out into the jar several spoonfuls of the clearest fat, being particularly careful not to remove any of the real gravy or brown particles at the bottom of the dripping pan (a flat dripping pan is preferable), baste again, and lightly flour. (This was done.) Now, my children, as the meat is within ten minutes of being done enough, baste the joints well, remove with the ladle all the clear fat remaining in each pan, and dredge all the unbrown places on the joints carefully. (This was done.) Now that 1 see the joints are nicely and thoroughly brown, take from the tea-kettle which is boiling on Nelly Chester's fire, each of you a full tea-cupful of water, pour immediately into the pan, stir in all the brown gathered round, and sprinkling in another pinch of salt, as well as a small pinch of brown sugar, baste your meat well for the last time. (This was done, the meat was richly brown and frothed, and there was, instead of hot water, a dish of gravy to pour over each joint worthy of the most learned epicure.)   And this," concluded Mrs. Dumple, "is, with small difference, the art of roasting."

During the period of this roasting the several girls had each one some half dozen potatoes in a small saucepan over her own fire; first, putting a little salt in the water, next watching them so that they only boiled gently, and when enough pouring the water very carefully off, then drying them for a second or two over the fire, and lastly, setting the saucepan at a distance on the hob, pressing down within each a clean folded cloth, by which means the vegetables were kept hot, whilst the steam had room to escape. In this way, when the cloth was laid for dinner, which it was in the larger kitchen, the several joints put on one dish and the potatoes in another, so pleased was Mrs. Dumple with her scholars' progress as to promise them a holiday that very afternoon, to which was joined the permission that for an hour previous to tea-time they should go up-stairs with her, and help her to arrange the great linen chest. And to show how much she was in earnest, no sooner was dinner over than Cicely was ordered to make a due number of rich short cakes, well-filled with currants and nicely sweet with sugar, so that the tea when set forth should look quite in holiday fashion.

This kind desire was carried out, and evening sinking on the faded glories of the "Dolphin," the good landlady retired to her little parlour, and sitting down quietly by the window—to which, the minute he saw the shadow of her cap, Billy the goat trotted across the yard, to rest his old gray beard upon the window-sill—it pleased her to hear the children's merry voices from the kitchen as they played at blind-man's-buff with Tummus, for it brought back in some degree the pleasure of her own childish days. However, it was not long before Becky came in to say that the schoolmistress of the neighbouring Ragged School would like to speak with Mrs. Dumple concerning the child she had so kindly noticed.

"Dear me, dear me," said Mrs. Dumple, apologetically, as the schoolmistress entered and took the chair the old servant had placed for her;

"it is very remiss in me, after my promise, to have thus——"

"Do not apologize, madam," interrupted the mistress, respectfully, "our obligations to you are already great; but the poor child is now even worse off than when she attracted your notice, as she had then a nightly shelter, but that is lost to her now, as the woman who gave it has been obliged, through extreme poverty, to go into one of the Union-houses. I think too, ma'am, you will the more readily help the poor child, as, from what I have learnt since your visit, your conjectures are right, and the child's grandmother was named Lockly before she married."

"I knew it—I knew it!"— and Mrs. Dumple listened breathlessly.

"It appears," continued the schoolmistress, "that, some year or two after you had left the country, she married a person named Field, and went with her husband to keep an inn in the North of England. For some years this flourished exceedingly, but afterwards, owing to the opening of so many railways in the neighbourhood, the business so fell of as at last to compel them to quit it, and with the little property they had saved to retire to a small cottage in a neighbouring village. Their only child, a girl of then about seventeen, would, in order to assist her parents, go out to service, which she did as barmaid in an inn. Here she remained till she was about twenty. Then, at the solicitation of her mistress, who loved Emma as her own child, she accepted a

situation as housekeeper to a gentleman of large
fortune, living not many miles from here in the
most beautiful part of Epping Forest, who had
written down to this mistress of the inn to procure
him a clever country servant, capable of conducting a house like his own.   Emma went, and stayed
two years, and then suddenly made her way to
London, carefully concealing her name, and
never, from what I hear, again corresponding with
either those in the place she had left, or her
parents.   Soon after this, this poor child was
born; but though she had a home to go to she
never went, but supported herself by the needle,
till her health gradually declined, and she fell
into a rapid consumption.   Though thus needing
assistance, she did not make known her condition
to a living soul, but lived upon the sale of her
clothes, and what few things she possessed.   At
her death, which happened suddenly, this poor
child was left utterly destitute, and it was not
till the other day that her landlady, in moving
some few old things from a closet in the room her
lodger had occupied, found the packet of letters
which give such little information as I possess.   I
have written to the North, but find the child's
grandparents are both dead."

"And the father?" questioned Mrs. Dumple.

"He is wealthy, and lives in Epping Forest, as
I have said. He is wealthy, as many things
stated in this poor girl's letters show, as they
speak of his going to Ascot, to Newmarket, and

to Doncaster, and of his spending large sums of money in collecting old things belonging to post chaises and stage-coaches. But rich as he was, and perhaps yet is, it appears the poor girl scorned to apply to him."

"As was doubtless right," said Mrs. Dumple; "so bring the child to-night, and she shall not want a friend."

Though that old homestead-orchard in the weald of Kent now showed its ruddy treasures in the summer, and its russet tints in autumn, to a newer generation, those of so many years ago were not altogether faded, but still flickered on the leaves, or hung in scarlet glory far up among the boughs. Thus, as the rich fruit hung, the overladen boughs drooped low, and the sun's rays, slanting through the leaves, fell on the mossied paths, a group of merry rustic children played up and down, two in closer companionship than the rest; who, now that the ruddy cherries peeped out so thickly from the boughs, sat hour-by-hour together through the summer days. One of these same children, Margery Dumple, living mentally again through all the beauty and inno-cent happiness of those long past days, took, that very night of the schoolmistress's visit, the grand-child of her once little playfellow to her heart, just as if no years, many of them tearful ones, had swept along her path; but that the boughs again were green, the cherries scarlet, the sunlight fall-ing through the leaves, and this the little childish friend she turned to. Good must be the nature that could do this so genuinely as Margery Dumple!

Perusing the poor faded letters till her spectacles were dim with tears, Mrs. Dumple found little, beyond what the schoolmistress had told her, which threw further light upon Emma Field's history. There was, however, in one letter, incidental reference made to a box, as if left for a time in a distant relation's care; and though the hope was vague that such a box could be found, still, as the place of deposit was not far distant, Mrs. Dumple sent Tummus, who, to her astonishment, in no great while returned bearing a little paper trunk upon his shoulder, which was still tied by an old worn cord, and had a faded direction on its lid. The relation, as Tummus ascertained, had gone abroad, and the poor woman with whom it had been left had scrupulously preserved it. When opened, it was found to contain a few clothes, and some further letters, out of which what appeared to be uniformly one name had been carefully erased with a penknife. But enough was clear to show what had been the wretched girl's fate; how her beauty, her gentleness, her usefulness, had won this rich man's love; how from the very first few months of her entrance into his service he had talked of marriage, and, to make her more fitted for her place as his wife, she had taken occasional lessons in various accomplishments. These facts were testified by his several letters when absent at places like Doncaster and Newmarket. Then there was a break of many months, and when the letters began again, they told—vehemently told—the wreck which in the interval had been made; for they showed that the unhappy girl had fled in her great sorrow, never to return ; and though letter after letter was there, expressing contrition, passionate grief, and yet more passionate love, and gave, if possible, yet more earnest promises, it was evident that such had never been replied to, or again trusted in; but, in an enduring, and a sort of expiating silence, the girl had sunk to her early grave. And Margery Dumple, in her pure, meek goodness, was the last one in the world to lift the veil the mother had thought fit to draw around the parent of her child.

In a short time, Emma was as much at home as if reared beneath the "Dolphin," Tummus taking to her with vast affection, and Billy likewise; for hitherto the renowned goat had treated the kitchen, the cooking, and the scholars with much disrespect, and would have even waged war with the latter, had a fitting opportunity occurred, and turned over with much *sang froid* any stewpan or saucepan which fell in his way; but no nice little opportunity of this sort occurring, he relapsed into a state of sullen dignity, never lessened even in the society of Mope, his great ally.

As the weeks passed on, and the elder scholars were further led through the admirable mysteries of plain and savoury cooking, it began to be pretty apparent what were Alderman Rudberry's intentions with respect to the desolate piece of waste land at the rear of the old inn. For now the dusty nettles, the dock leaves, the mouldy lichens, the old piles of wood and heaps of rubbish were cleared away, there began to rise from the foundation the skeleton walls of a large and stately iron building, intended—as Tummus, who had meditated much upon the matter, soon ascertained—as a model lodging-house for young men "like hisself, vithout encumbrances." This was probable, as the Alderman took a vast delight in its progress; and coming once or twice a week after his dinner-hour, now that the days were long, he would go over it with his great friend the poor gentleman of the Charter-house, and Mrs. Dumple, and then returning into the pleasantest parlour of the "Dolphin," there take a cup of tea and listen to Margery's cheerful stories concerning her scholars, or on rare occasions tell one himself.

"My dear Margery," said Mr. Rudberry one evening, as he and the poor gentleman sat with the tender-hearted landlady, and when such time had elapsed as to bring the great lodging-house to the eve of completion, "my satin-weaver, Boncœur, sought me out yesterday and poured forth such an abundance of praise concerning a half shoulder of mutton and some onion sauce which Henriette cooked for them in her visit home last Sunday, as to quite surprise as well as please me, for he said, 'You, sir, and Mrs. Dumple—God bless her!—*have* made a woman of my girl.'"

The landlady said nothing—only lifted up her white pocket-handkerchief; but the act preached a sermon.

"And further good," continued Mr. Rudberry, "is likely to arise out of this day's cooking. For a neighbour of the Boncœurs, a small but respectable master weaver of the name of Gregory, happening to dine there that day, was so well pleased as to propose taking Henriette as servant and housekeeper; for his sister, who keeps his house, can spare little time from her employment as a pattern-drawer."

"I am glad of this," replied Mrs. Dumple, "though I shall part reluctantly with *my children* (Heaven bless her! Margery said this from her heart), and with some of them I think I cannot. Yet you will hardly think it, but Henriette is the least forward of my pupils, and from the first has been the most difficult to instruct, on account of the thriftless, dirty habits of which, with rare exceptions, poverty and ignorance are the mother. One thing is, however, strange. If I need dishes nicely ornamented with flowers, or gracefully arranged—as was the case, Alderman, with those little sweets I made and sent for your last dinner-party —Henriette is the one to do it; for, whilst the others would stick, for instance, a white rose into a colourless blanc-mange—Henriette would dress the dish like a flower-garden. The same thing holds good with respect to fireside duties. It is, therefore, strange."

"Not at all, my dear Mrs. Dumple, not at all,"

replied Alderman Rudberry, " Boncœur comes of the good old Nantes stock of Frenchmen, and is one of the finest pattern-weavers I have. He would, if left to himself, no more blend inharmonious colours than nature herself! Henriette, therefore, inherits what comes of past cultivation and bright skies. The same rule holds good in a hundred cases throughout Spitalfields; and the poorest faded gown and shawl of many a needy weaver's wife would show a difference between the red-top knots of Shadwell or Limehouse.

" Well," replied Mrs. Dumple, kindly, " considering the chances that were against me in taking these untrained, untutored children under my care, I have succeeded beyond any reasonable expectation, and believing with you that there is much in this idea of fitness and propriety, in small things as in large, I have striven to teach these poor children such things of this sort as seemed well. For instance, many have laughed at my baby-house of a kitchen, wherein I have sought to make each separate girl perfect mistress of a humble home. But the result will, I hope, prove the old landlady of the Southwark ' Dolphin ' to have been wiser than they; for each separate girl has gone through the duties of a humble home, its cleaning, its setting forth, its order, its management. I have said, ' My dears, when I was a young married woman, though I was never poor, and through life have had servants to wait on me, still there were many things which I considered it my right and duty to attend to. For instance, that the morning's hearth was scrupulously clean, the fire bright, and myself in no slipshod attire. That the dinner at all times was ready at the due hour, but especially if my husband had been absent—and the same rule holds good, my dears, if the meal were but of potatoes—and that all should be set forth with propriety and cleanliness. Then, as your case may be, my dears, when nights are wintry, wet, and dark, let the coat by the fire, the dry shoes in the fender, and the steaming tea-kettle testify to love and care; for depend upon it, my dears, that small things like these bring full-grown angels to our hearths'—"

"My dear Margery," interrupted the Alderman, as smilingly he touched Mrs. Dumple's hand, "I see you are preparing for the siege of my lodging-house."

"No," replied the landlady, "you mistake me. I mean these womanly duties to hold in many other relations of life besides that of wife; and I do not think that much can be done for the moral life of the lower classes till they more prudently regard marriage than they do at present. No, I sincerely hope that the larger part of my poor girls will perform rather the part of good servants, good housekeepers, good sisters, good daughters, than that of wives—these first are more wanted."

"Be this as it may," replied Mr. Rudberry, gravely, "it seems you will not want for scholars, Margery, for the Board of Guardians of two of the city parishes have made an application to me, asking at what charge you will take twenty or thirty pauper girls to instruct in housewifery and cooking. And this brings me to a subject upon which for several weeks I have been desirous of speaking—that is, the sale of that mass of what I must not offend you, Margery, if I call *rubbish*, which takes up so much room that might be turned to better account."

"Dear me, dear me," said Mrs. Dumple, pettishly, if ever in her life she spoke so—"this would so interfere with my poor Thomas!"

"Still, my dear madam," was the answer, "if half these things are really rubbish, are in the way, and yet would sell for a good price—for an old-fashioned snaffle, with a Brentford saddler's mark on it, was advertised for yesterday in the *Times* at the price of five guineas—of course they would be better sold and the room they take up made useful."

"Mr. Rudberry," replied Margery, with a solemn firmness, which plainly showed that her goodness and justice of character had their strong as well as their weak side, "the answer to your question must be made by my good and faithful old servant, Thomas. For the value of a few pounds shall never make me unjust to the harmless tastes of one who has served me and mine so long, so honestly, and so well. But if you like to ring for him you can; his consent is mine."

This Alderman Rudberry did—and after a due visitation to the pump, and to his "chist" for the "second best vaiskit," Tummus appeared, full as usual of humour, respect, and faithful attachment to his mistress.

"Thomas," began the Alderman.

"Tummus, if you please, sir. T-u-m-m-u-s D-o-l-f-i-n—that's the vay I spell it ven I write—vich aren't often, sir."

"Tummus, then," went on the Alderman, smiling good-humouredly, "you of course know that the committees of many Ragged Schools in distant parts of London have asked to be supplied with food from this Cooking School, as also that several parishes are desirous of sending pauper children here for instruction. Attention to these requests will for one thing require further room; I have therefore been suggesting to your mistress that much of the old lumber of post-chaises, harness, and saddles might be sold."

For the instant one deaf, or looking through the window, without hearing what was said within, might have fancied that the renowned hostler had been struck by some secret projectile, so sudden was his change of respectful, good-humoured deference to another really expressive of pain and disappointment. But recovering his old manner by an effort, apparent, at least, to his good mistress, he said, with a mournful slowness that touched Margery to the very soul. "Is it your vishes, mum, that the Dolfin should go off to the coffin-maker's this werry minnit—because, mum, the selling o' things that is nat'ral to him is putting out his last light with a pritty certain extinguisher."

"My good, excellent, much-respected Thomas," pleaded the good landlady apologetically, "you shall do as you like—I'm sure you shall—only—only—Mr. Rudberry being so much our friend, why—"

"Dear missis," interrupted the hostler, with a genuine pathos which would have done honour to the written immortality of Sterne, " through life your vill has bin a law, and it shall be so now, though it vos to the putting my vinders up and going my last journey. But I must have time to think on it, missis—as a man ought to have that's got to the writing o' his last vill and testament."

" Thomas," spoke his mistress, after a due pause—for though a keen observer might have seen divers wicked twinkles in the most secret corners of Alderman Rudberry's kindly eyes, still the two most interested in this discussion were pretty fairly in earnest—" I mean, most certainly mean, that nothing should be parted with that you particularly care for, or that once belonged to your honoured master and my dear husband, Jonathan Dumple. But, fully considering the change made in any future plan I once thought to adopt, by my voluntary charge of my dead playfellow's little grand-daughter, and my growing attachment to her and Nelly Chester, this good gentleman's little favourite, I think it is not improbable that when once the school is fully established, and some fitting persons found to carry it on under my occasional superintendence, I shall remove to some secluded country place, not too far from town,

and there with my two children (the poor gentleman looked here at Mrs. Dumple in a way which
said, ' Ay, now you've won my heart '), with you,
and such other of my dear servants as like to accompany me, farm a little, and supply vegetables
to the school.   As such may be the case, my good
and excellent Thomas, you must see that there
are many things here that we could not necessarily
take with us, and therefore, there is a show of
reason in what Alderman Rudberry proposes ; as
many such things as you have been hoarding up
are inquired for at a large price.   But as there is
no immediate necessity for this change, take your
own time to think it over, my good and excellent
Thomas, and if, when fully thought over, you cannot make up your mind to—"

" I'll try, mum, I'll try, mum," interrupted the
hostler, with a mournfulness which was quaint,
though profoundly genuine, " but on course,
missis, as I said afore, a last vill and testament is
a solemn thing, and therefore, vith your leave, I
von't be in a hurry."   So saying, with a respectful bow, he hurried from the room, evidently not
willing to be drawn into any further concession
respecting the faded signs of the once " Dolphin "
glory.

Thomas was quite right in his conjecture, for
the Alderman was too much a man of the world
to deal in anything like sentiment ; so, if he had
had his own will, the hostler would have been
called back and the nail struck on the head at
once ; but Margery's negative too plainly said, " I

am mistress of the 'Dolphin,'" though she only gently said, "No, no, Alderman, this subject must never be mentioned again, unless prompted by my servant himself, for the experience of a long life has taught me that leniency and gentleness towards the innocent weaknesses of our fellow-creatures is the way of taking them by the hand, and leading them in matters of nobler and larger consequence."

Miss Hazlehurst makes a pause here, for her voice is spent.

END OF VOL. I.

R. BORN, PRINTER, GLOUCESTER STREET, REGENT'S PARK.